Hell is empty and all the devils are here.

William Shakespeare, *The Tempest*

A
BRUTAL
SEASON

An absolutely gripping crime thriller

JUDI DAYKIN

DS Sara Hirst Book 3

Joffe Books, London
www.joffebooks.com

First published in Great Britain in 2021

This paperback edition first published
in Great Britain in 2023

Cover art by Dee Dee Book Covers

ISBN: 978-1-80405-911-1

AUTHOR'S NOTE

It has been my great delight to call Norfolk my home for the last forty years. As with all regions, we have our own way of doing and saying things here. The accent is lyrical and open, just like the countryside and skies. If you would like to pronounce some of the real place names in this book like a local, the following may help:

Happisburgh = Haze-bruh
Wymondham = Wind-am
Norwich hides its 'w'
Cromer (Crow-mah) is a real place, the pier and its theatre iconic landmarks. It was my pleasure to work there for several years, doing Jessie's job. The people described are fictional, but the layout of the venue is accurate. At the time of writing, the Seaside Special Show is still a feature and well worth a visit.

PROLOGUE

He was sure that they couldn't see him hiding in the gap between the beach huts at the end of the prom. Not that they would have cared. Being the slapper she was, the woman had opened her legs for the Untermensch right there on the sand. Knickers off, skirt lifted. The bitch. He'd watched as the couple went at it behind the wooden groyne, where they thought no one would see them. How wrong could they be?

What a whore, he thought. His hands clenched open and shut. He could feel his body responding to watching the live porn show in front of him. The temptation to rub his crotch until he exploded was huge. *Wait, don't lose it now.*

With a sigh, the couple climaxed. The watcher shook his head in frustration. It didn't matter if she enjoyed it. Women should be grateful for anything they got.

'Best get back,' she said. She pulled on her high-heeled strappy sandals, grabbed her bag, and started to walk away. Then she stopped and looked back over her shoulder. 'I'll think about it.' She held out her hand. He hesitated for a moment, then smiled and took it. Their arms swinging, they drifted up the ramp to the promenade in a post-coital haze.

Young love, the watcher sneered to himself. *How delightful. Stupid twats.*

1

They'd pass him in seconds, he realised, and eased quickly behind the beach hut where it stood against the concrete wall. He waited until he heard them go past, the man murmuring something, the girl responding with a light laugh. He watched them from the shadows until they reached the café and museum, then followed them at a distance, keeping out of sight. His erection hadn't quite subsided and was rubbing on the inside of his trousers.

The couple stopped at the bottom of the cliff steps up to the town.

'If you're sure, then I can go back this way,' the man said. They kissed passionately as he massaged her breast. She responded by rubbing the front of his trousers. 'No more. Not tonight.'

That should be me. In the shadow of the cream walls of the café, the watcher groaned gently. *She should be doing that for me*.

The man walked off along the prom. The young woman climbed the steps up to East Cliff alone. That might be a mistake he could capitalize on. The town was busy tonight — it always was in carnival week. Lots of the pubs had late-running bars, and drinkers often congregated outside. No one would notice him. He smiled. When she had reached the top of the steep stairs, he silently ran up after her.

At the top, he checked for revellers. A group stood in the doorway of the White Lion, far too engrossed in their own partying to notice the young woman pass with him tailing her. She pattered unevenly past the shops behind the church, pausing to sit on the low boundary wall. He pulled himself into a shadowy doorway and waited. She unfastened and pulled off her useless shoes, then wandered on until she reached the cobbled street that ran between the fisherman's cottages.

Here the road divided into two small streets that went in parallel along the top of the cliff. The front street overlooked the promenade and soon petered out into a path. The other ran one row of buildings back, past shops, cafés, the rear of the Hotel De Paris and holiday lets. He knew where she lived. She would be heading up to the clifftop gardens.

He lengthened his stride. There were several small alleys between the two streets. He knew how to get ahead of her without being seen. Choosing the narrowest alley, he squeezed past the big blue wheelie bin that the restaurants used for food waste.

The woman was walking slowly along the cobbled street. A group of lads outside The Duke wolf-whistled as she passed. Unfazed, she replied with a laugh and walked on. The lads laughed in return, then jeered as she stuck up a middle finger at them. Amplified music roared out of the open pub doors, voices raised as they sang to Bon Jovi.

'Get back to your band,' she called with a smile.

'Dirty bitch,' he muttered under his breath. 'Got it coming.'

He waited, his erection returning with full force in anticipation. She weaved towards him, oblivious. All anyone watching might have seen was his arm reaching out to grab hers as she passed the alley.

CHAPTER 1

The Pavilion Theatre stood at the end of Cromer Pier, a Victorian structure that stretched nearly five hundred feet out over the North Sea. A wide wooden boardwalk ran from the promenade below the town at the land end to the five-hundred seat theatre. A café and bar provided drinks, ice creams and cakes during the day and acted as the foyer for the theatre when a show was on. The boardwalk circled the theatre on all sides, with the RNLI lifeboat station at the tip.

As usual, on a show night, Jessie Dobson would be one of the last to leave the theatre. She operated and mixed the sound for the shows from her workstation on the left of the entrance stairs at the back of the auditorium. Known as the soundbox, it was surrounded by a waist-high wooden wall with a half-door in it. During shows, Jessie perched on a high stool behind the mixing desk, watching the stage and hearing exactly what the audience did. Sitting out there also made her the last one backstage at the end of the show.

This was Jessie's tenth summer season, and at the end of it, she would be celebrating a decade of working and living in Cromer. She rarely paid much attention to who was performing. She looked after whomever was booked, without let or favour. So, when she had arrived for the meet-and-greet on the first day of rehearsals in June, Jessie had been horrified to watch Ricky Easton walk along the pier and into the theatre bar.

By the look on Ricky's face, he hadn't known she would be there either. He would be in his mid-forties now, and in the harsh world of musical theatre, that meant he was on the slide. Sixteen weeks by the seaside was a very nice contract to have. As the theatre manager had introduced the cast to the crew and one another, Ricky had feigned not knowing Jessie. She acknowledged it was a great acting job, but she saw the hooded look in his eyes.

Here they were, in the middle week in August, ten weeks into the season, and it had been as horrible as Jessie had feared. Ricky never spoke to her unless it was for professional reasons, which they could hardly avoid, while he lost no opportunity to complain about her and the standard of her work. Predictably, Ricky had also started chatting up several of the female cast before settling on an affair with the lead female vocalist. Unfortunately, Hallie was married with a toddler son, and the romance was making her deeply unhappy and conflicted. Jessie longed to warn her about Ricky.

Jessie's only means of defence was to avoid the man, which was what she was doing now. Once the auditorium was empty, she took her time tidying up the box and turning off the equipment. She slipped through the pass door to the stage's prompt side and closed down the emergency mics, listening out for Ricky's voice. It was coming from Hallie's dressing room. She was able to make it into the green room, where the lockers were.

The posse of girl dancers giggled their way along the backstage corridor in their pretty dresses. Yazza, Jessie's housemate, leaned around the green room door. 'You joining us? We're off to try that new cocktail place.'

Jessie was pulling her rucksack and coat from her locker. Her immediate reaction was to say no, but she felt stressed about Ricky and could do with a drink. 'Is everyone going?'

5

'Nah, just us girls.'

'OK then, I'll catch you up.' She always helped Pete, the stage manager, lock up backstage once it was clear.

Ricky pushed past Yazza from the corridor. 'Move up, Yazza.'

The dancer rolled her eyes as Ricky slapped her, none too kindly, on the backside. He glanced at Jessie as he headed for the back door, pulling the hood of his black sweat jacket over his shock of blonde hair.

'We'll see you up there,' said Yazza and scuttled after the other three girls who had left via the auditorium.

The performers usually went that way, as audience members would hang around in the bar waiting to chat or collect autographs and selfies. Jessie was surprised Ricky was leaving the back way. He liked to have his ego massaged more than most.

She joined Pete, and they checked all the dressing rooms were empty, then drew in the main stage curtains. Jessie left by the stage door, locking it behind her. It led directly out onto the boardwalk as it passed in its circuit around the rear of the theatre, lit by the lifeboat station, whose lights were always on, and the theatre building's fire exit lighting. The usual selection of intrepid blokes who spent the evening fishing off the pier's side were leaning on the rails, their rods dangling lines over the metal barriers, their kit boxes littering the boards.

She deadlocked the door as the outside lights were switched off by the house manager, and this side of the pier was plunged into darkness.

Typical of Charlotte to be so efficient, she thought of the house manager, reaching into her pocket for her mobile.

Somewhere around the back, she heard a crash and the sound of two men's voices raised in argument. The light from the lifeboat station ought to have been sufficient to see by, but it sounded like someone had fallen over some fishing equipment. Flicking on her torch, she looked around the corner in case they needed any help.

Ricky Easton was pinned against the theatre's back wall by a man in a dark padded jacket. He was big and bulky, with a shaven head that seemed to grow up from his shoulders without the necessity of a neck. He held Ricky with one hand on the chest, the other gripping the singer's jawline, jamming it upwards. It looked painful — enough to damage his face. Jessie's loyalty to the show came before her feelings about Ricky. There was no understudy should Ricky be injured.

'What's going on?' she yelled, flashing the torchlight along the boards. The beam wasn't strong enough to fully illuminate the pair, and Jessie wasn't going any closer.

The bald man glanced in her direction, then pushed Ricky sideways onto the decking. The singer landed with an unhealthy thump, crying out in pain. His assailant marched off into the dark, kicking the pile of plastic fishing crates out of the way as he went around the opposite corner of the building. Waiting until the sound of his footsteps faded, Jessie went to help Ricky.

'Are you hurt?'

Ricky had rolled up into a sitting position, his back against the theatre wall. He was rubbing his jaw with one hand.

'Fuck off, Jessie.'

'I can't leave you like this. I'll fetch help.'

'Don't you dare,' Ricky snarled. 'And don't bother to ask what it was all about.'

'I won't, then.'

Ricky didn't reply, and feeling less than charitable, Jessie headed around the theatre, leaving him to it. As she passed the lights of the bar, she could see that the girls were conspicuous by their absence. They must have already headed up to the cocktail place. Jessie waved through the window to Pete and set off.

Under the dim lights of the promenade, she could see the man who had attacked Ricky hovering by a bench. She reached the landward end of the boardwalk and walked between the box office and Waves restaurant that formed the entrance to the pier. From the top of the steps, she watched as the man climbed into a taxi.

Grateful that she didn't have to walk past him, Jessie headed up the zigzag pedestrian ramps that led up the cliff to the town. Whatever Ricky had done to deserve that, as far as she was concerned, it couldn't have happened to a better person.

CHAPTER 2

The sun was already shining when Detective Sergeant Sara Hirst's mobile rang loudly enough to wake her up before cutting out. Her alarm clock said 6.58 a.m. Surely, she hadn't set the thing by mistake. It was Saturday, and she wasn't due at work.

Confused and yawning, Sara pulled the mobile onto the pillow next to her and tapped the screen. DI Edwards had been the culprit. That made her sit up. Her boss wouldn't be ringing this early unless it was important. She hastily pulled on a longline T-shirt and was halfway downstairs by the time his voicemail rang through. *Good morning. Get dressed and get to Cromer. I'll meet you there.*

It looked as if their long, easy-going summer was about to get busy. She flicked on the kettle and got out her travel mug to make a coffee. The mobile signal was flaky inside the kitchen. It was better at the bottom of her garden. Sara rang him back as she reached the drunkenly leaning garden shed, which she had yet to fix. Just one more outstanding job on the country cottage she had inherited from her father the previous winter.

'Morning, boss.'

'Got you up? Good thing. Don't head for the office — go straight to Cromer. I'm on my way there. Mike's gone to pick up Ian.'

'What have we got?'

'Young woman's body in an alley near the bus station. Right in the middle of town.'

'I'll be away in ten minutes,' Sara said.

'Uniform already have it shut off. We're going to cause chaos.'

She knew he was right. Work had taken her to Cromer on a handful of previous occasions. The streets were narrow and the town usually busy. The one-way traffic system got backed up all too easily.

As a London girl, Sara had found adapting to rural life something of a challenge. The smallness of everything, the lack of facilities and the insular nature of country living took some getting used to. There were also the sudden bursts of activity that accompanied the holiday visitors who flocked to the villages and caravan parks from Easter onwards. Now it was the middle of August, and the high season was in full swing. If it was busy here in the small coastal village of Happisburgh, what was it like in a seaside resort like Cromer?

Showered and dressed, Sara knotted her braided hair into a tight bun. The braiding kept it neat, with a nod to her Jamaican heritage. She still relied on her mum to look after her hair, which was her mum's speciality as a hairdresser in London, and besides, Sara hadn't wanted to offend her by switching to a local hairdresser, not since they had made up their differences last year.

She secured the coffee mug in its holder in the front of her car and stuffed a slice of toast into her mouth. Cromer was only fifteen miles away. She would probably be the first to arrive. The coast road twisted through Mundesley and Overstrand before it dropped out partway down the Norwich road to the north of the Cromer shops, where traffic was already building up. There was no alternative route unless you drove back several miles out of your way, so the town spent much of the summer choked with traffic, just not usually this early in the day.

Sara soon realised why. There were already a number of buses parked in the one-way system, forcing other vehicles into a bottleneck which a uniformed officer was trying to organize. In the distance, she heard sirens wailing. They would need more help to shut down the middle of the town and clear the traffic jam.

She flashed her warrant card through the windscreen. Someone had strung crime scene tape across both the entrance and the side road, which also had bus stops and shelters. Two police cars were parked in the station, with a coach that said *Norwich X99* on the front. A man she assumed to be the driver was standing in front of his bus, smoking in a distracted way.

As she got out of her car, Sara tried to get her bearings. Opposite the bus station, a small, narrow alley ran towards the seafront at right angles to the side road. Just about wide enough to drive a small car down, the cobbled path was the service road to the flats that backed onto it. A café on a wooden platform was raised above the street at the alley's entrance. Commercial waste bins labelled *Pat's Café* blocked the access. A pair of officers were struggling to rig a temporary screen out of a blue-and-white striped beach windbreak to shield whichever poor soul now lay behind the waste bins.

'More help on its way?' Sara asked one of the officers struggling with the windbreak.

'Yes,' he said. He was trying to fasten one end of the plastic sheeting to a drainpipe with cable ties. 'Hold that for me, will you? Despatch are sending more patrol cars to help seal off the area. It's going to be hell. Sod's law this would all happen right in the middle of the transport hub.'

'And it's Saturday.'

'Indeed. And it's Carnival.'

'What?'

'Start of Cromer Carnival today.' He pointed to a large banner across the street outside. 'It's the busiest week of the entire year.'

Sara had zoned out the banners and posters in her desire to reach the scene as quickly as possible. Now she looked at them with growing dread. On the wall behind her, Sara could see a poster with a long list of events. There were dozens of them scheduled across eight days. Today had more than most.

'There we are.' The officer finally seemed satisfied that he had succeeded. 'Poor girl. No dignity in being looked at. Rest of your team on their way?'

'They are.' *And the sooner, the better*, she thought.

The two officers hurried away to help with the gathering traffic. Sara was tall and had no difficulty looking over the top of the striped screen. She couldn't help but feel a momentary sadness at what she saw. It didn't seem to matter how many of these cases Sara ended up working on, the victims still touched her heart.

Stretched out on the cobbles was a young woman. In her early twenties, her long blonde hair was matted and dishevelled around her head. Her face had the remnants of heavy make-up, the eyes were staring open, and the jaw had slackened. Something had trickled from her mouth and dried to a crust on her cheek. The girl's left arm was lying by her side. The other hand lay on her stomach, the fingers clutching a sparkly plastic tiara. She was wearing a pale green, strappy dress made of shiny, silky fabric and looked as if she had been going out for the evening somewhere. Perhaps it had been a hen party. It looked like that sort of silly headgear.

Sirens sounded from the one-way system. DI Edwards and a couple of patrol cars were arriving, forcing their way through the gridlock. Sara was relieved to see the first CSI van with them.

'Morning, Sara. What's this thing?' Edwards tapped on the windbreak.

'They were just trying to shield her from prying eyes,' she explained. 'We've got a young woman dressed up to the nines.'

Edwards peered over and let out a low whistle. 'I'm not surprised she was dressed up. She's the Carnival Queen.'

CHAPTER 3

Jessie's job at the pier had allowed her to put down roots and to buy her own place in the middle of Cromer. It was one of the old-fashioned fisherman's terraced cottages on a small street that stretched between the two roads forming the town's circular one-way traffic system. The street was pedestrianised, and apart from early-morning delivery vans heading for the local shops, it was quiet enough.

Her season routine was now firmly established, and she had been looking forward to her Saturday morning lie-in. So, Jessie wondered why she was being woken so early by cars bibbing their horns and revving their engines. Was that really a bus?

With a yawn, Jessie checked her bedside clock. It was only eight, but she was unlikely to get back to sleep with the traffic noise. She rolled over, pulled on an old pair of PJs and headed downstairs to make coffee. There was no sound of movement from Yazza in the front bedroom. *How is she sleeping through the racket?* Jessie thought.

Mind you, a brass band could be playing outside the front door, and normally Yazza wouldn't be disturbed before 11 a.m. on a Saturday. Especially not after the dancers had been partying. Jessie smiled at the idea. She loved having

13

Yazza for company, but it did make her feel her age sometimes. It was a long time since she had waited impatiently to be eighteen and move to the city from her rural Yorkshire upbringing. She had trained in Manchester, then moved to London for work. Nowadays she enjoyed the quieter pace of life that Norfolk offered.

She took her coffee through to the lounge and drew back the curtains. Beyond the nets — a necessary evil given that the pavement ran directly outside the window — a queue of cars moved with a staccato rhythm, each vehicle starting and halting with a jerk after only a few yards. Tempers were surely fraying.

Jessie tried the television for the local news. Whatever was going on didn't seem to have reached them yet. She flipped open her MacBook Pro. The Norfolk Police site had nothing, nor did the Fire Service. Finally, she tracked down a brief paragraph on the local newspaper's Facebook page. There was a problem near the bus station, and traffic was being diverted.

Right, she thought. *Diverted outside my bloody window.*

A thump above her head warned Jessie that Yazza might be stirring. When the slight, dark-haired dancer joined her in the living room, she looked sleepy.

'Why is there all this traffic?' Pulling the belt on her pink, fluffy dressing gown tightly, Yazza slumped into the armchair.

'Something is wrong at the bus station,' said Jessie. She turned the laptop around for Yazza to see. 'Doesn't say what. The coffee should still be warm.'

'You didn't stay out long last night.'

'It was kind of you to ask me,' said Jessie. 'It's not really my scene, though. Not at my age.'

'Cocktails were nice, weren't they?'

'I confess to being partial to a Bellini, and they made a nice one.'

Yazza wandered to the kitchen, returning with a mug.

'I'm going to get a shower,' Jessie told Yazza. 'Then I'll go as far as the bakery for some croissants if you fancy?'

14

For a moment, the dancer looked a little green. Sipping her coffee seemed to help. 'That will be nice, I think.'

Jessie wasn't going to tell Yazza off for having a hangover. She was young enough to get over it, and none of them ever gave less than their best when showtime came — good old Doctor Theatre. She wondered if the same could be said of Ricky Easton. His jaw would probably be sore or bruised this morning, not a good move for a singer. Knowing Ricky of old, he would be up to something. Hopefully, she'd never find out what.

Jessie made her bed and laid out her clothes for the day. Black jeans, a black polo shirt with a Cromer Pier Theatre Staff logo, with a black hoodie. Her job required that she wear black clothes every day. For the morning, she selected a lightweight easy-cut blouse in bright colours. It made a change and hid a multitude of sins. Her figure wasn't bad for someone her age, and she had long since given up the battle of the bulge with her stomach. At five foot two, she reasoned that if the flubber couldn't stretch up and down, then it had to go forward. Jessie liked her food, assumed she would never be seen naked by a man ever again and consequently enjoyed the cakes and pies from the bakery regularly. Tight jeans helped keep the wobbles at bay. Her work shirts had gone up a size recently, but what the hell.

Clean and dressed, she grabbed her bag and went out. Cross Street was still jammed with vehicles, and the exhaust fumes tickled her throat. Jessie turned towards the bus station to see what she could find out.

CHAPTER 4

'Did you know her, sir?' Sara asked DI Edwards in surprise. They had moved away from the stripey windbreak and were standing by their cars in the bus station.

'Not personally,' he said. 'I just recognise her from the newspaper. A pretty young thing, a local girl. They like to choose someone who lives in the town if they can.'

'Do you remember her name?'

'Not immediately.' He stood, chewing his lip for a moment. 'Nope, I just remember the picture.'

The sound of a man's voice getting stroppy with the young traffic cop at the entrance made them turn. It was DC Bowen, with DC Noble sitting in the passenger seat. Noble was looking out of the side window, pretending that he wasn't at all embarrassed by Bowen's performance. Sara smiled to herself as the DI went over to let them in.

She had been working in the Norfolk Police's Serious Crimes Unit team for a year now, and Mike Bowen didn't seem to get any less argumentative than he had been when they'd met on her first day. Sara smiled briefly at the memory of their early arguments and sparring. Bowen was in his early fifties, and she sometimes felt a generational gap of understanding between them that would never be bridged. They had learned to appreciate each other, nonetheless. Young Ian Noble was relatively new to being a detective and had a tendency to get embarrassed, though he was learning to control his facial reactions these days. The four of them made a good team.

If you could park a car grumpily, Bowen managed it. Sara assumed Bowen was tetchy because they'd been called directly out to Cromer, and he was missing his morning cake from their admin, Aggie. He probably hadn't remembered that it was Saturday. She wouldn't be in the office unless they had asked her to be.

The DI gestured for his team to gather around, and he filled the two DCs in. 'I think the poor lass is this year's Carnival Queen. Mike, got any contacts at the local paper?'

'Of course.'

'See if you can get her name or information about her, like her home address. It may be quicker that way.'

'Daisy Shaw,' said Sara. She had a strong signal on her mobile for once and had been checking the newspaper's website. She kept her voice low so that the growing number of gawping onlookers couldn't hear. 'Her name is Daisy Shaw.'

'I'm on it,' said Bowen, and he wandered off, scrolling through his phone.

'Ian, give the locals a hand to get these people cleared. See if you can get hold of someone to sort the buses out. People will still need them.'

Noble nodded and headed for the side street. A forensic investigator was unloading the CSI van while his teammate was putting up the standard white tent behind the waste bins. They left the windbreak where it was, providing extra cover from prying eyes. Edwards and Sara joined the anxious-looking bus driver.

'David Briggs,' he said, then lit another cigarette as if on autopilot. He glanced up at Edwards. 'Sorry, I should have asked. Do you mind?'

'Not at all.'

Briggs shivered, despite the warmth of the morning. 'Her legs were sticking out, and at first, I thought it might be a shop dummy or something.'

'Run me through it from the beginning,' said Edwards. 'What time did you get here?'

Briggs's hand shook as he put the cigarette to his lips again. 'About half past six.'

'Was anyone waiting for you? Passengers?'

'No, I was a bit early. I'm not due to leave until seven.'

'You didn't see anyone else?'

'Just the despatch lady at the depot when I picked up the coach.'

Edwards nodded. 'You drove straight here?'

'Yes,' said Briggs. He sucked on his smoke again.

'Then what happened?' Sara prompted him.

Briggs pointed to the side street where two additional bus stops stood outside the raised café. 'Our stop is over there. Pat doesn't like us parking in front of the café for long, or customers can't see it, she says.'

The picnic tables on the veranda outside the café were empty. It should have been doing a brisk trade, Sara realised, except now it was behind the exclusion tape. The owner was standing on the deck watching proceedings with her arms folded and a sour look on her face.

'So, I parked the bus in here and went for a drink and a butty,' said Briggs. He gestured at the woman on the deck. 'Pat gives us drivers a discount.'

'Did that take long?'

'Few minutes. I didn't hang about because Pat doesn't have much to say for herself first thing in the morning.' Briggs pointed to a picnic table on the edge of the veranda. 'I sat there. Then I thought I'd sit on the wall and have a smoke.'

He indicated the low perimeter wall that ran around all four sides of the station, which, no doubt, marked the boundary of the bus company's property. Tall walls hemmed in two sides of the bus station — one hiding an old warehouse, whose ancient asbestos roof peeked over the top of the bricks, the other hiding the backs of a row of Victorian terraced houses, which were the mainstay of the town's bed-and-breakfast trade. The other two sides of the bus station were open to the street.

'That's when I saw her. At first, I thought it was just rubbish because she was between the bins.'

'But you went to have a look anyway?' Sara confirmed.

Briggs nodded, and his eyes glittered. 'I saw the dress flapping in the breeze, and the colour of the skin was wrong.'

'In what way?'

'It was grey.' He sighed. 'I'm glad I did. Poor girl. It might have been Pat or even a child that found her if I hadn't.'

'Did you touch her at all?'

'Not likely,' said Briggs. He pulled the last drag from his cigarette and stubbed it out on the floor. 'I knew she was dead. I'm lifeboat crew. I know a body when I see one.'

CHAPTER 5

Adele was the first of the family to get up — hardly surprising, given how much her husband and eighteen-year-old son,
Xander, had seemed intent on drinking last night at the ball.
Greg had slid into bed next to her a couple of hours after
she'd climbed in, falling asleep quickly and snoring loudly,
as he always did when he'd had too many Whiskey Macs.
It had been a much-disturbed night, and Adele felt groggy
from lack of sleep.

The evening had been one of celebration, both personal
and for the carnival committee. Xander had his two best
friends visiting for carnival week, and they had all received
good A level results on Thursday, paving the way to Oxford
or Cambridge Universities for all three. Greg had also sold an
impressively expensive house to a celebrity, the commission
from which would buy them a holiday in the Caribbean. If
her husband deigned to invite her.

While they had all been getting drunk on the free wine,
Adele had limited herself to one glass of champagne. The
carnival's opening ball was the first in a long series of events
that stretched out in front of the committee for the next eight
days. The whole thing was a feat of organization that she felt
ought to be beyond their capabilities, since the committee

was only made up of local people from the town. Some were small business owners, like the chair, Henry Lacey, one of the small group of inshore fishermen. But somehow they had managed it.

After the speeches, she discreetly left early enough to get some sleep and late enough not to offend anyone. Adele considered herself to be 'only a housewife' these days, and she kept herself to herself. She'd been pleased when she had been invited to join the committee three years before, just when her husband and his partner had relieved her of her part-time job at their estate agency by taking on a full-time administrator, something she still felt aggrieved about. Greg had not objected to her having an interest outside the home, as it seemed he felt that it reflected well on him as a local businessman. So long as Adele never put the committee before his needs or those of their son.

'If I'd wanted you to work full-time, I would have kept you on at the agency,' he'd said. 'I wanted you to take early retirement and look after us at home instead.' But Adele hadn't wanted to take early retirement at forty-five.

There were no easy seats on the committee. Everyone had to work on a project. Adele was in charge of the soap-box derby. Their big day was tomorrow. There were already more than forty entries, and more people always turned up at the start.

She was tucking into a bowl of muesli when her mobile rang. It was Henry Lacey.

'Mornin', Adele. You up, my woman?' Henry's broad Norfolk brogue was well to the fore, which usually meant that he was worried about something. 'You bin watchin' the news?'

'Morning, Henry. No, I haven't. Why?'

'Suthin's up near the bus station. Town's locked solid. Real bad, they say.'

'Hang on.' Adele turned on the small television, which sat at one end of the kitchen island. Tucking her long mousey-brown hair behind her ears, she watched for a moment before picking up the phone again. 'Can't see anything on the news.'

Henry sniffed. 'Dun't matter. I'm goin' down to see, and I want you to join me.'

'I'll drive down in a few minutes.'

'No point. You wun't get any farther than the end of your road. Everywhere is jammed. If you walk, I'll meet you at the top of the Gangway.'

Adele lived halfway up the hill on Roughton Road. The house had been brand new when they had moved here a couple of years ago, Greg insisting that it would be a good investment. She had thought the estate and the expensive detached houses were soulless, but her view hadn't been sought. Naturally non-confrontational, Adele had learned to keep her thoughts to herself over the years, especially in company. Greg had a habit of running her down, especially when he'd been drinking.

Grabbing a cardigan, she set off down the hill, her slim figure moving lightly. Her summer dress flapped around her knees, and she squinted in the sunshine. Sometimes she wished she could wear those tough, long summer shorts that suited a woman of her age, or a pair of trainers. Greg would throw a fit if she wore anything that wasn't 'ladylike', in his opinion, and Adele simply didn't want the argument.

The noise from the traffic jam reached her long before she got to the main road. Some vehicles were turning and heading back the way they had come. A tiny trickle of cars came towards her with each change of the traffic lights. As Adele reached the Gangway, she saw Henry huffing and puffing up the steep incline of the narrow cobbled street. It stretched down the hill to the area on the seafront where the crab fishermen beached their boats to unload their catch. The promenade stretched to either side, leading to the pier one way and beach huts the other.

With little more than a nod in greeting, they set off past the bakery behind the church. Everyone expected the town to be busy at this time of year, but the honking horns, revving engines, shouting and swearing that was echoing up and down the street was not the atmosphere most people would have had in mind. The pavements were packed with grumpy sightseers. Cutting through the supermarket, they got past some of the crowds and reached the coast road. It was shut off. Police were turning vehicles and sending them back out of the town.

'This is chaos,' said Adele. 'Have you spoken to anyone else?'

'Nope. I was up early for the tide.'

Adele knew he would have been lifting and resetting his crab and lobster baskets as soon as the tide and daylight allowed. It was a lucrative time of year for the fishermen as well as everyone else. She felt a quiet pride that Henry had called her first. They pushed through the crowd milling about on the pavement.

'Did you enjoy the dance last night?'

'It was all right,' said Henry. He glanced sideways at her. 'I left just after you.'

'I thought it was a lovely start. I had a word with Karen. She was so proud. Daisy gave such a wonderful speech, and I wanted to congratulate them both.'

'Knew I was right to pick her. She's a good 'un.'

They had reached an exclusion tape stretched across the road. A police officer held up a hand to stop them.

'Can you tell us what's happening?' Adele asked. 'I can see it's an "incident", but can you say if it's serious? How long will the town be closed?'

'What's your interest, madam?' The officer's tone was antagonistic.

'We represent the carnival committee,' said Adele.

Henry nodded in agreement. 'This is a busy day for the town. It'd be grand if we had some idea what's goin' on.'

The officer considered this for a minute, then spoke into a radio. Though he must have understood it, the static obscured the reply, as he explained the need for someone senior to come over. They waited some time before an older man in a suit joined them, with a tall, gangly-looking younger man in tow.

'I'm DC Bowen,' said the older man. 'This is DC Noble.'

'Can you tell us what's going on? Adele asked.

'No, madam,' said DC Bowen. 'I'm afraid the area will be closed for quite some time.'

'Meaning what?' Henry demanded. 'It's Saturday. There's events for the kiddies on the prom and the sandcastle-building competition.'

'Yes, sir. I've looked at your poster with the lists. I'm sorry about the impact on the carnival. However, people will still be able to access the town, and the bus company are organizing themselves as we speak.'

'Who you found, then?' Henry's face turned white under his outdoor summer tan. 'And dun't say that you can't talk about it.'

'I think you should be careful not to spread rumours, sir.' The DC frowned at Henry. 'Now, move along.'

CHAPTER 6

The pavements were becoming crowded. Jessie couldn't complain — she was rubbernecking too. Despite several police officers trying to keep things moving on the roads, it didn't bode well for the day proper. A high-season Saturday was always a big day for the town. Holidaymakers would be leaving their bed and breakfasts by ten and the next set arriving around lunchtime. The daytrippers would also be descending. It was a pleasant sunny day, and the beach would be popular. Carnival events along the prom and on the beach would draw extra crowds. It was madness now, and it could only get worse.

The bus station was shut by that blue-and-white tape the police used. There was a coach in there, along with several cars and two CSI vans. Jessie pursed her lips as she decided what to do next.

A dark saloon car pushed its way across the lines of traffic. It joined the other vehicles in the bus station, and an older man got out. Despite the early hour, the man was wearing a suit with a waistcoat and a jaunty bow tie.

Two people approached the newcomer. Jessie assumed they were detectives. One was a middle-aged man, the other a tall woman. The pair looked relieved to see the suited man. They began to talk.

A sudden honking of vehicle horns was followed by the sound of shouting voices and doors slamming. A traffic queue dispute was about to turn into a fight. Three or four men were yelling obscenities at one another. One marched round to another driver, and they began to go head-to-head, the swearing continuing unabated. Two traffic officers moved swiftly to break it up.

Jessie appreciated a bit of street theatre as much as the next person. She smiled as the officers tried to get everyone back into their respective cars. Turning back to the bus station, she could see that the man in the bow tie had pulled on protective overalls. He collected a large, square leather bag, and the three walked into the alley by Pat's Café.

He must be from Forensics, she thought. *Out in force, someone must be dead.*

If there was a body, it felt macabre to be standing there watching. Whoever it was deserved some privacy. Her stomach grumbled. The bakery was at the other end of the high street.

She had almost reached the top end when she heard more voices. This time it was a distraught woman. Jessie looked up the side road past the café.

'I must see,' said the woman loudly. 'Don't you dare stop me!'

A female uniformed officer was trying to talk to her. Her voice was low, but the woman was getting more hysterical by the second.

'I rang your lot last night,' she shouted. 'Told you my daughter was missing. But you wouldn't listen to me.'

The tall female detective walked quickly over to the sobbing woman, showed her ID and spoke to her.

'I want to see her,' the woman screamed. 'Don't do this to me.' The detective pointed to one of the official cars in the station. The sobbing woman slumped down onto the floor. 'I'm not leaving.'

The older male detective joined them. He also pointed to a car. The woman shook her head again, so the man knelt beside the woman, talking quietly. She watched him with a transfixed stare. When he finished, he helped her up. The female detective drove over in one of the cars and tried to guide the woman into the back seat. Suddenly, the woman let out a howl. The sound was primal.

It cut through Jessie's thoughts and churned her stomach. It also made her angry. No one should have been able to witness that, whatever was going on. Feeling like a voyeur, Jessie pushed through the crowd and hurried away.

CHAPTER 7

Sara felt guilty that they had not tried harder to persuade Karen Shaw to sit in DI Edwards's car. Even though they could not show Mrs Shaw the body, there seemed little doubt that the victim was her daughter from the mother's description. When the woman had started to wail, Sara had pulled her into a hug out of instinct, even though they weren't supposed to touch people these days. Mrs Shaw had allowed herself to be guided into the back seat, and they were taking her home.

'I can't believe it,' sobbed Mrs Shaw. 'Who can have done this to her?'

The Shaws' house was in a side street off the Runton Road. Edwards pulled into the drive as there was no room to park on the street — random cars were driving up and down, trying to avoid the jam. Sara helped Mrs Shaw inside.

'Karen? What's going on, love?' Mr Shaw was in the kitchen. His wife rushed to him, flinging herself into his arms. He glanced at Sara, who was following discreetly. 'Who are you?'

'Fred! Oh, Fred! It's our Daisy.'

Fred shushed his wife as if she were a child. 'There, there.'

'I'm DS Sara Hirst.' Sara showed her warrant card and introduced the DI behind her. 'Mrs Shaw was down at the bus station. I take it you've heard the news this morning?'

'About the town being closed? Yes. What has that to do with us? What's happened?' The colour drained from his face. His wife wailed again, and he hugged her tightly.

'Perhaps we could sit down?' Sara asked.

Fred steered them all into the living room. He sat on the sofa, pulling his weeping wife down with him and into his arms. There were photographs everywhere. Portraits of the family, landscapes, seascapes, close-ups of animals and birds. Most of all, there were pictures of Daisy Shaw — smiling, running in races, playing on the beach as a child, as an adult leaning on the balustrade of the pier.

'It's my hobby,' said Fred, as Sara looked at the dozens of framed photos. 'Sell them to calendar or postcard people sometimes. Go on then. Say it.'

Sara said it. She sat opposite the couple and told them that a body had been found. A body that was very likely to be that of their daughter. The DI hovered in the doorway. Karen moaned quietly. Her wailing and sobbing had played out for now. Fred turned ashen, and he rocked his wife in his arms as though to comfort himself as much as her.

'I'm afraid we will need you to formally identify her,' finished Sara.

'Are you sure it's her?'

'This is your daughter?' She pointed to a beautiful portrait, taken on the beach, backlit by a setting sun. Fred nodded. Sara glanced at the DI, who also nodded. 'Then I'm as sure as I can be, without your confirmation.'

'Karen said something was wrong when Daisy didn't come home last night. I just thought she'd gone on somewhere with a friend, and who could blame her? She's not a child.'

'When did you last see Daisy?' Edwards asked. Karen groaned and leaned into her husband even harder.

'We all went to the ball last night,' said Fred. 'Daisy is Carnival Queen this year. We're so proud of her. She looked so beautiful.'

'I treated her to a special dress.' Karen turned to her husband. 'Daisy looked so lovely in it. Like one of those old film stars you're so fond of.'

'Like Marlene Dietrich or Bette Davis in their heyday.' Fred leaned down the side of the sofa and pulled up a camera bag stuffed with equipment. He pulled out an expensive-looking digital camera, turned it on and concentrated on the screen, flicking through images. He handed over the camera to Sara. 'Like this.'

Sara looked at the small image. Daisy looked elegant in a long sheath dress in a pale green, silky fabric, which clung in folds against her neat figure. Her hair had been put up into a soft topknot, with some strands woven into a small plastic tiara, and wispy tendrils falling around her chin and shoulders. She did indeed look beautiful.

'Where did you take the picture?' Sara asked.

'In the marquee on Carnival Field.' Fred waved vaguely towards the main road. 'The ball is the first event. Daisy's first task as Carnival Queen was to make a speech and open the carnival.'

'May I keep the camera for a while? Have a look at your photos?'

'If it will help.' Fred's voice trailed away into a gulp.

'We bought her a bottle of champagne,' said Karen. Her tone sounded wistful. 'To congratulate her. She was dancing with boy after boy. Young men, really, I suppose. We left the ball just after ten.'

'Daisy can do as she wants, even though she lives with us,' said Fred. 'But she's a good girl. If she thinks we might worry, she lets us know. Tells us where she's staying, like at a friend's house.'

'Not last night?' Sara wasn't going to mention that Fred was still speaking of his daughter in the present tense. Let the poor couple come to terms with things in their own time.

Karen fiddled with the ball of damp tissues in her hand. 'I sent her a text to say we'd gone home and to let us know how she was.'

'How long was it before you began to worry about her?' Sara asked.

'I got up for the loo in the night. I looked into Daisy's bedroom, and it was empty. My mobile was in the kitchen, so I checked it.'

'No message?'

'No. I tried to call her phone, but it just kept switching to voicemail. That's when I woke Fred up.'

'I walked back to the field.' Fred took up their story. 'The place was deserted. I walked down as far as the pier. I didn't see a soul.'

'And since then?'

'We've rung and rung her mobile. She never answered.' Karen was shaking now. Fred took her hand in his. Tears were streaming down his face. 'I've kept ringing her and ringing her. Making cups of tea and waiting. When I heard it on the radio, I just knew.'

Karen leaned towards Sara. 'She's our only child. You have to catch whoever did this.'

CHAPTER 8

Adele and Henry were moved politely but firmly away from the cordon. As they struggled through the crowd, Henry placed a hand on Adele's arm.

'Look,' he said. They watched as a car drove from the bus station to the tape and was let out.

'Was that Mrs Shaw?' asked Henry.

Adele had recognised the white, frozen face, too and nodded, as sure as she could be. 'My God,' she breathed. 'I hope that doesn't mean what I think it does.'

Without speaking, Henry led her gently through the gossiping people, down to the prom and along to the pier. The first of the children's events was starting soon. The committee ran most events with volunteers, but with some grant money, they had employed a couple of local young women to work with the children this year.

This morning, the pair had set up trestle tables at the top of the steps that formed part of the pier entrance. Hundreds of small pebbles and beach rocks were laid out, along with pots of paint, brushes and plastic aprons. On the prom itself, they had set up child-sized tables and chairs. A tinny megaphone crackled and announced the pebble-painting competition.

A steady stream of children and parents chose pebbles and collected paint equipment. The organizers filled out entry forms to sit under the completed artwork until a guest judge, a local teacher, would pick her favourites later in the day. A large pile of packets of baby wipes stood waiting at one end of the trestle tables.

The walk had helped clear Adele's head, and she was pleased to see things were progressing as they ought to be. Henry walked beside her. His rolling fisherman's gait was somehow calming. His companionable silence demanded nothing of her.

'Let's go for a coffee,' suggested Henry.

They wove their way along the boardwalk. It was busy with people of all ages enjoying an old-fashioned airing and the summer sunshine. Henry queued for their drink in the theatre bar, while Adele managed to grab two seats at a picnic table outside.

'What do you think is goin' on, then?' Henry asked as he put down their cups.

'I'm not sure.'

Henry tipped several sachets of sugar into his latte and stirred it thoughtfully. Adele gazed out across the bay to the Overstrand Cliffs. The beach was full of laughing families laying out picnics, buckets and spades. There were groups windsurfing or paddle-boarding, and the beach lifeguards' hut was manned as always at this time of year. It was a far cry from the chaos in the town.

'I think it's suthin' to do with Daisy. Which is gonna be real sad if I'm right. She's a lovely lass.'

'You suggested her for Carnival Queen, didn't you?'

'That I did. Thought she would be good at it, and I was right.'

'What will we do if it is her?'

'Speak to her parents first. That's only right. Maybe you could?'

Henry let the question hang. Adele knew that he meant that it might be easier to talk to a woman, but it wasn't easier for her. She was too shy. Nor could she imagine what Daisy's parents might be going through now.

'I think we should wait a bit,' she said with a shudder. 'Until we know more.'

'Fair enough. You enjoy last night, then?'

'Yes, I did.'

'Who were those other boys you brought?'

'They're Xander's friends. He's known them for years.'

'I didn't recognise 'em.'

'They were roommates at Langton Hall. Jacob's going to Oxford with Xander. Benji opted for Cambridge.'

Adele realised she had just made the boys sound like the privileged kids that they were. Her husband had insisted on Xander being privately educated and boasted of his ability to pay the expensive fees. Adele's own schooling had ended after training to be a secretary at Norwich City College back in the nineties.

'Drank a fair bit.'

Adele squirmed uncomfortably at the implied criticism, though she knew Henry was right. All of them had been getting loud before she had left the ball, encouraged by her husband. 'They're all eighteen.'

'Made a bit of a fuss, I hear.'

'I'll have a word,' she said, knowing she wouldn't.

'You all sorted for tomorrow?' Henry had made his point and was changing the subject.

'I hope so. Look, I'd better get home.'

'So soon? Will I see you tonight at the karaoke?'

Karaoke was not her thing, even it if was Henry's. He had a splendid voice and took every opportunity to sing. He was also a staunch member of the Sheringham Shantymen folk choir, who would be giving a concert in the marquee on Tuesday night.

'Maybe. Bye Henry.' Suddenly, Adele felt glad to get away. Henry was a good friend, possibly her only friend. But she couldn't afford to be seen spending too much time with him, or there would be hell to pay at home.

The pebble-painting was in full swing on the prom, and Adele was pleased to see the theatre's stage manager, Pete Wheeler, there with his two toddlers. His wife leaned wearily on the beach wall as Pete sat painting with the boys at a table. She was expecting their third in a few weeks. Adele headed home up the hill. Unused to walking that much, she was breathing heavily by the time she let herself into the kitchen.

'Where have you been?' her husband demanded. He was slumped on a high stool at the breakfast bar, clutching a half-finished glass of orange juice. An open packet of paracetamol told her all she needed to know.

'Up long?'

'No.'

'The boys?'

'Not a peep. Make some coffee.' It wasn't a request. It was a demand. Greg glowered at her.

Adele busied herself with cleaning the cafetière and making a fresh pot to avoid the critical comment that might follow. While it brewed, she went upstairs to rouse Xander and his guests. She knocked at the first spare bedroom. A grunt gave her permission to pop her head around the door. Benji lay tangled in a sheet on one of the single beds. The other hadn't been used.

'Coffee downstairs,' she said. 'When you're ready.'

Benji blinked blearily at her before mustering a smile. 'Sure. I'll be down in a few minutes.'

Jacob was supposed to be sharing the spare room with Benji, but after knocking on her son's door, she was unsurprised to see the two young men passed out on the sofa. Several empty beer cans lay scattered on the carpet in front of them. Xander's television flickered random frozen images from the computer console attached to it.

'Morning,' she said with a cheerfulness she didn't really feel. All she could think of was Karen Shaw's ashen face. Jacob groaned as she opened the curtains to let in the sunshine. 'Coffee's ready downstairs.'

Xander muttered a selection of expletives that Adele didn't approve of him using, though she said nothing. She gathered up some of the dirty clothes from her son's bedroom floor and left them to it.

In the kitchen, Greg had his head in his hands. Adele walked past him into the utility room to load the washing machine. Only she couldn't, as there was already a set of washing in there.

CHAPTER 9

DI Edwards and Sara left the grieving Shaws' house with the promise of appointing a family liaison officer and providing regular updates. They crossed the Runton Road through the traffic inching around the diversion. On the other side, they walked past the pitch-and-putt green to reach the wide footpath that ran the length of the resort. It wound above sandy cliffs, which fell steeply down to the promenade and beach almost a hundred metres below.

'Carnival Field is up there,' said Edwards, and they turned away from the town.

At the end of the footpath, a wooden café with a thatched roof stood above a large grassy field. It was used as an overflow car park, and there was a steady stream of vehicles manoeuvring or unpacking families laden down with beach clutter. It was difficult to watch a typical family fun day out when Sara had left two bewildered and bereft parents to their grief a few minutes ago. She pulled herself up to her full height and strode across the grass.

At the far end of the field, a funfair had been set up. Sara could see various rides and stalls, lights blazing in the sunshine advertising that the place was open for business. A large white marquee had been pitched between the funfair

37

and the car park. It looked shut, until they got closer. There was a van at the cliff end, and a man was moving between its open back doors and a flap at the rear of the tent.

'Good morning,' said DI Edwards, as the man emerged. They both opened their warrant cards.

'How can I help you?'

'Do you help to run the carnival?'

'I do.' The man held out his hand to each of them in turn. 'Brian Medler. Call me Brian. I'm in charge of the bar and dances.'

'Like last night? Was it busy?'

'Sold out.' Brian picked up a shrink-wrapped tray of beer cans. 'Come on in.'

The bar that Brian was restocking stood at one end of the marquee. At the other was a stage with tables on it. Around the edges, there were stacks of plastic chairs. Tables with their folding legs tucked away lay in a pile. The air inside smelled of trampled grass and spilled booze.

'Is it ticket holders only?' Sara asked.

'On the first and last nights,' said Brian. He offered tins of cheap cola to them, then opened one for himself. 'We're supposed to be self-financing, you see.'

'I thought most of the events were free.'

'So they are. We get a bit of sponsorship from local firms and help for the children's events from the council. We need to make what money we can on official dances like last night. Ticket money and bar takings from the events we have up here make all the difference.'

'How many would there be, and is there a list of who attended?'

'Capacity is four hundred,' said Brian. 'I have the names of who bought the tickets at any rate, if not who they were all for. I can send you a copy.'

Sara pulled out a card with her contact details. 'Thank you, that would be helpful. So how did the evening go?'

'Well enough. It's an odd night, in as much as some people pay to get in, and the rest are local bigwigs. Or at least, that's how they think of themselves. Freeloaders, I call them.'

'Freeloaders?' Edwards sounded surprised.

Brian frowned. 'Sorry, shouldn't call them that, I suppose — our beloved district councillors, the mayor and so forth. Always first at the buffet and the free drinks.'

'The same last night?'

Brian nodded. He put the tray of beers on top of a pile of identical ones. They obviously sold a lot of the stuff.

'And did it all go to plan?'

'Pretty much. Young Daisy made a lovely speech and opened the carnival. The disco played until closing.'

'How was Daisy?'

'Oh, she was having a fine old time. Drinking that champagne her mum had asked me to get for her and dancing with those boys who came with the Haywards.'

'Did you notice her leave?'

'No, not after those buggers from the funfair turned up.'

'Funfair?' Edwards asked sharply. 'Did they have tickets?'

'No, they bloody didn't. You see, the funfair shuts at eleven. Our licence runs until midnight. By that time, it's mostly the diehards and the youngsters.'

'People came here after visiting the funfair?'

'Not their customers, the Traveller boys. The little sods unlaced a section of the tent over there and let themselves in. We didn't realise because it was behind the disco.' Brian pointed to a corner of the tent behind the stage.

Sara winced at the prejudice in Brian's tone. 'They caused a problem?'

'We only have a couple of security guys. Anyway, the lads bought some drinks, so I thought that was fair enough. It was late, and "every little helps", as they say. It was when they started dancing with Daisy that the trouble started.'

'Daisy didn't like it?'

'No, quite the opposite. I think she'd had a bit by then, and she likes a dance. One of the Traveller lads cut in and pushed Xander out of the way.'

'Xander?' Sara asked.

'Mrs Hayward's son. He didn't like it much.'

39

'I can imagine.' Edwards shrugged. 'And then?'

'She was getting a bit wiggly,' said Brian. He looked embarrassed. 'If you get my meaning.'

'Not really.'

'You know, getting wiggly with it. Isn't that what they say?' Brian looked at Sara as if she should be able to answer.

She raised an eyebrow. 'I'm afraid my clubbing days are over.'

'Mine too,' said Edwards. 'And this caused a problem?'

'I didn't see exactly. There was a rush on at the bar. I heard a bit of shouting and name-calling. When I surfaced, they had all gone.'

'All of them?'

'Xander, his mates and his dad, the funfair lads and Daisy. I think Joe and Phil threw the lot of them out.'

CHAPTER 10

Greg was talking on his mobile when Adele returned to the kitchen. Although he kept his voice low, he made no attempt to turn away. She felt her heart sinking. Who could Greg be talking to now? Sometimes she wondered where on earth the handsome, caring man she'd married had vanished to.

Some of it might be stress, she admitted to herself. Greg and his partner had expanded their estate agency three years ago. It was the reason they had taken on a full-time assistant, and Adele had been dismissed. They had become so successful at selling high-end country retreats to wealthy Londoners that his partner had taken early retirement last year. The older man had headed off to Florida after Greg had bought him out, but her husband clearly missed his guiding hand. Certainly, his behaviour had begun to change from the moment Eric had jetted off to warmer climes. Or at least, not long afterwards.

Perhaps it was her fault, as he so often suggested. It was the excuse he used when he yelled at her, or even slapped or punched her. *Look what you made me do.* Not that she ever had. Adele never spoke back or opposed anything he said. She didn't question where he went or how much he drank. Nor did she object when he began to treat Xander like a protégé

41

rather than his son. The house was immaculate, the chores always done and food on the table whenever he expected it. She tried to give him no excuse to criticise her. Adele knew she ought to find some courage and talk to him about things, to stand up for herself. But it wasn't as simple as that. It never was. She couldn't anticipate his reactions, and his temper was becoming ever more extreme. Fear kept her silent.

'You'll have to wait,' Greg said into the phone. He took a mouthful of the coffee Adele had placed in front of him and then spat it out. 'For fuck's sake, woman. It burned my mouth.'

He slammed the cup down, slopping the contents onto the countertop and floor. Adele flinched and stepped backwards. When Greg carried on his call, she moved away to the sink.

'I'm on holiday. Tell them I'll get back to them next week.'

Adele heard a female voice speaking heatedly enough for the sound to escape from where her husband held the mobile lightly against his cheek. Something about an extremely good sale.

'You deal with it then. That's what I pay you for.'

Greg dropped the mobile with a clatter onto the breakfast bar. The back of Adele's neck prickled with anxiety as her husband stepped up behind her. She had been foolish to turn her back on him when he was in this sort of mood.

Adele was five-and-a-half feet tall. Greg was nearly six inches taller and well-built from his rugby playing days. He leaned heavily against her, pinning her to the sink, his hips grinding against the small of her back. He reached past her and took a clean mug from the draining board. The pressure drove most of the air from Adele's lungs, making her gasp for breath.

'I should punish you,' he murmured. 'You hurt me. Say sorry.'

'Sorry,' she wheezed. Greg pushed even harder against her. The handle on the cupboard door drove into the front of her thigh. 'I'm sorry. Really.'

He laughed, dropped his head and pecked a kiss into the nape of her neck. The sound of one of their young guests coming down the stairs made Greg turn away. He poured himself another coffee. Adele picked up a cleaning cloth and began to clear up the spilled drink. The atmosphere in the room was so obvious that Benji halted in the kitchen doorway, unsure if he should come in.

Greg pointed to the cafetière. 'Coffee? Help yourself.' He smiled at Adele as if nothing had just happened, then went upstairs. Adele waited until she heard their bedroom door close, then went into the utility room.

The dirty clothes she had brought from Xander's room lay in a basket. Adele opened the washing machine and pulled out the wet items. She couldn't remember putting these on to wash, especially not a load like this. Greg's black sweatshirts and tracksuit bottoms were mixed with Xander's smartest clothes. She tutted to herself, knowing that some of this should have been dry cleaned. Sorting the items out, she put some into the tumble dryer and hung the rest on a drying rack before putting on the second load.

Adele went into the downstairs toilet and locked herself in. Pulling up her skirt, she checked the front of her legs. A bruise was already forming where the kitchen cabinet handle had been forced against her thigh. She winced when she touched it. At least no one would be able to see it there. She returned to the kitchen.

Benji was perched on one of the high stools at the breakfast bar. 'Lovely coffee.'

'Would you like something to eat? A croissant or cereal?'

He smiled, accepting a croissant without any butter or jam. He pulled the end from it, dipped the morsel into his coffee and dropped the melting mass into his mouth clumsily. She poured herself a glass of orange juice and began to potter around the kitchen.

'Do you have any idea what you three might be doing today?'

'Not really.' Benji dipped more pastry and ate it. The caffeine and sugar seemed to be perking him up.

'I'm just wondering about meals, that's all. Maybe I should just do something simple that you could heat up if you wanted it. Shepherd's pie?'

'Lovely.' Benji finished his croissant and reached for another before looking at her. 'Is that OK? Can I have two?'

'Of course,' said Adele. He had far better manners than her own son, she reflected. Or her husband. The other thing that struck her was how, at eighteen, their physiques were dominated by their choice of sports at school. Benji was tall and slim, a middle-distance runner of considerable promise, Xander had told her. Jacob was shorter, well-built and strong, while Xander was between the two in height, thickset and heavily muscled. The pair owed their bulkier physiques to rugby training.

Greg breezed through the kitchen, his hair still wet from the shower. Grabbing his keys and mobile, he pecked her on the cheek. 'Back soon.'

When she was certain his car had driven down the road, Adele sat opposite Benji and smiled at him. 'Another?'

'No, thank you, Mrs Hayward.' Shaking his head, Benji pushed the plate towards her, and she casually took a croissant.

'You can call me Adele. Better ask Xander's dad what he prefers you to call him.'

'Sure thing.' Benji smiled at her.

'Did you enjoy last night? I'm sorry I had to leave so early. I have committee things to do today.'

'No problem. It was good,' said Benji with a shrug.

'You stayed out late?' Adele felt like she was grilling the poor lad.

'Yeah, for a while. To be honest, the marquee thing was a bit . . . you know.'

'Old-fashioned?'

'I guess. When Greg said they were going down the pub, I wasn't surprised.'

'Only Henry said something to me about a disturbance,' Adele probed.

'Henry?'

'One of the carnival committee.'

'I didn't see anything.' Benji's eyes flickered over her shoulder, avoiding contact with hers. 'They said there was this band on at the pub.'

'Did you enjoy the band more?'

'Oh, well, I . . .' Benji mangled his words, trying to formulate his reply. 'To be honest, I didn't go. I don't really drink. It doesn't suit me. I have my running to think of.'

Almost too sensible for eighteen, Adele thought.

'I said I'd be all right to drive. Greg gave me his keys, and I went back to the car park to fetch his motor.'

Greg had insisted on driving them up to Carnival Field the previous evening. The monstrous Porsche Cayenne was his pride and joy. Adele was surprised that Benji had been allowed to drive it. No one was usually allowed to even touch it. 'You brought them all back here?'

'Well, no,' admitted Benji. The colour was rising on his forehead under his floppy blonde fringe. 'Just me. There's a door key with the car set.' Benji pulled the key ring from his pocket and placed it on the breakfast bar. 'I thought you would be asleep and didn't want to disturb you. So, I just let myself in and went to bed.'

CHAPTER 11

Sara and DI Edwards walked down the clifftop path towards the town.

'We'd better get an update,' said Edwards. 'See what the Doc has to say.'

The Runton Road turned at the corner by the petrol station owned by the supermarket. The traffic had eased, and Sara assumed that the roadblocks were now functioning better outside the town. Crowds of families were still roaming around the streets, looking in the shop windows or heading for the beach. As they went beyond the cordon, Sara could hear the bustle of the town behind the four-storey houses, which lined most of the streets near the seafront.

The roads around the bus station were eerily quiet in comparison. A discreet private ambulance stood in the yard. Dr Taylor was supervising the removal of their victim. She was zipped up in a black body bag and laid on a gurney. The crew lifted her with care inside the vehicle. A group of FIs were on their hands and knees, doing a fingertip search of the floor around Pat's Café and in the alley. Bowen and Noble were sat on a bench on the veranda, mugs of tea in their hands, deep in conversation. Sara waved them over.

'Inspector,' Dr Taylor said curtly. 'How are the parents?'

'Not good,' Edwards admitted. 'Couldn't be otherwise. Can you tell us anything yet?'

'You've already identified our victim. I'll run the usual checks to confirm.'

'Her father will do the formal ID,' Sara said.

'Give me until Monday before you bring him over, will you? There are some things I want to do first.'

'Preliminary report? I assume it's murder?' Edwards spoke quietly as the other detectives gathered around to listen.

'Daisy has been attacked, certainly.'

'Time of death?'

'I would say sometime between 10 p.m. and 2 a.m. last night. She has been out here in the open for several hours, lying on her back. Rigor has set in, and she has distinct signs of livor mortis. The blood has pooled in her back, her calf muscles and the underside of her arms.'

Sara recollected the grey pallor of Daisy's face. Next to her, DC Noble shuffled uncomfortably. DC Bowen took the younger detective a few yards away and spoke quietly with him.

'What kind of attack. Can you be more specific?'

'I can see red marks on her neck and face, bruising to her arms, and sand embedded in her hair on the back of her head. Her fingernails have debris under them, which I'll get analysed.'

'Blood or wounds?'

'No.' Dr Taylor shook his head. 'At least, not on the first inspection.'

'Has she been . . .' DI Edwards faltered.

'I didn't feel it appropriate to check in situ,' replied Dr Taylor. 'Another job for the lab. Her clothes are intact, but there is one thing I suggest you start with.'

'What?'

'She isn't wearing any shoes. The soles of her feet are dirty, as if she walked barefoot somewhere. The tops of her toes are covered in grazes, which is very odd.'

'We need to find her shoes urgently, then,' agreed Edwards.

'And no handbag. I don't believe Daisy would have been out without one. We've checked the alley, including the bins, and no joy.'

'Sir,' Sara interrupted. She brought out the camera that she had taken from Fred Shaw. 'We have that picture of her.'

She fiddled with the buttons, unable to do more than turn it on.

'I might be able to do it.' DC Noble held out his hand. 'It's like the one my Dad has.'

Dr Taylor gave the all-clear to the ambulance crew, who set off back to the mortuary in Norwich. He stripped off his protective layers, gathered up his work bag and dumped them in his car. 'I'll be in touch as soon as I can. Give me a few hours, and I'll be able to confirm some more details.'

Noble examined the back of the camera, pressed a couple of buttons, and the picture of Daisy in her ballgown appeared in the viewing aperture. He shielded it from the sunlight so they could all see the image.

'There's a handbag,' Sara pointed at the edge of the picture, where a bag lay on a table. 'I bet that's hers. It's green like her dress.'

'Shoes?' Edwards asked.

'Hard to see,' said Noble. 'Her dress is rather long. Let me zoom in.'

Sara took the camera and examined the magnified image. 'I can see spikey heels. And straps on her toes. The straps are green, I think. Evening shoes, to go with her outfit. Fit for a queen.'

'Noble, can you download that image and get it circulated?'

He nodded. 'I'd need to do it in the office.'

Sara handed over the camera.

'I'll take you,' said Bowen.

'Mike, you track down any town CCTV while you're waiting for Noble to be clever. Whoever it belongs to. From 8 p.m. to 8 a.m., after our driver found the body.'

Bowen pulled the car keys from his pocket. Noble returned the camera to the evidence bag.

'When you've done it, Ian,' continued Edwards, 'let me know. I'll arrange for local backup to go round the shops and restaurants. We need to ask them to check their backyards and bins. Best we do that today, so get a move on.'

'Sir!' snapped the pair and headed off.

'Lunch?' Edwards asked Sara. She was startled by this. He pointed up to the café on its decking. 'Pat may have seen something or have CCTV and will know the area better than most.'

The owner was putting dirty mugs on a tray when they approached.

'Can we have a word?' asked Sara. 'And a sandwich, if you've got one.'

'Dozens of the bloody things,' said Pat grumpily. 'All going to waste. You'd best come inside.'

CHAPTER 12

The shelves in Pat's fridge were stacked with wrapped sand-wiches, all *freshly made on the premises*, said a handwritten sign. Sara selected some for herself and the DI, ordered drinks and settled down at a table inside, opposite her boss. When Pat appeared with mugs of tea, Edwards invited her to join them. She took off her tabard, which covered her ample figure. Her face and arms were tanned, Sara noticed as Pat settled on a spare chair. There was no make-up in evidence, and the café owner could have been any age from forty to sixty.

'Do you have CCTV at all?' Edwards asked, unwrap-ping a roll stuffed with chicken and salad.

'Sorry, no. There are cameras all over the bus station, so I don't need it really. Too expensive for me.'

'What time did you get here this morning?'

'Six.' Pat indicated the sandwich display. 'I open at seven. It takes me an hour to get enough stuff ready.'

'You run the place on your own?' Sara looked around the café. With the benches outside and the tables inside, it would seat at least fifty people.

'Some of the time. Not in the summer. I have a couple of girls help me when it's the holiday season and on Saturdays.'

'Casual staff?'

'Yeah, teenagers mostly. During their holidays from school or college. Most of them don't stay long. One season, maybe two.'

'Not today?'

'When I saw what was going on, I rang the pair of them and said not to come in.'

'You didn't go home yourself?'

'I thought I'd stay.' Pat folded her arms and looked at Edwards, who ignored the challenge. 'You never know, I might be able to salvage some opening time later. I'll need to. I've lost a good day's trade as it is.'

'Tell me about this morning,' Edwards said, turning his full attention to Pat. Sara knew he had been listening closely — it just wouldn't seem that way to the café owner.

'I had done quite a bit when David came in. I let the early drivers have something if they want it, even if I'm not officially open. He bought a butty and a drink and went back out. I had the radio on, so I didn't realise anything had happened until I heard the siren.'

'Were you surprised that something might be wrong?'

'Not at first,' she admitted. 'We get the occasional tramp sleeping in the alley or the bus station. I thought it was that sort of thing.'

'It isn't a homeless person,' said Sara. She folded the film from her roll and left it on her plate.

'Daisy Shaw?' asked Pat. Sara kept her face neutral under Pat's stare. 'I saw her mum. Is it Daisy? Because she was a nice kid. She started working for me when she was at school.'

'Does she still work for you now?' Edwards asked.

'Not for years. She's now assistant manager at Waves, the restaurant on the pier. Doing well for herself. Carnival Queen. Looked lovely last night.'

'You went to the ball?'

'All the local business owners go,' said Pat.

'So, you saw Daisy last night? Who was she with?'

51

'Her mum and dad to start with. Then she danced with those young lads who came with Greg Hayward. When those funfair lads came in, it got a bit nasty.'

'In what way?'

'Daisy seemed to know one of them.' Pat chewed her lip thoughtfully. 'I don't pay much attention to the funfair. It's not my thing. But it's popular, and the same family come each summer. Maybe she had met him before.'

Pat seemed to prefer talking to Edwards. Sara leaned back in her chair and watched.

'What happened then?'

'It kicked off when Daisy refused to dance with Hayward's son again. The lads started getting loud and shoving one another about. His dad just stood there laughing.'

'A fight broke out?'

'Not really. The security guards appeared and chucked them all out. When I left, there was no sign of any of them.'

'Do you think you would be able to identify them again?'

'Maybe. The youngsters were with Hayward, so he'll know who they were. Don't know about the funfair people.'

Sara took the details for Greg Hayward.

'He's an estate agent, really,' said Pat with a smirk. 'Gives it a fancy name, but that's what he does. Has a posh office in Holt. Thinks he's too good for the likes of us in Cromer. His wife is nice, though. She's on the carnival committee.'

Edwards thanked Pat, then waved at the piles of food. 'Why don't you take a selection of this lot round the officers and forensic people? Then you won't lose all your stock.' He dropped three twenty-pound notes on the table.

Pat beamed at him. Sara looked at the DI in surprise. Being sensitive to witnesses was not one of his strong points in her experience. He didn't meet her look as she piled up their crockery.

'That was kind, sir,' said Sara as they left.

'Self-interest,' replied Edwards. 'Keep her on side.'

'Not to mention the team, who will be getting free sandwiches.'

Edwards grunted. 'I think we should go to the pier, don't you?'

It was no more than a couple of minutes' walk to the ramps that led down to the promenade. The pier stretched out over the North Sea, its wooden boards and gleaming white wind-shelters crammed with holidaymakers. Families crowded around the entrance, where a PA system blared out children's songs, and someone dressed as a clown encouraged people to join in silly actions and dance moves. There were hundreds of people down there. More groups were walking up and down the promenade itself. They sat outside cafés having lunch or ran in and out of the amusement arcade.

'Traditional British summer scene,' said Edwards as they wove down the zigzag path. Sara wasn't sure if he was being sarcastic or if he enjoyed the idea.

The noise increased as they hit the prom. The clown began singing, seriously out of tune, and the group around him joined in or screamed with laughter. Trestle tables overloaded with painted pebbles blocked part of the walkway. Families bickered — some laughed, others tried to calm overemotional children who were crying. You either loved this or hated it, Sara reasoned. Brought up on Sundays at Camden Lock, Sara loved it.

'Half of them will be drinking,' said Edwards.

Hates it, Sara thought.

'The rest will be caught up in the events and not paying any attention. It's not going to be easy finding Daisy's shoes and bag in all of this.'

CHAPTER 13

Unlike on weekdays, the Saturday matinée didn't start until 4 p.m. Something to do with guest house changeover times, Jessie had always assumed. It meant that there was precious little time between the end of the first show and the second at 8 p.m. Despite living ten minutes' walk away, she always took a packed lunch on Saturdays. She dumped her bags in her locker in the green room and ran two steps at a time up the wide stairs to the soundbox. There was something she loved about being there on her own, doing the setup and sound checks in the empty auditorium and dressing rooms.

Jessie removed and folded the cover that protected the mixing desk and pushed it under the table. Following her routine, she fired up the racks in the gallery's lighting box, turned on the rest of the equipment, and ran her checks. Then, taking a handful of batteries, she went backstage through the pass door. The dressing rooms were unlocked, which meant that Pete was already in his office. Each artiste with a speaking or singing part had a head mic attached to a battery pack, which they hid underneath their costumes. Jessie went from room to room, checking each individual set and changing the batteries.

The two lead singers had their own rooms. Ricky Easton's door was open, his mirror lights on. When she knocked, there was no response. She poked her head around, saw gratefully that the singer was absent and checked the mic. Hallie was next in line. Her door was closed. Jessie could see electric light under the door, and voices murmured inside.

Don't they have digs to go to? she thought sarcastically. *I hope they aren't having sex in the bloody dressing rooms. That carpet never gets cleaned.* She rapped sharply at the door. 'Only me. Mic check.'

Jessie waited for a moment, then opened the door a few inches. Hallie was sitting in front of her mirror, still in her street clothes and without a scrap of make-up. Her beautiful face was rigid with what looked like shock. The mic pack sat on the end of her dressing table. There was a frigid atmosphere in the room, and someone was seated on a chair behind the door.

'Can I just check your pack?' Jessie reached through the door and easily picked it up. She pulled the door closed and stood in the corridor to run her checks, then knocked again. 'All done.'

Opening the door just wide enough for her arm, she lay the set back on the table.

'Thank you,' croaked Hallie.

Jessie smiled and closed the door. Neither occupant of the room took into account that the full-length mirror for that room was on the far wall, where Jessie could see quite clearly who was behind the door. Ricky Easton was sitting on the chair, his head bowed and his arms around himself. In the brief glimpse she got, his face was drawn and ashen. There might have been a neat pair of bruises on his chin, or it might have been stubble.

'I don't know why I do it,' she heard Ricky mutter. 'But I can't seem to stop.'

Hallie made a shushing sound. Jessie made a point of opening the next dressing room door noisily to show she'd moved on.

Something to do with their damn affair, she thought, checking the last pack. *Or whatever last night was about. He'll be dumping her soon, just like he did me.*

Checks completed, she popped into Pete's office. 'Afternoon. How are you? Had a nice morning with the kids?'

'Took them to the pebble decorating. Paint got everywhere.'

'They're only little.'

He swivelled around on his chair to face her. He looked grim. 'Have you heard? It's all over town.'

'They found someone near the bus station, didn't they?'

'Daisy Shaw.'

Jessie let out a grunt. 'Our Daisy? From the restaurant?'

'And Carnival Queen.'

'Oh my God.' Jessie sat on a spare office chair with a thump. She couldn't remember if she had ever met Daisy's mother, but the sound of the poor woman's cry still rang in her head.

'Killed and dumped, I've heard. Sometime during the night. The first bus driver into the station this morning found her.'

'Murdered?'

'Sounds like it.'

'In Cromer? That sort of thing never happens here.'

'Well, it has now, and this week of all weeks.' His voice wobbled with emotion.

Jessie stared at Pete. His eyes were focused in the middle distance. Daisy was part of the permanent pier staff. They all knew one another, liked one another. Some of them had even been at school together.

'Do you know what I've been thinking?' Pete asked.

Jessie shook her head.

'What if it had been my wife?' Pete snuffled, then blew his nose and cleared his throat.

'Joy wouldn't have been out late,' said Jessie.

'This week is different. The streets are noisy, pubs open late. If the kids can't sleep, she takes them out for a walk in

56

the double buggy. It's warm enough at this time of year, and the fresh air helps.'

Pete lived with his family in a small terrace house on one of the side streets in the middle of the town, not that far from Jessie's cottage. 'Last night?'

'She was just coming in with them when I got home.'

Jessie digested this information in silence. Pete and Joy were both local, had known each other since they were in their teens. Carnival week was as exciting for this young couple as it was for everyone else. She couldn't blame Joy for wanting to take in some of the atmosphere while her husband worked late. 'Maybe she should wait for you in future. Until this is sorted out.'

He nodded. 'Anyway, we have to brace ourselves. I think they'll want to speak to all the staff here.'

'In case it's someone she knew? They say it often is, don't they? And the performers as well?'

'I expect so. They'll be wrong, though.'

'Why?'

'It will be some incomer,' said Pete vehemently. 'No one around here would do such a thing. It will be someone here for the carnival.'

CHAPTER 14

By the time Greg returned, Xander and Jacob had also surfaced. Adele was grateful that they had managed to shower and put on clean clothes before reconvening in the kitchen. She handed out croissants, coffee and juice, as Greg loaded tins of beer and a bottle of vodka onto the kitchen island.

'What's planned for today?' Xander asked his dad.

'How about taking out the jet ski?' Greg grinned.

Xander squealed in delight. 'Really?'

'Yes, really. You all up for that?'

The three nodded and exclaimed their willingness, although Benji seemed less enthusiastic than the rest.

'You will be careful, won't you?' Adele murmured.

'Don't be a killjoy.' Greg snapped at her. 'You'll need your swimming gear, lads. Best you go and get changed.'

Xander and Jacob raced for the stairs, laughing and joking. Benji hovered behind.

'Problem?' demanded Greg. Adele knew he would be offended if Benji didn't want to go.

'No.' Benji seemed embarrassed. 'Should we take anything else?'

'It's a holiday. No need to plan the hell out of everything. You need to relax, son. Enjoy yourself.' Benji looked at the floor as Greg continued. 'Seems like a bit of drinking action was too much for you as well, eh? At least you got the motor back here in one piece.'

'Yes, Mr Hayward.' Benji flushed bright red.

'Bloody soft,' muttered Greg.

Benji looked at Adele. 'Thanks for breakfast.'

'My pleasure,' she said. The young man leaped up the stairs two at a time, as if he couldn't get away from the kitchen fast enough. Adele began to load the dirty pots into the dishwasher.

'What will you do?' asked Greg.

She looked up in surprise. 'I have some committee stuff to get ready for tomorrow morning.'

'Good. Stay in the house today and don't speak to anyone unless I'm with you.'

Adele stood with a dirty mug dripping coffee onto the floor, her mouth open. 'What? Why? I don't understand.'

Greg stepped round the kitchen island and grabbed Adele by the wrist. She dropped the mug in surprise, and it bounced away across the floor. 'I don't want you talking to strangers. And I don't want the boys getting into trouble just because they got rat-arsed last night.'

'Why would they be in trouble?'

'This girl, in town.' He tightened his grip, making her squirm in discomfort. 'You've heard?'

'Yes, of course.'

'I don't want the police fitting them up for anything just because they were enjoying themselves.'

'All right.' There was little point in arguing with Greg when he had arrived at some fixed idea. He had no time for debate or willingness to change his views once his opinion was formed.

Greg let go of her and went upstairs to join the boys, shouting at them to hurry. Adele rubbed her wrist before retrieving the mug and returning to the dishwasher. As she dropped a washing capsule into the machine, she could hear all four male voices raised in excitement. She was grateful that they were leaving her in peace to get ready for the soapbox derby tomorrow. It would be so much easier on her own.

Heavy footsteps came down the stairs, and Xander bounced into the kitchen.

'Where are you off to?'

'To the beach gap. Dad says we can take the jet ski out on our own.' Xander sounded excited.

'You will take care of your guests, won't you?'

'Of course, what do you take me for?'

An overexcited teenager with no sense of danger, Adele thought, then said, 'Do you want me to do you a picnic?'

'No time, we'll buy something.' Xander dropped a kiss on her cheek. 'Thanks for offering. Where's my tracksuit? My club one?'

'In your room.'

'Can't find it. What have you done with it?'

Adele sighed quietly and went upstairs. It didn't take her long to extract the suit he wanted from the piles of clean clothes that she left for him regularly in his bedroom but never made it to drawers or cupboards.

'Cheers, Mum.' Xander grabbed the things from her hands and headed for his en-suite.

She went back to the kitchen, where Greg was stuffing the cans of beer and the bottle of vodka into a sports holdall. He ignored her, instead yelling up the stairs, 'Come on, you lot.'

It took several more minutes of shouting, door slamming and quarrelling outside before Greg managed to hook the jet ski trailer onto the back of his car. Adele watched them from the living room window as they left, wondering why Greg was worried about her talking to anyone else. After all, he'd been out all night with the boys himself. He had taken Xander drinking before. He hadn't waited until their son was eighteen to begin this initiation. The pair saw these sessions as some kind of rite of passage, an entry into manhood. It was a mystery to her what they saw in any of it.

Adele shook her head and went to the utility room. She needed to get some mince out of the freezer if she was going to make a shepherd's pie for their evening meal. Looking around in surprise, she saw that the washing machine was still sloshing its current load around in the drum. But the tumble dryer and the drying racks were empty.

CHAPTER 15

Edwards queued in the box office behind excited audience members collecting tickets for the show. When he flipped his warrant card, the lady behind the counter fought back tears.

'It's true then? It's our Daisy? I'll fetch the general manager.'

Sara followed her boss into the manager's tiny office. It was the size of a broom cupboard, and every available surface was stacked with office files or boxes holding seaside souvenirs for the shop. A pile of programmes marked *Seaside Summer Special* sat in the middle of his desk. They weren't invited to sit down — there wasn't anywhere available.

A tall bearded man in his forties introduced himself as Donal Byrne and assured them that all the staff were willing to help in any way that they could. 'We're a family here,' he said. 'Daisy has been with us for three years and was a highly valued member of staff. We were so proud when she was asked to be Carnival Queen.'

'Did she have a boyfriend?' asked Edwards.

'Not that I know of. You'd have to ask the others.'

'Would you say her behaviour recently had changed? Perhaps she was looking forward to seeing someone or even afraid of something?'

'Nervous about her carnival duties,' confirmed Donal. 'I wouldn't call it afraid. We all did what we could in our own way. Her mum bought her a lovely dress, and the wardrobe mistress fitted it to her. The girl dancers helped her with her make-up. My assistant manager gave her advice on the speech for last night.'

'We will need to speak to your team. Especially those who leave late at night.'

'That would be the theatre staff and front of house people. The show finishes at about half past ten. I'm afraid that you'd have to work around the performance times, but I am sure they would be happy to chat.'

'Thank you.'

'Is there anything else for now? I really need to get these down to the theatre. They're waiting.'

'A list of staff who were here last night, please.' Sara handed the manager her card. 'If you could get someone to email it to me.'

'Sure, no problem.' Donal gathered up an armful of programmes, and Sara held the door open for him. They watched as he wove his way among the crowds down the boardwalk.

'What do you think of that?' Edwards asked as they pushed their way back to the promenade.

'They sound like a close-knit bunch,' said Sara. 'I suspect it's the job and the hours.'

'Like us, you mean? I think it would be worth interviewing them all.'

'They may not have seen anything. Depends on the timing. What about the funfair people?'

'Oh, we're definitely going to speak to them. We just need to figure out which ones.'

Edwards mobile shrilled. Answering it, he put one hand over his free ear to cut out the noise of the crowds around them. His pace slowed, and he looked at Sara, his lips pursed. 'Excellent,' he said. 'Can you email it to me? I can open it on my phone, I think.'

Sara nodded in confirmation, gesturing to her own phone.

'Did they? That's helpful. We'll go there now.'

'Sir?'

'Ian is sending that picture over now, smart lad.' Edwards sounded proud of his most junior team member. 'And Mike has had some joy with the petrol station. They have three cameras that record twenty-four seven. We can collect a copy of last night's footage if we go up there.'

Sara's mobile pinged with the picture of Daisy. As she collected the memory stick from the station's cashier, Edwards was haranguing someone on the phone. 'This is a murder inquiry,' he said. 'You'll release all the manpower I need, and you'll do it now.'

They headed back to Pat's Café, where the FIs were packing up.

'I think we've got everything we can,' said their team leader. 'They could open the place up once we've moved the vehicles.'

'Much joy?'

'I'm afraid not. I'd hazard an opinion and say that I don't think our victim was killed in the alley. Just dumped here.'

'Next to the waste bins, like a piece of rubbish,' said Sara. She felt herself flushing with anger. As the FIs packed up, three police cars arrived.

'That's everyone I have at the Cromer station,' said a sergeant, who introduced himself as Matthews. 'If you want any more, we'll have to contact Sheringham.'

'It will do for a start,' replied Edwards. 'Get them together.'

The uniformed officers moved into a huddle around the DI so that his voice wouldn't have to carry too far.

'You all know what we've found,' he said. 'We suspect that our victim was not murdered here at the bus station. Someone has moved her. Although I can't rule out the use of a car, we need to check the town first. Speak to my sergeant in a moment, and she will forward you a picture, which shows our victim as she was dressed last night. Her shoes and handbag were not at the scene, and we need to find them. Get yourselves into teams, and ask all the businesses in the town if anyone remembers seeing her last night. Get them to check their rubbish bins for the missing items. Check every public waste bin, commercial bins, and recycling drop-off points. Oh, and move your vehicles. We're opening up the bus station again in a few minutes.'

It took Sara several minutes to deal with the officers and send them the picture. Edwards was talking to Sergeant Matthews.

'I'll go back to the station,' he said. 'Print off copies of this to hand out as a reminder.'

The cordons were being removed, and traffic was filling the roads. They swivelled their heads at a familiar engine sound. A rubbish truck pulled up outside Pat's Café. A worker in a hi-vis outfit jumped out, collected the food waste bin from the alley and hooked it onto the back. With a familiar whining sound, mechanical arms lifted the bin over the open back, and waste tumbled into the crusher. The contents vanished into the belly of the vehicle.

'It's Saturday,' said Sara in surprise.

'Bugger,' said DI Edwards.

CHAPTER 16

The turnaround time between the late matinée and the evening show at 8 p.m. was tight. The cast generally went into the theatre bar as soon as the earlier audience had left, sitting around one of the bigger tables in a group to eat their salads and drink their energy drinks. The crew rehung and reset the scenery for the opening number while Jessie double-checked the mic packs. They were left with little more than twenty minutes to eat their food before the half-hour warning was due to be called, and everyone would be swept backstage so the auditorium could be opened to the public again. The cleaner was bustling between the rows of seats, picking up the litter and hoovering up trampled debris and glitter from the finale cannon.

Jessie stayed in her operator's box to eat. She took large bites of her sandwich as she unpacked a new headset for Hallie. The current one had begun to cut in and out during the last show. Jessie preferred to change it now than risk it ceasing to transmit during the second show. It wasn't a difficult job, but it was several minutes of fiddly work, which needed concentration. She hung the old mic on a rail in the box to dry. Sometimes it was just sweat that caused the problem, and the headset could be used again. It was worth a try.

With five minutes to spare, she dropped the pack in Hallie's dressing room, grabbed her mug from the green room and went into the bar for a coffee. Ricky and Hallie were sitting at a separate table from everyone else. Ricky had his back to the room, and Hallie was looking at him with big doe-eyes, not speaking. Yazza glanced at Jessie, followed her gaze, then rolled her eyes with a smile.

Jessie took her things backstage when the half-hour was called and flopped on the sofa in the green room. Unwrapping an energy bar, Jessie swigged on her coffee and watched as Hallie and Ricky were the last to arrive. Hallie's back was ramrod straight, while Ricky swayed with a casual nonchalance. He swung into his dressing room. Hallie slammed the door of hers so hard that Jessie thought she might have broken it.

Guess they just broke up, Jessie thought. She put her lunch box in her locker and went to check the emergency mics backstage. *I'll give her a few minutes.*

There was a moment backstage which, when she felt it, Jessie knew meant that she was still in love with the theatre. Her ex-husband had told her once that some French chap had called this love "red-and-gold disease". Once it gripped you, it never died. Theatre might leave you, the work might dry up, or you become too ill to carry on. But you never left the theatre once it got into your blood. *Bugger Ricky Easton*, she vowed. *He won't get me sacked. I won't let him. This is my place too.*

'Just going to make sure Hallie's new mic is OK,' she said to Pete. The stage manager waved in acknowledgement, although his attention was on listening to some voice on the cans, as the internal comms system was called. Jessie dropped down to the corridor and knocked on Hallie's door.

'Come in,' called a shaky voice.

'I just wanted to let you know that I've changed your headset,' said Jessie. 'Do you want me to adjust the back for you?'

Hallie nodded, and Jessie went in, closing out the noisy corridor as she did. Hallie hooked the headset around her ears while Jessie stood behind her and fiddled with the fitting until it was snug. Then she flicked on the battery pack and smiled at Hallie in the brightly lit mirror. 'All done. Comfortable?' There were tears in the pretty singer's eyes. 'Are you all right?'

Hallie shook her head. Tears began to make her mascara run. She grabbed a tissue and dabbed at the goo before it could set. 'Mustn't cry, bad for my voice,' she muttered.

'I know. Can I get you some water or anything?'

'Got some.' Hallie pointed to a drinking bottle.

'Cool. Have a good show.'

Not only did Jessie not want to encourage Hallie to spoil her lovely vocals, she wasn't very good at emotions. All her life, Jessie had tended to overreact. Once her marriage had broken down, she had worked hard to discipline herself to show as little emotion as possible. While she often seethed inside or felt sentimental tears welling, Jessie would shout at herself inwardly until the feelings went away.

She left via the stage door and walked around the outside of the theatre on the boardwalk. It was still light, and there were plenty of people taking the evening air. Working her way through the audience in the bar to the back of the auditorium, she reached her soundbox and carefully locked herself in.

To her right, in a stack that reached towards the ceiling, the receivers for each head mic winked and glowed. Apart from the occasional out-of-range red flicker, the bank twinkled green. All the mics were constantly live while the show was running, and it was part of her job to protect each user's privacy when they were not on stage.

Jessie pulled on a pair of noise-cancelling headphones, which were plugged into the mixing desk. At the top of each input was a button that allowed her to listen in to the head mic and check it was working. She didn't know if the performers knew she could do this. Or if they did, they didn't always remember. It was a matter of trust that neither she nor any other sound tech would linger on the line longer than the few seconds it took to make sure there was no interference. They called it "making sure the line was clean". She'd heard many odd things over the years. People swearing, or running scales, or using the toilet. Now, as she worked her way down the inputs one by one, she reached Hallie's mic.

'Why would you do that to her?' Hallie sobbed.

Damn the woman, Jessie thought. *She'll spoil her solos.*

Another voice spoke in the background. No doubt it was Ricky bloody Easton, wreaking havoc among the cast. It cost Jessie some hesitation before she decided to betray a lifetime of trust. She flicked the interrupt on Ricky's mic as well.

'I didn't mean to hurt her,' his voice cut in against Hallie's sobs. 'But she was only a waitress.'

CHAPTER 17

As Sara had gone to the crime scene in her own car, she headed directly home. DI Edwards had called a halt to their part of the investigation for the day.

'There isn't much more we can do,' he'd said. 'I think it's better that Uniform deal with the local businesses.'

There was quite a queue of traffic leaving Cromer, no doubt people who had been enjoying a day at the seaside and the carnival fun. Waiting for the traffic lights to change, Sara fired up her mobile in the hands-free slot and rang Chris.

'Hello, you,' he said. She could hear the till for his café chuntering in the background. 'How are you doing?'

'Just on my way home.'

'I thought it was your weekend off?'

'It was. That's why I'm ringing.'

'Ah, something has come up.' Chris sounded resigned. 'A problem in Cromer perhaps?'

'Exactly. I'm sorry. I'll be working every day for a while.'

'Do you still want me to come over this evening? I could cook for us.'

Sara felt that her relationship with Chris was muddling along at best because they saw so little of each other these days. They were both too busy and worked long hours. When they'd lived in the same building, in flats that were just one floor apart, it had been easier to make time. She had even introduced Chris to her mum and stepfather, and everyone had seemed to get on well. For a few months, it had all seemed so promising. 'It would be nice to see you. It's been a while.'

'Rehearsals and all that, you know how it is.'

Chris not only ran his own independent café, but was also a regular performer at Norwich's prestigious Maddermarket Theatre. Although the place was technically amateur, the performers were treated as semi-professional actors, expected to spend long hours rehearsing in their spare time. Now that Sara lived on the coast, the time they could spend together was rapidly diminishing. She wasn't sure if there was anything either of them was prepared to do about it.

'Are your mum and Javed still coming up to visit?' Chris asked when Sara hesitated.

'In theory. If this investigation doesn't spoil it.'

'I've got tomorrow off. I could do a bit of weeding, make the garden look a bit tidier.'

'Sounds like a plan.' The traffic had moved sufficiently for Sara to be driving out of Cromer and along the coast road. 'See you later then.'

'Give me an hour. Love you.' Chris cancelled the call before Sara could reply.

Would she have said it in reply? Or meant it? *Love you, too.* It seemed that they were comfortable with each other, happy together part-time. Wasn't that enough? She shook her head. She didn't need to be thinking about this now, not with the Daisy Shaw case to deal with.

As she joined another traffic queue, Sara rang her mum.

I live my life on the phone, she thought, as the number rang. *Or at work or on my own. How sad am I?*

Tegan sounded cheerful when she answered. 'You busy?'

Sara explained that they had a new big case. 'Have you decided about visiting at the end of the month?'

There was a long silence, and Sara steeled herself for the reply. 'We would be in the way. If you've got a lot to do.'

'You wouldn't, Mum.' She tried to keep her tone light. 'I just might not be able to get the whole week off to be with you like I planned to. You could still go for days out.'

'I don't like Norwich. It wasn't good to me.'

'That was more than thirty years ago.' Sara sighed. 'Things have changed. You won't be in Norwich anyway. We're miles away and near the beach.'

'I'm still thinking about it.'

'You won't be staying in Dad's cottage,' she reminded her mother. 'You'll be at the other end of the terrace. You don't have to come into his house if you don't feel up to it.'

'Will that nice boy, Chris, be there?'

'I hope so. He's trying to get cover for the café. Please say you'll come.'

'I'll talk to Javed,' was all that Tegan would promise. Sara bit her lip in frustration, dropping that bit of the conversation. The holiday cottage had cost her a lot of money to rent for the last week in August.

They swapped affectionate goodbyes as Sara reached the turning for Happisburgh. There was still plenty of evening left. She would sort out some salad to go with whatever Chris intended to cook and open a bottle of wine. They could sit out in the garden if Sara lit the citronella candles. Perhaps a quiet evening and some alcohol would banish the image of Daisy's greying face and the sound of Mrs Shaw crying.

CHAPTER 18

Greg had taken the boys drinking again after their jet ski outing. Adele was grateful they stayed out late, even though it meant that the shepherd's pie she'd so carefully made for them went into the fridge with just her own helping eaten. She lay in bed listening to all four of them messing around in the kitchen when they came back, until the sound of a large dish smashing on the floor was followed by hoots of laughter and the noise of them stumbling upstairs.

Weaving unsteadily, Greg crossed their bedroom to the en-suite bathroom, leaving the door open onto the landing. Adele kept as still as she dare, her breathing shallow, trying to mimic sleeping.

On the landing, teasing and backslapping between the boys had ended with Benji asking, 'Shouldn't we clear up the mess before we go to bed?'

'Why bother?' Xander's voice was slurred and uneven. 'My mother can clean it up in the morning.'

'She made it for us, especially.'

Xander laughed, there was a moment of scuffling, and when Adele peeked cautiously from under the duvet, she could see that her son had Benji in a headlock. Xander pushed him towards the guest room.

'Why should we help her?' Xander demanded. 'It's not like she's got anything else to do all day. Dad does all the work around here. He pays all the bloody bills. She's a kept woman.' Her son roared out another laugh at his own wit.

How Benji reacted to this, Adele couldn't see, though she heard his bedroom door close. With a loud belch, her son spun quickly on his heel and ran for his own room. Left alone, Jacob hesitated, then followed Benji.

Greg came out of their en-suite before Adele had time to snap shut her eyelids. He looked at her, then slammed the bedroom door and climbed into bed next to her. 'No point in pretending,' he slurred. He dragged Adele over to face him. 'You're not asleep. Open them up, my lady.'

His hands pulled at her nightie, struggling with the flimsy cotton material as it caught around her legs. She didn't resist. It only made him worse. When he got like this, passivity was her only resort. Parting her legs with his knees, he trapped one thigh under his bony kneecap and levered himself over her, pinching the vulnerable soft inner flesh painfully. She winced. He smiled. With one hand, he dragged Adele's wrist high above her head, while with the other, he explored her private parts.

It wasn't foreplay. Her gratification was not a consideration. He was checking that she had no tampons inside her. With his free hand, he began to stroke and tease himself. As Adele lay waiting for him to push inside her, she realised that something was going wrong. His manhood was not responding.

'Your bloody fault,' he slurred as he tried to pump his penis into action. 'Lying there like a beached whale. Who'd fancy that?'

Greg rolled off her, collapsing onto his own side of the bed, still trying to force action from something that obviously didn't want to come out to play. After a few moments, his hand stilled, and his breathing deepened. The amount of booze consumed had not only taken away his performance, but it had also knocked him out.

Adele tiptoed to the bathroom, locked herself in and wiped between her legs with toilet tissue. Rearranging her nightdress, she returned to lie on the very edge of the double bed, as far away from her husband as she could manage.

She drifted to sleep at some point, waking to the sound of her alarm at 6 a.m., stiff from keeping as still as possible. She gathered up the clothes she wanted for the day and locked herself in the family bathroom to shower as quietly as she could manage. Dragging on her clothes, she could hear that Greg was snoring like the pig he was. Adele crept downstairs, trying desperately not to wake anyone else.

She closed the kitchen door to mask her movements and put a pot of coffee on to steep while she cleaned the floor. Someone had dropped the shepherd's pie in its baking dish near the fridge. It was smashed, and there were fragments of glass everywhere. The pie had stained the light wood laminate floor. Having picked up all the mess she could find, Adele took a floor wipe and tried unsuccessfully to remove the mark. She offered a silent prayer that Greg wouldn't notice.

Gulping down a bowl of cereal and the hot coffee, she slipped on a pair of comfy shoes. It was going to be a long day for her. She needed all the comfort she could get. The paperwork for the soapbox derby was ready in a shoulder bag where Adele had left it the previous evening.

She let herself out of the house, carefully turning the key so that it didn't make too much noise. Her small car waited on the drive. She dropped the bag onto the passenger seat and started the car, grateful it started the first time. The engine purred gently. Adele reversed out and headed for the car park at Carnival Field.

She was at least three hours too early, but the morning was warm and sunny. In an hour or two, the Big Sky Café or one of the food vans would be open. Perhaps she might go for a walk, see if Henry was bringing his catch in down on the Gangway. Or she might just sit on a bench and watch the sea for a while. That was always something that soothed her.

Adele needed time to think. If people knew how Greg treated her, they would just shrug and ask why she allowed it, why she didn't leave. If she was sure of only one thing, it was that the answer was far more complicated than she could explain, and any solution far from simple. Her husband was well-liked. His friends wouldn't believe her if she spoke out. She had no girlfriends of her own to turn to.

She took a snap of the bruises on her wrist, then saved it to the special file on her phone, the only one that she kept carefully password protected. It held several photos of the results of Greg's increasing violence towards her. Some months back, Adele had paid a visit to the library in Norwich and spent an interesting hour on a computer. One women's support website had suggested keeping such a record in case of prosecutions or police action, and since then, she had kept the evidence just in case.

The trouble was, Adele didn't know how to find the courage to do something with it.

CHAPTER 19

When Sara got to the office first thing on Sunday morning, their civilian admin, Aggie Hewett, was already at her desk. Her eyes were focused on a computer screen, and her hand gripped the mouse, fingers clicking. The two women were the first to arrive. She glanced up distractedly as Sara said good morning to point at a cake tin on the spare desk.

'Morning. I didn't have much notice, so it's only scones. Haven't made the coffee yet.'

Sara unravelled the statement as she brought water for the filter machine. Aggie regularly brought in the most luscious sponges, tray bakes, muffins or brownies. A fact which showed on all their waistlines, especially Aggie's, whose plump, homely figure belied her eagle eyes and sharp brain with computer databases. Her "only scones" were the best in the county. This morning she was wearing a sleeveless floral dress that was a little unforgiving on her older figure, especially as she leaned in closer to examine the screen.

Sara flicked on the coffee machine. 'What have you got?'

For a moment, Aggie didn't reply, then she stretched back in her chair. 'I'm not sure,' she sighed. 'It's right on the edge of the camera's range. You have a look.'

Sara examined the image. It was grainy and mainly focused on the forecourt of the petrol station. There were no cars, and chains were pulled across the visible entrance in the wall next to the pavement. The forecourt lights were off, but there were streetlights on the road beyond. The timestamp indicated the footage was recorded just before 1 a.m., if it was accurate.

'I'm not sure I can see anything important,' said Sara.

Aggie pointed at the top edge of the screen, where the side road next to the station was visible. 'Watch there.' Aggie clicked her mouse, sending the recording backwards frame by frame for thirty or so seconds.

Sara concentrated. 'There are some people walking.'

'Not just walking. It may be wishful thinking, but to me, it looks like two people helping a third.'

Aggie froze the screen again and zoomed in as close as she could. The image became even more indistinct. Sara pulled back to try and make sense of it.

'Like two people carrying a drunk, maybe?' Aggie asked hopefully.

'Perhaps. Is this all the footage there is?'

'Yes, for now. There are three cameras, though. This one looks over the pumps. The road it clips is New Street. It comes up from the town past the pubs.'

'Why are you here doing this, anyway? It should be DC Noble. Where is everyone else?'

'I saw Mike last night,' said Aggie. She sounded a bit embarrassed. 'I offered to come in early to get started.'

Bowen and Aggie were enjoying a second-time-around friendship or romance, which the rest of the team was not supposed to know about. Sara was pleased for them. There was nothing wrong with finding a partner later in life, in her opinion. The pair were doing better than she was with Chris.

'Show it to the DI when the rest get in. Coffee?'

When he arrived, Edwards was inclined to believe Aggie, even though the image was unclear. Bowen patted Aggie on the shoulder proprietorially.

'Good work,' the DI said, brushing at the scone crumbs on his tie. 'Could be interesting. Where do you think they've come from?'

'Could be up New Street,' said Aggie. 'Or from the foot-path behind the houses. I've looked at the times on either side of this. I can't see anyone else in the fifteen minutes before.'

'And after?' asked Edwards.

'There's quite a crowd goes past about five minutes later. The pub must have shut by then, even with its carnival week licence extension. They seem to head up the hill to the gardens. The same direction these three were going.'

'They could all just be drunks,' said Noble. Bowen shot him a disapproving scowl, and Noble dropped his gaze.

Edwards took another bite of scone to cover his amusement. 'What we need is something from New Street. What about the local council?'

'I've tried them, sir,' said Aggie. 'There's an out-of-hours number for the weekend, and I left a message. But I'm not holding my breath.'

'Other businesses? Who is there?'

'The Duke is on the corner,' said Bowen. 'There's an amusement arcade part way along. They might have something.'

'And the posh chippie,' suggested Noble.

'That would be Graham Bradley's award-winning "Feast in the East fish restaurant" to you,' said Edwards with a grin. Noble grinned back.

'Worth a try,' said Bowen.

'You and Noble can start with that,' said Edwards. 'Aggie, try the council again, then have a look at any other camera views that we can turn up. Sara, you're with me.'

She followed him into his office, where he dialled the Cromer Police Station in search of Sergeant Matthews. He wasn't on duty.

'Did they find anything in the bins?' Edwards asked the duty sergeant. His fingers began to drum on the desk. 'Is there no report for me?'

The phone was on speaker mode, so the desk officer in Cromer could surely hear the tapping. He spluttered that he would have a look, and the line went dead.

'What do they get up to in these little stations?' he asked, with a roll of his eyes. Sara suspected that the answer was traffic, moving on drunks and the occasional fight or break-in. It was hardly going to be high-octane stuff, though she didn't say so.

The line crackled back into life. 'Found it, sir,' he said. 'It was sent to you last night. Did you not get it?'

Edwards looked at his computer, which he had yet to turn on. 'No. Save me some time and read it out.'

The officer read out the basic report. 'We asked them to check their bins and yards. They have our contact details, sir, and those pictures that Sergeant Matthews printed out. Not much else we can do.'

'Tell me about bin collections in the town.'

'Sir?'

'Do you know when the commercial bins are emptied in the town? I don't mean household waste.'

'Oh, I see. Well, it's peak holiday season, so at least once a day. Especially the food waste.'

'And the rest?'

'Council empties the litter bins twice a day in August.'

'OK, thanks. I'll check for the report.' Edwards put down the phone. 'It's not looking good for finding the shoes or handbag, is it?'

'I'm afraid not, sir. If they were put in a bin Friday night, they would have gone before we started the search.'

CHAPTER 20

Sara followed DI Edwards in her own car when they headed up to Cromer again. Runton Road was closed to traffic from the Carnival Field down the hill to the petrol station.

'This is nothing to do with us, I hope,' he grumbled after they parked behind the marquee at the bar end, next to a catering van. The flap of the tent opened briefly as Brian Medler looked out at them. Edwards waved, and Brian nodded before dropping the canvas back into place.

Sara followed the DI into the tent, which was already open for business and crammed with people, some carrying crash helmets, elbow pads and thick gloves. The sound of voices was almost overwhelming, and it was still before ten in the morning.

'Soapbox derby,' explained Brian when they managed to get to the bar. 'Very popular. Soft drinks, tea and coffee only until midday, before you ask. Breakfast baps over there.'

'Who is in charge of this event?'

'That would be Mrs Hayward.' The barman pointed to a mousey-haired woman dressed in a floaty skirt and a pretty floral blouse. She stood gripping a clipboard behind a table covered in a pile of paperwork. Entrants were lining up to sign in and receive their numbers. Another man stood next to her in a hi-vis vest that said *Cromer Carnival* on it. 'And that's Henry, our chairman.'

'We need a word with both of them,' said Sara to Edwards. 'They look very busy, don't they?'

'Let's try the funfair workers first. Brian?'

'Yep? Can I offer you a tea or anything?'

'When we get back, that would be great. I wanted to ask you about Friday night.'

'Sure, carry on.' Brian turned to serve the next person in the queue.

'Do you know any of the funfair workers you mentioned when we spoke before?'

'Nope. I'd probably recognise the one who was making a fuss of Daisy.'

'It has been suggested to us that Daisy might have known this young man,' said Sara.

Brian set the coffee grinder rattling as he thought about this. 'Well, she might have, now you say that. Besides, "he was handsome, she was pretty".' Brian sang these last couple of lines with a smile. 'Sorry, I'm a Shantyman, like Henry. It's one of the better-known folk songs we do.'

'Can you describe him?'

'Tall, about six foot. Dark hair, short round the back, with a floppy fringe. Dark eyes as well. Well-muscled — it's physical work on the funfairs. Handsome, like I said. Can't say I blame Daisy. They made a good-looking couple. Chocolate?' Brian put two cappuccinos on the counter for the customer and rang the money for them into the till. 'The families live in the vans beyond the stalls. They'll be up by now.'

The funfair was closed. Brightly coloured boards or tarpaulins were fastened up to hide the various rides and attractions. All the same, it looked like fun to Sara. There was even an old-fashioned Ferris wheel, orientated to look out to sea.

What a view that must be from up there, thought Sara, as they made their way to the living vans, which were parked against a white panel fence at the back of the site. Most of the vans had their doors open. People, young and old, moved between them. Several men stood talking in a group near a four-by-four with its bonnet up. A group of teenage boys were tinkering with a cart for the soapbox derby. One of them wore his starting number and looked on rather uncertainly as his friends made adjustments. The vans themselves looked modern and pristine. Batteries supplied the power, large water barrels were hooked up, most had television satellite dishes on their roofs.

As Sara and Edwards approached, group by group, the activity stilled until all eyes were turned towards them. The silence drew several women to the doors of their vans to watch with carefully blank faces. A short man in his late fifties detached from the group by the vehicle to intercept them.

'Mornin', officers,' he said in a broad Norfolk accent. 'What can I do for you?'

'Good morning.' Edwards introduced himself and Sara, they showed their warrant cards. 'Are you a spokesman?'

'I'm Will Grice.' He folded his arms rather than offering a handshake of introduction. 'By way of bein' the father of the firm.'

'I'm grateful for your time.' Edwards didn't manage to sound as if he was. 'I take it you've heard about what happened in the town on Friday night?'

'We have. Rum old thing, ain't it. Poor lass.'

'Indeed. We're trying to trace what happened to our victim after she left the marquee on Friday evening.'

'We would all have been working.'

'You close at eleven?'

'Jus' as our licence says.' Grice shifted his weight so that he stood evenly balanced, ready for anything that might happen. Sara thought he managed to look aggressive without moving his face out of neutral. Edwards glanced at her, and she took over.

'We believe that a few of your younger workers went to the marquee once you had closed up.'

'Now, why would they do that?'

'For a drink and a dance? It is carnival time, after all.'

'Always showtime for us. It's our business to be other people's good time.'

'It's all right, Dad. I'll deal with this.'

A twenty-something young man joined them. Brian Medler's description was pretty accurate. No one feature of the face stood out as particularly well-formed, but the whole was indeed handsome. His smile was captivating as it spread to wrinkle the bronzed skin around his exceptionally dark eyes.

'I'm Kit Grice,' he said, and this time a hand was extended, which Sara shook before Edwards could get to it. Kit turned to his father with a smile. 'You wouldn't have realised because you went straight to bed. Me and a couple of the others went over for a drink once we'd closed up. We don't often get the chance, working so late.'

Kit's accent was less broad than his father's. There was even a hint of street-estuary in it. There was no defensiveness in his stance as he placed his hand protectively on his father's shoulder.

'It's about this dead girl,' said the older Grice. 'Nothing to do with us. Who is she anyway?'

'You haven't heard?' Sara was surprised. 'It seems to have gone round the town rather quickly.'

'We be visitors, though we come here every year. They don't tell us much.'

Nor had the name of the victim been released to the press, Sara knew.

'Local girl, is it?'

'Indeed. In fact, she was the Carnival Queen, and . . .'

Before Sara could finish, Kit Grice let out a cry. His face pulled tight in anguish, and his fists clenched in front of his chest. He staggered backwards as if his legs were giving out from under him. Will Grice moved after him, catching him before he could fall. 'Son? What's this?'

Edwards brushed past Sara to face the young man. 'They told us you were dancing with her,' he said. 'Intimately.'

The men near the four-by-four began to talk angrily as they strode forward and surrounded Edwards and the Grices. Sara pushed through the ring that was forming, holding up her hands in a pacifying gesture. 'It's OK,' she said loudly. 'We're only asking a few questions.'

'That's what you lot always say,' called one man.

'Kit,' snapped Edwards. 'Were you dancing with Daisy Shaw on Friday night?'

'Yes, I was.' Kit straightened up to face the DI. 'Why the hell not? She was my bloody girlfriend.'

CHAPTER 21

The cast and crew had two days off each week. Once the Saturday shows were over, they weren't due back in the venue until Tuesday. Some people drove home late into the night. Others celebrated with a few drinks before arranging social gatherings for one of the off-days.

Jessie might not have gone drinking last night, but she had sat up late. The words she'd overheard on the cans worried her. When Ricky had said "only a waitress", had he meant Daisy? Why hadn't he meant to hurt whoever it was? What had he done?

When she woke on Sunday morning, Jessie took her time brewing a coffee before she heard Yazza stirring upstairs. Jessie took her drink out into the warmth of her garden. It was going to be a beautiful day. The six houses stood in two blocks with a small alley between to access the back gardens, which formed a small private square. Each had a view of the others. For such a private person, Jessie found this almost communal space challenging at times. She was grateful that her immediate neighbour was Henry Lacey, one of the local fishermen, and a quiet single man. When Yazza joined Jessie ten minutes later, she sat blinking in the sunshine and sipping orange juice.

'We're going to watch the cart racing later on,' said Yazza. She stretched her dancer's muscled and slim figure luxuriously. Jessie felt a stab of envy, quickly tempered by the practicalities of not ever needing to go on a diet again. 'You want to come?'

'Maybe?'

'Are you going to have breakfast first, at the beach café? Full English, as they say.'

'I put my name on the list.'

'We're due at eleven thirty.'

'Best you get dressed then.' Jessie looked pointedly at Yazza's pyjamas. 'It's a quarter past.'

With a little squeal of laughter, she darted off inside, and ten minutes later, the pair were heading for the prom. The pavements were becoming crowded, and if one of the cast hadn't pre-booked, there would have been no free tables at the café. A children's event was being set up at the prom end of the pier, involving dancing and making pirate hats. Jessie didn't envy the organizers.

A couple of the cast and all the dancers joined them as they occupied the long table on the little terrace outside the café. Jessie reckoned there were one or two hangovers, as she made sure to sit as far away from Ricky Easton as she could. She kept her sunglasses on, though she had her back to the sun, covertly keeping an eye on the singer as they placed their orders.

People who didn't work in theatre didn't understand how close you got as a group during the sixteen weeks of rehearsal and performance. You became a temporary family, and many a tear was shed on the last night of the season. Not by Jessie, of course. She wouldn't allow herself that. But it was a pity that the camaraderie was being spoiled for her this year by Ricky's presence.

She watched the singer sharing a joke with one of the dancers. He looked completely at ease. Surely he couldn't look so casual if he'd had anything to do with Daisy's death? It didn't make sense. Perhaps the best thing she could do was forget about it. People who listen at doors always get into trouble, her mother had warned her when she was young. And that was what she had been doing, wasn't it? Secretly listening to things that didn't concern her. On the other hand, if she had some ammunition against Ricky, it might be useful should he try to get her sacked. Perhaps she should try to find out more.

Jessie turned to listen to Yazza talking about auditions and tried to relax. There was enough food to feed five dancers, she thought when her plate arrived. She ate it all, though. It was one of her favourite treats.

Afterwards, Jessie felt too full to join the rest standing on the roadside to watch the race. Ricky also declined to join them, and she made her mind up. Making sure that she appeared to leave for home, Jessie hung about on the prom as the group headed towards Carnival Field. She bought an ice cream she didn't want and leaned on the seawall, waiting. Ricky also waited until the rest had vanished into the crowds, then headed up the cliff steps towards the town.

Jessie dumped the melting cone into a rubbish bin and followed him. At the top, a quick glance in front of the pub confirmed the singer hadn't gone that way. She cut through a small alley behind some of the magnificent Victorian houses that these days were holiday flats. Ricky must have gone through here — it was the only other route. Cautiously weaving between the waste bins for the flats, she walked slowly until she spotted her quarry. Her trainers made no noise on the old flagged pavement, so Jessie didn't alert the two figures who were standing by a back gate behind the holiday apartments. She stopped moving, slipped into a gap behind a bay window and peered around.

Ricky was standing opposite a man in a bright purple polo shirt, who looked vaguely familiar. The man was speaking angrily, though his tone was low, and she couldn't hear what was being said. Suddenly, the man reached out and pulled Ricky towards him by the shirt front, until their noses almost met. The singer raised his hands in a pacifying gesture, his lips moving rapidly. No doubt, he was trying to sweet-talk the man. He had a gift for it, as Jessie knew to her cost. She sucked in her breath, fearing what she was about to witness, only releasing it when the man let Ricky go.

He pulled something small from his trouser pocket and passed it to Ricky, taking the money the singer was holding out. The money was slipped quickly into another pocket as the man walked away. It was the walk that did it. Jessie recognised that walk. This had to be the same man who had attacked the singer on Friday night.

Ricky turned down the alley towards Jessie. He was going to walk right past where she was hiding. There was no avoiding him. She panicked. She stepped out into the alley and jogged back towards the steps. When she heard footsteps running behind her, she increased her stride. It didn't help. Seconds later, Ricky snatched at her blouse and pulled her backwards. He grabbed her arm and spun her around.

'You'd make a rotten detective,' he snarled. 'I saw you before you hid behind that window.'

CHAPTER 22

They ended up inside the Show Man's living van, hoping for some privacy. It was a long, large vehicle and far more luxurious inside than Sara expected.

Mrs Grice watched her looking around as they settled in the living room. 'We live in it all year round,' she said. 'What did you expect?'

'You're on the road all year?'

'I didn't say that.' Mrs Grice sat next to her son, putting her arm around his shoulders. She glowered at Sara. 'We live in it even when we're in our winter quarters. Why are you upsetting my son?'

Kit looked at Sara with anxious eyes as she explained about Daisy. DI Edwards blocked the doorway, and Mr Grice stood in the kitchen leaning on a unit that formed both a work surface and waist-high divider to the seating area. The atmosphere was hostile. All eyes were trained on Sara, including those of several other show men looking through the van's panoramic window.

She shuffled uncomfortably. 'You went for a drink in the marquee? With a couple of friends?'

'Yes.'

'Then what?'

'Daisy and me went for a walk.'

'It wasn't as simple as that, was it?' Edwards butted in crossly. Sara wished he hadn't. It exasperated her that the DI could be so blunt sometimes. Being a northerner was no excuse in her book. 'We've spoken to the bar manager already.'

'It was nothing,' said Kit, his tone defensive. 'We're incomers. It can get like that.'

'Like what?' Mr Grice demanded.

'Kit got into a fight.' Edwards turned on the father. 'Didn't he say? At the dance. Got thrown out by the security guards.'

Sara knew they only had Brian Medler's word for this and wasn't surprised when Kit's view differed.

Shaking his head, Kit leaned forward to address Sara, ignoring her boss. 'You must know what it's like.' Kit pointed to her arm. 'That's not a suntan, is it? Bet you get racist crap sometimes.'

'Occasionally,' admitted Sara.

'Well, so do we. Especially from the likes of them.'

'Meaning?'

'Wet behind the ears. Privileged. White, male, posh accents, private schools. Can't hold their drink. Think the world owes them, and hard-working people are beneath them.'

No prejudice there either, thought Sara. 'What did they say to you?'

'One was the leader. He'd been trying it on with Daisy. When we turned up, he was well pissed.'

'And you took exception to this?'

'See?' Kit turned to his mother, his face full of frustration. 'It's going to be my fault, whatever I say.'

'What did he say or do, Kit?' Sara ignored Mrs Grice's muttered reply of 'As per bloody usual.'

'He told me to fuck off. Grabbed me by the arm and tried to pull me away.'

'What did Daisy think of that?'

'We both thought it was funny because he couldn't do it. Not really. For all his size, he didn't have the power. When I pushed him away, he fell on his arse on the grass. Everyone laughed at him then, even his own mates.'

91

'What did he think of that?'

'Not much.' Kit shrugged. 'He went for me. I was going to defend myself, wasn't I?'

'And that's when security got involved?'

'Yeah. They pulled him off, told us all to bugger off because the place was closing anyway.'

There was no CCTV in the marquee or the field to back any of this up. Sara had already checked. 'And when you got outside?'

'The lot of them were halfway across the field by the time Daisy had found her stuff.'

'How many of them were there?'

'Three. All about the same age, with an older man.'

'Then what did you do?'

'Keir and Ian came back here. Daisy and me went to get some privacy.'

'Where?' Edwards snapped. 'Where did you take her?'

Kit stood up and faced the DI, clearly riled by Edwards's tone. 'Why does it matter? We just wanted to be alone for a bit.'

'We'll find you on the town CCTV. You might as well save us the bother.'

'Why would I want to save you any bother?' Kit demanded.

'Because if you don't, I'll arrest you on suspicion of murder and take you in for questioning.'

All hell broke loose. Sara sat with her head in her hands as Mr Grice yelled at the DI and Mrs Grice held Kit back from lunging at him. The men watching outside began to shout. Other families hurried out of their living vans and gathered angrily in front of the Grice's door.

'Let's all calm down,' she yelled. 'Please be quiet.'

The hubbub died down. Kit's chest was heaving, his mother grasping his right hand to stop it from moving. Mr Grice and the DI were staring at each other, their faces bright red. Sara wished her boss would have remembered that they were dealing with a bereaved person, just like Daisy's parents, until they knew otherwise.

She stood up slowly and moved between Kit and Edwards. 'Kit,' she said gently, 'you may have been the last person to see Daisy alive.'

'You saying I murdered her? Because I didn't.'

'No, I'm not saying that,' said Sara as calmly as she could. 'What we need to do is trace your girlfriend's movements and find out why she never got home. Will you help us?'

Kit slumped back onto the sofa, tears forming in his eyes. He made a guttural noise as he opened his mouth. Mrs Grice flopped next to him, seeming unsure what to do.

'We went to the beach.' Kit choked out the words. 'To get some privacy. It's usually quiet at night. Except it wasn't. Something was going on at the café.'

'And then?' Sara sat down again so that she wasn't towering over him.

'We had to go further along, past the beach huts.'

'Did you stay there long?'

'I'm not sure.'

'Why didn't you walk her home?'

'Oh Jeez, I wish to God I had. She didn't want me to.'

'Whyever not?'

'I'd just asked her to marry me.' Kit's eyes widened at the memory, his face crumpled.

Mrs Grice sucked in a sudden breath. Sara glanced at the mother, who was visibly shocked. This was as much news to her as it was to everyone else.

'Did she say yes?'

'She said she wanted to think about it, to be on her own. It's no easy life, being on the move all the time. I understood.'

'Where did you see her last?'

'At the RNLI café. I walked back along the prom. She went up the steps to the main street. Said it was quicker for her that way.'

Sara sat forward. 'Was Daisy wearing her shoes? Was she still carrying her handbag?'

'I think so. Oh God, this is all my fault. I should never have let her go alone.'

CHAPTER 23

One o'clock had arrived far too quickly for Adele. The soapbox derby was her biggest responsibility during carnival week, and here it was. Carnival Field car park was full of competitors' vans, cars and trailers. Since the idea had been taken up on television several years ago, the number of entrants and the standard of the carts had grown exponentially. She'd felt sorry for the local teams, who still tended to treat it like the bit of fun it was originally intended to be. Consequently, the committee had agreed to divide the competition in two, with the standard of the buggy's construction being the deciding factor. There was also a prize for under sixteens. With Henry's guidance, Adele had inspected every entrant and placed them in their category.

The road down the hill from the field to the petrol station had been closed off. Straw bales lined the route, forming chicanes and protecting the onlookers from the inevitable crashes. There was even an electronic timing system for those carts that made it from start to finish. Adele's planning all seemed to be working, and it looked fantastic. She walked to the roped-off area at the top and allowed herself a moment to look around in enjoyment. There was rarely anything in her life that she could be proud of, but this was definitely one.

'All in place?' Henry asked. He had been at her side all morning, his quiet support giving her courage. She nodded. 'It's looking good. Well done, Adele.'

Crowds stood closely packed on the pavements behind rope barriers, patrolled by volunteer stewards and uniformed police officers. Food vans were doing a brisk trade. The scent of burgers, onions, chips, candy floss and doughnuts filled the air. The atmosphere was jovial, and the town would be reaping the rewards, selling everything from takeaway pints to seaside tea towels. The PA system crackled into life, and their celebrity for the day was introduced.

'So happy to be here in sunny Cromer,' the voice of a local television newsreader cut in and out. There was a squeal from the microphone before it settled down. 'Let's give three cheers for the brave competitors of the soapbox derby!'

She handed the final list of entrants to the timekeeper, who stood on the start line next to the newsreader. There were cheers from the crowd as the first team was escorted to the line by one of the other volunteers. A name was announced to whoops and whistles, the newsreader counted down, the flag dropped, and the first team pushed themselves off. The cart's wheels rumbled on the tarmac as a group of young men from a local pub wove their unsteady way down the course until gravity, lack of preparation and beer steered them into the third set of straw bales. The crowd laughed and clapped. The afternoon had begun.

'Not much else you can do now,' suggested Henry. 'Shall we get some lunch?'

'Lovely,' said Adele. 'I'd be glad of a sit-down. Then I must have a walk up and down the course. Say thank you to the volunteers.'

They went back to the marquee. Brian had the bar open for the steady stream of competitors and helpers wandering in and out. The hot sandwich man was still going great guns. After being in a state of high anxiety all morning, Adele felt her appetite returning. The sausages were from the local butchers and cooked to perfection. Henry brought two mugs of tea as they selected a table near the marquee entrance and tucked in.

'Another success for you.' He smiled at Adele. 'We've bin lucky to have you on the committee, I reckon.'

Adele blushed, took another bite of food and glanced at him shyly.

'That's a pity you can't do a bit more,' Henry continued. He turned his gaze outside, his expression thoughtful. 'You could start a little business, organizing events, maybe?'

'I don't need my own business.'

'Give you a bit of independence.' Henry seemed to have something on his mind and was determined to say it. 'Get you out the house. Now your lad is away to university.'

Adele rubbed the marks on her wrist. Being so busy all morning, she had forgotten about them. Hadn't realised that they were visible. She dropped her gaze to the table, the remnants of the sandwich on its paper plate. Her appetite vanished again, and she began to feel sick. 'I don't think my husband would like that.'

'P'rhaps not,' mumbled Henry. He ran a gentle finger over the bruise. 'You bin a good wife and mother. P'rhaps it's time to do suthin' for yourself.'

Adele wondered how much Henry suspected. He had been the one to invite her onto the committee, had pointed out to Greg how good it looked for a local businessman to have his wife involved in one of the town's biggest events. She valued Henry's friendship. It seemed he appreciated hers in return. She felt a blush rising up her neck, which seemed a ridiculously teenager-like reaction given her age. Her heart began to beat faster, but before she could reply, a shadow fell over the table.

'Mrs Adele Hayward?' The woman was tall and smartly dressed. She proffered a warrant card to Adele. 'I'm Detective Sergeant Hirst. This is Detective Inspector Edwards.'

The man standing next to Hirst opened his own warrant card. 'I wondered if we might have a few words? About the ball on Friday night?'

'This be about poor Daisy?' asked Henry. He introduced himself. Adele was grateful that he hadn't moved from his seat. Her heart was pounding so loudly she could barely focus on what was being said. The woman nodded. 'Best you sit down.'

The two detectives pulled up chairs. The man sat back in his and let the DS ask the questions. To Adele's relief, it all seemed simple enough.

'She looked so pretty,' said Adele. 'Like a princess. I wasn't surprised my son asked her for a dance. All three of them did, I think.'

The DS shifted her attention when Adele explained that she had left early. 'Mr Lacey, did you see what happened later?'

Henry was just about to answer when Adele felt a hand slap onto her shoulder. It gripped the muscle, pinching it painfully. She winced, not needing to look to see who it was.

'What's all this?' asked Greg. She could hear the suspicion in his tone, feel the anger in his grip. 'Who are you? What do you want with my wife?'

The woman glanced between Adele and Henry, then looked at Greg and stood to offer her warrant card again. Her boss remained seated, his eyes locked on Adele's husband.

'I can tell you anything you need to know,' said Greg. 'My wife wasn't there.'

'We'd also like to have a word with your son and his friends,' said DS Hirst.

Greg let go of Adele and stepped forward. 'That won't be necessary. I'd be happy to give a statement.'

Adele watched with wide eyes. Greg and the detective were of similar height. The DS looked him in the eye and didn't back away. This was an unusual situation for her husband. Women didn't usually stand up to him. She could also smell the alcohol on his breath from where she was sitting. No doubt the detective could as well.

DS Hirst held her ground as the DI stood up behind her. They made a formidable pair.

'Any reason why they wouldn't want to talk to us?' Hirst asked politely.

'Of course not, they're just . . .' Greg stumbled over his words. 'Well, they're young. They'd been drinking. They won't remember.'

'Were you with them all night?' Edwards cut in.

'Yes, of course,' Greg was blustering now, his face beginning to go red. He wasn't used to having to justify his actions.

'Are they here this afternoon? Could we speak to them now?'

'It would be very helpful.' DS Hirst kept her tone more polite than her boss.

'I suppose so.' Greg shrugged, pulling a roll of ten-pound notes from his pocket. 'I was just getting some drinks in, then we're off to see the race. I left them outside.'

'Why don't you do that, sir? Mrs Hayward can introduce us.'

DS Hirst turned her polite smile to Adele, who glanced at Henry. Too late, Adele realised that Greg would have noticed this and would make her pay for it later. She nodded to her husband, who stamped off to the bar.

'I'll be here if you need me,' said Henry, although who he said this for wasn't clear. The DS thanked him, and the three went out of the marquee.

Adele thought they might have to search for Xander and his friends, that, tired of waiting for Greg to get the booze, they might already have disappeared into the crowds watching the race. In fact, they were about twenty yards away and beating the hell out of one another — at least Xander was punching Benji, who was trying to defend himself. Jacob was screaming with laughter and pointing at Benji. 'Serves you right,' he shouted. 'Bloody lightweight.'

Xander planted a heavy punch into Benji's stomach. Adele heard the sound of it connecting and the whoosh of air leaving Benji's lungs as he doubled over. She screamed and began to run. 'Xander, stop it. What are you doing?'

DS Hirst ran past her, grabbing Xander as he swivelled to hit his friend again. Benji staggered a few steps away, leaning on a car bonnet to catch his breath.

Xander struggled in the detective's grip. 'Who the fuck are you?' he demanded. 'What you doing?'

'Detective Sergeant Hirst of Norfolk Police,' she snapped. She had Xander in an armlock as her boss caught up and slapped handcuffs on her son's wrists. 'And right now, I'm breaking up an affray.'

This announcement sobered all three boys. As Adele reached them, she heard Jacob muttering to Benji. 'The fucking police. Now you've done it, runner boy.'

CHAPTER 24

The day hadn't been an unqualified success so far. Sara had arranged for Kit Grice to make a witness statement later in the day when he had recovered his composure. Will Grice was already on the phone to find some legal help. The funfair families had surrounded them in a passive-aggressive cordon when they'd left the living quarters.

Now, here they were, with another possible witness, Xander Hayward, in cuffs while his mother stood open-mouthed and his father berated them loudly. His two friends looked on, one with his arms folded and a frown on his face, the other still leaning with one hand on a car bonnet and wheezing from the blow to the stomach that Xander had dealt him.

'How are you doing?' Sara asked him. The young man made a dismissive gesture with his free hand. 'What's your name?'

'I'm all right. Don't worry about me. It's Benji. Benji Wilder.'

'Just a bust-up between mates?'

'That's it.'

She patted Benji on the shoulder. DI Edwards was holding Xander by the handcuffs, his arms pinned behind his back.

'Don't you worry, boy,' Mr Hayward was yelling. 'I'll prosecute them for wrongful arrest. Put in a complaint.'

Sara addressed Xander, putting herself carefully between the blustering father and the now shamefaced son. 'Have you calmed down?'

'Yeah,' he muttered. 'Won't do it again.'

'I'll take your word for that.' Sara smiled at Edwards. 'OK, sir. All over now.'

Edwards unlocked the cuffs, and Xander's arms dropped to his sides. He rubbed his wrists with a deliberate gesture, though there were no marks on them that Sara could see.

'All we want to do is ask a few questions about Friday night. But let's start with why you were hitting your friend there.'

'Don't say anything,' shouted Mr Hayward.

'No comment,' muttered the son.

'You know what, sir?' Sara looked up at the DI. 'We have so many statements to take, I think we should acquire ourselves a room at the local station. I'm sure Sergeant Matthews will be able to arrange that.'

'Good idea.'

'I'll need all your details.' She swung round to look at Mr Hayward. His face was so red, she wondered if he was about to have a heart attack. 'Then we'll arrange a time for you to come in and make a statement.'

'That poor girl's been murdered,' Mrs Hayward said quietly. 'I'm sure we'll be happy to help if we can.'

It was enough to take the wind out of her husband's sails. The family gave their details to Sara before they walked away, Mrs Hayward to resume her duties and the four men to the beer tent.

The soapbox derby was in full swing. The pavements were crowded, so Sara and the DI turned along the cliff path through the gardens. They had almost reached the posh chippie when DC Noble came striding out of the restaurant door, his head down and punching his mobile phone. Edwards's mobile rang.

'Sir, you need to come to the posh chippie, sir,' he said, oblivious to the fact that Edwards stood a few yards away. 'Will you be long?'

'Oooh, about five seconds, I reckon.' Edwards smiled at Sara. 'Good line, isn't it?'

'Two bean tins and a piece of string would work at this distance.' She laughed as Noble swung round in a panic. 'What's up?'

'You need to see this, sir.'

Noble nodded to the waitress at the door as he led them through the restaurant seating area, across a working kitchen that could, fashionably, be seen by the diners and through a pass door. A flight of stairs led them to a basement area. In the first room, kitchen staff paused from dealing with fish and chopping salad on their stainless-steel counters, watching them curiously as Noble walked through another door.

A row of large chest freezers stood against one wall of the second room. Against the other wall, shelving held boxes of every possible necessity for a fish and chip supper. At the far end of this room, Sara could see DC Bowen. He was talking to a tall, thin, middle-aged man. His face was familiar, and under the circumstances, she took it to be the chef, Graham Bradley. There was a work desk with a computer and baskets of office papers. Several filing cabinets stood in a row behind the office chair, on which a teenager in a staff uniform was sitting looking glum.

'God, that was quick,' said Bowen.

Edwards smiled. 'What is it?'

Noble indicated the desk and stepped aside to make way for Sara, who had already noticed the pair of green, high-heeled, strappy sandals and small pale green handbag. Both items were covered in food debris. The photo they had circulated lay on the desk.

The glum youngster looked at her and said, 'I'm sorry.'

Graham Bradley seemed more exasperated than annoyed with the youngster. He also appeared keen to ensure no one got into trouble. 'Wayne's only sixteen. This is his first job.'

Sara wondered how much of the town's tourism indus-
try ran on kids and students doing summer jobs.

Bradley spoke over the youngster whenever the DI or
Sara asked a question. 'He was on first thing yesterday. Eight
until twelve. Not back on until this afternoon.'

'Tell us about your find,' said Sara. She raised her hand
in a gentle warning gesture as Bradley opened his mouth to
speak again. 'What happened, Wayne?'

'First thing, I always put the rubbish out,' mumbled
Wayne in a strong local accent. His face was red with embarrassment. ''Specially the food waste.'

'Which bins?'

'They're the blue ones.' Wayne waved above his head.
'They gets emptied every morning in the summer. I took the
bags up, like normal. When I lifts the lid, there they were.'

'In the food waste bin?'

'Yeah.'

'What did you do?'

'Can't leave 'em there. It mucks up the system.'

Sara glanced at Graham Bradley. 'That's right. If we put
non-food items in a food waste bin, we can be fined.'

'And other rubbish? Wayne?'

'There's a general rubbish one and a recycling one.'

'When had you last checked them?'

'Night before.' Wayne frowned in concentration. 'I got
done at six, and they weren't there then.'

'To be clear,' said DI Edwards, 'you checked the bin just
before six on Friday night, and these items were not there.
When you checked the bin again at eight on Saturday morning, they were.'

'Yeah. So, I picked them out and put 'em by the back
door.'

'Why would you do that?' Sara couldn't help noticing that
DI Edwards spoke far more gently to this local teenager than
he had to Kit Grice. 'Why not throw them in the rubbish bin?'

'I thought they looked expensive. P'rhaps somebody had
done it as a joke, and somebody else might come looking

for them. I left them in my locker when I was done for the morning.'

'He produced them when he saw your picture on the staff noticeboard,' said Bradley.

Sara looked at the shoes and bag. Although they were stained from where they had lain among the food, they did look like costly items. 'Can you show me where the bins were that morning?'

'Same place as always.' Wayne glanced at Graham, who nodded his permission for the boy to lead the way.

At the end of the storeroom and office, an outside door stood propped open. Sara expected to find some sort of yard until she saw the legs of people walking past on the pavement outside. A set of stone steps led up to ground level, where an old cast-iron railing and gate cut off the basement entrance from the public. A walkway ran between the terrace of tall Victorian houses and a set of railings on the cliff-edge. Below them stretched the promenade, beach and pier. The restaurant for the posh chippie stood at one end of the terrace, the kitchens underneath, and the takeaway on the opposite side of the building.

Wayne showed Sara to the first cut-through from the footpath to the road on the other side. Edwards remained on the seaward footpath, talking to Graham Bradley. He had already sent Bowen and Noble off to reserve an interview room with Sergeant Matthews.

The alley was narrow. Commercial rubbish bins with *FEAST* stencilled on them lined one wall, making the gap even narrower. Wayne lifted the lid on one of the blue ones.

'Do people often put stuff in your bins?' Sara stepped back. The bin stank.

'Yeah, sometimes.' Wayne dropped the lid and moved on to the next one. Sara didn't follow. 'They can't be locked, you see. People use them as litter bins. That's why I check.'

'Is this how you always keep them lined up?'

'People get cross if the bins block the alley. But it's where the council say we should keep them.'

'Were they in the right place yesterday morning when you found the shoes?'

Wayne thought about his. He pointed at an old black drainpipe that ran from a gutter in the roof to a small grate in the path. 'I put them on each side of the drain, see? Keep them as tight as I can.'

'And that morning?'

'They weren't where I'd left them. Like someone had been messing about with them. It happens.'

Sara stood as far back as she could, which was only a couple of feet. Her back against the windowless wall of the neighbouring bed and breakfast, she scanned up and down the alley. She couldn't see any local council CCTV cameras trained down the gap. She could see the sparkling of coloured bulbs outside the amusement arcade at the land end, hear the machines rattling and playing assorted music to lure players inside. Bowen had mentioned the place before. Hopefully, they had cameras. Edwards and Bradley were leaning over the railings at the other end, looking down at the prom.

'Wayne—' she kept her voice low — 'do you find other things here sometimes?'

He shuffled uncomfortably. 'What like?'

'Things you might not know exactly what they were for?'

'Oh, you mean needles and stuff? Yeah, I find them sometimes. There's an emergency needle bin round the back of the petrol station. I just dump the rest. They teach us about that in school.'

Poor teachers, Sara thought. 'Anything more personal?'

'I don't understand.'

'Condoms. Underwear. Anything like that?'

Wayne blushed red to the roots of his mousey-brown hair and shook his head. He chewed his bottom lip, then paced forward to move two of the waste bins out of their regimented row.

'There was this, though.' He pointed to the restaurant's white painted wall. 'I'd never seen that before yesterday.'

On the wall at about hip height, a series of scratches had been gouged out of the plasterwork.

CHAPTER 25

'Are you following me?' Ricky demanded. Jessie shrank away from him, pressing her back against the brick wall of the guest house.

'No, of course not,' she stammered. 'Why would I be doing that?'

'You tell me. First on Friday and now this. What are you up to?'

This ought to be her question. What was Ricky up to? Knowing would put her in danger, of that she no longer had any doubt. She'd been stupid to follow him.

'I was taking a shortcut.' She pointed down the street. 'I'm on my way home. Why would I think you were here?'

'Why come this way, then?'

'None of your bloody business.'

Ricky placed one hand on the wall behind her shoulder and leaned in so that his face was close to hers. He grabbed the fingers of her right hand and squeezed so hard, Jessie gasped at the pain.

'Stop following me.' His voice was low and menacing. 'Or I'll make sure that you never work again.'

Ricky pushed himself upright, deliberately catching Jessie on the side of her face with his signet ring as he did it. He winked at her, turned away and strode off.

Jessie felt faint. She rubbed her cheek, more for the unwanted physical contact than the damage Ricky had done. There was blood between her fingers. Shaking her hand to restore circulation, she headed out of the alley. She was more rattled than she wanted to admit.

There was no sign of Ricky when she reached the busy high street. Dodging through the holiday crowds, Jessie reached her side street and the sanctuary of home.

There was a bottle of white wine in the fridge. Jessie poured herself a large glass before sitting in her garden. It was remarkably quiet in the sun-trapped square, the bustle of the town muted by the houses. The sound of crowds and the PA at the soapbox derby floated in the air.

The wine vanished rapidly. To save her legs, she brought the bottle back out with her. Her fingers were still aching as she poured another large glass. And then another.

The sun sank behind the buildings, and the garden began to cool as Jessie sat, trying to decide what to do. The race must have finished. The traffic built up then faded, the crowds drifted past and away. Maybe she dozed for a while. Or perhaps the wine made her lose all sense of time. Either way, Yazza startled her.

'Did you drink all that on your own? You're a dark horse.' Yazza waggled the empty wine bottle. 'I'll get the other one.'

She brought a second bottle and another glass. She filled her own and held out the bottle to Jessie with a questioning look. When Jessie nodded, she half-filled the other glass. Settling on the other garden chair, Yazza watched as Jessie lifted the glass to her lips. Suddenly the wine tasted sour, making her choke and cough.

Yazza patted Jessie on the back, pulling her into a hug afterwards. Overwhelmed, Jessie began to cry.

'What's this?' Yazza asked in amazement. 'Have you been drinking all afternoon? That's not like you.'

'Went for a walk after you all left.' Jessie snuffled into a crumpled tissue she had pulled from her trouser pocket.

Yazza held Jessie by the shoulders and examined her face. She ran a gentle finger down Jessie's cheek. 'And where did you get this?'

Jessie's hand flew up to cover the mark. She could feel crusted lumps of blood on the soft flesh.

'What's going on, Jessie? I've been staying with you for three years now. We're friends, yeah?'

Jessie plonked the wine glass down onto the garden table and blew her nose. With a trembling finger, she picked at the scabs of blood.

'This is about Ricky Easton, isn't it?'

'What?' Jessie was stunned. She thought she had been hiding it so well.

'What is it between you two? You can't bear to be near him. He complains about you all the time, makes your life really difficult.'

'Oh, God. Is it that obvious?'

'Well, the complaining is.' Yazza smiled. 'Especially as he is the only one doing it. You know how the other performers all love what you do for them. Did he do that?'

Jessie stared at Yazza. She desperately wanted to confide in someone. 'If I explain, you have to promise to keep this to yourself. I could lose my job again.'

'Again?' Yazza looked surprised. 'Why again? And, yes, I promise. I can't bear to see you like this.'

Jessie looked at the little scabs of blood under her nails. She thought about Daisy and her suspicions that Ricky might be somehow involved. She couldn't tell Yazza about that — she had no proof. Sharing the old stuff might help.

'Well?'

'I knew Ricky years ago when he was first starting out. You know I used to work in the West End?'

'Yes. To be honest, if you were on *Phantom* and *Les Mis*, I never understood how you ended up out here.'

'I *was* on *Phantom*, and *Les Mis*, and several other big shows over the years. I met and married my husband working on those shows.'

'I didn't know you had been married.'

'For just over ten years. To Malcolm Bell.'

Yazza nearly dropped her glass in surprise. They all knew who Malcolm Bell was. They all wanted to work on one of his famous West End productions. 'God, what happened?'

'Ricky Easton happened. He was young, fit and handsome. Malc was away, taking a production to Broadway. I couldn't go with him, you know, union rules. I didn't mind, his career was way more important than mine. He was flying, and I was bumbling along. There was less and less time for me.'

'And then?'

'Ricky wasn't long out of drama school, got into the chorus on the show I was on. I was forty-two, he was twenty-three. I was stupid, he was ambitious. We had an affair.'

'You slept with him?' Yazza sounded horrified.

That made Jessie smile a little. 'I wasn't that bad looking, you know. I was stupid, though. He flattered me, told me it wasn't fair that I'd given up my career and been left behind. I got into the whole clandestine thing of it. Then suddenly, Malc was back, and it turned out that Ricky was a bastard.'

'What did he do?' Yazza's voice came out as a squeal.

'He told Malc about us. Demanded a lead role to keep it quiet. And that was the end of that. Turned out I wasn't the only one. Malc had been shagging his leading lady in New York and wanted rid of me anyway. He palmed Ricky off onto another producer to get his "big break". He paid me off with a divorce settlement. On the condition that I left London. I was embarrassing to him, apparently. A middle-aged woman having a fling with a young dancer.'

Yazza gasped. 'Wasn't he doing the same?'

'You know damn well that the rules are different for men. He gets to be the one the other men envy. I get to be the sad middle-aged slut,' Jessie said bitterly. 'They destroyed me, between them. Two men colluding to hide their embarrassment that an ordinary middle-aged woman found sex enjoyable.'

Jessie paused, the old scenes running like a bad movie in her mind. Usually, she could bury these thoughts, the memories of the rows and the looks on Malc and Ricky's faces. The way they had laughed together about her behind her back, then to her face when she'd tried to negotiate. 'Anyway, here I am. Do you know what? I've never told anyone here why I ended up in Cromer.'

'You still haven't. You could have gone anywhere.'

'I know. I did for a while. Freelance contracts on tours, pantos that needed extra staff. When I hit fifty, I realised I was alone, with no home and no partner and that if I didn't do something about it, I could die in some hotel room and no one would even notice.'

Yazza laughed. 'A bit overdramatic!'

Jessie laughed with her. 'Yeah, it was. Anyway, someone suggested they were looking for a sound op for the season here. I came up, loved the job and the town. Bought the cottage and settled down.'

'Until this season.'

'Yes.'

'So, what is he threatening to do?'

'Convince the bosses I can't do my job.'

'That's spiteful, but you could ride that out. We all know that you're great.'

Jessie gulped at her wine again. She flexed her fingers, the ones Ricky had crushed. If they didn't work properly, she couldn't do her job. It was all about delicacy on the sliders. Would Ricky really crush her hands to make her keep his secrets? 'I thought it would be easier just to ignore him and get through the season. Until Friday night.'

'Oh?'

'When I locked up, I saw Ricky with some bloke behind the theatre.'

'Ricky's not gay? He *is* a shag bandit. He tried it on with Daisy and with me before he got his hooks into Hallie.'

'No, I don't mean that. The man attacked him. I saw them together again this afternoon.' Jessie rubbed at her cheek. 'Ricky was buying something. I think this bloke is a drug dealer.'

CHAPTER 26

DI Edwards called for an FI team to check the area around the bins. Sara taped off the alley at each end as they waited for them to arrive. Bowen and Noble had sorted out the interview room at the local nick, but when they had approached the Hayward group, the men had all been drunk. Statements given under the influence were not admissible in court, so they would attend the following morning. Kit Grice had been working on the waltzers and agreed to do the same.

'There's no one about at the theatre,' said DC Bowen grumpily. 'Your friend, the general manager, failed to tell you that all the theatre staff have Sunday and Monday off.'

'They sent a contact list,' said Noble. 'Staff are mostly local. We could see them tomorrow. Performers are staying in digs for the season and might have gone home for the weekend.'

'Set up what you can.' DI Edwards sighed. 'You two work from the local station tomorrow and get some staff statements. I'll have to go to headquarters first thing. Sara, you better start in the office with Aggie, and we'll take it from there. Let's call it a day.'

With the forensic investigators in place, Sara headed home in her car. When she called Chris, he was working in the garden.

'I've got something ready to cook,' he said. He sounded anxious to please. 'We can eat as soon as you get back.'

'See you in half an hour, then.' Sara ended the call. Sitting at the traffic lights waiting for them to change, she gazed up the hill out of the town. It being late on Sunday afternoon, she hadn't expected there to be much traffic. But as far as she could see up the hill, there was a queue coming towards her. It was a line of caravans and horseboxes being towed by an assortment of broken-down four-wheel drive vehicles, interspersed with several white vans that had seen better days. She glanced at them individually as she drove out of town. None of the things looked legal or roadworthy. In fact, it looked like a convoy of hard-up Travellers, the sort that got moved from town to town.

She tapped on her mobile and called the office. The switchboard was answered by the ever-on-duty and always reliable Sergeant Trevor Jones. 'Good afternoon, Sara. What would you like?'

'Trev, are we expecting any Traveller groups in the county?'

'Haven't you heard? We've been watching for them all day. Have they got to Cromer?'

'Just arriving, I think. What do you know?'

'Seem to be a group from the south coast. Rocked up in Lowestoft about a week ago. Illegally camped on a playing field behind the high school. Evicted this morning. Lots of petty thefts in the meantime.'

'Is there an official Travellers' site up here?'

'Nope.' Jones recited a list that he obviously knew by heart. 'We have five in the county. Nearest ones to Cromer are Yarmouth, King's Lynn or Norwich.'

'Do you think they'll keep moving then?'

'I doubt it. They've probably come for the carnival. I'll let Uniform know.'

'Where is the site in Norwich?'

'There's two. Either at Mile Cross or out near the Norfolk showground. Why?'

'We've been talking to the Grices. They've got their funfair up on Carnival Field. Do you know which site they usually live on?'

'Neither,' said Jones. 'They're not Travellers. They're Show People. They have their own grounds off Wroxham Road. Been there for at least three generations.'

'In the middle of suburbia?' Sara was surprised.

'You can't see it from the main road. That land would be worth a fortune if they wanted to sell it for building.'

'Thanks, Sarge.' She signed off.

Sara knew what it was like to be the victim of prejudice, and wanted to treat the Travellers with fairness and respect. But the sight of this group heading into Cromer in the middle of a murder inquiry had made her hackles rise. *SCU have enough work to do*, she thought as she parked outside her cottage.

Chris had been busy in the garden. The grass was cut. The flower beds near the kitchen had been weeded, and some pretty bedding plants now filled the border in a simple pattern. Even the pots at the front had been cleared up and trimmed.

'Wow! You've been going at it. It's great.'

'I can't do all that lot.' The garden was long and narrow. A footpath staggered unevenly past the broken-down garden shed to the farmer's field behind the little terrace of cottages. It was a weed-infested wilderness, or "wildlife garden", as Sara preferred to think of it. 'That would take a couple of weeks.'

Chris had also cleaned up the garden furniture. He'd wiped off the plastic chairs and levelled up the table, which was set with plates, cutlery, napkins and a vase of wildflowers. 'You sit down and relax,' he said. 'I won't be a minute.'

Sara did as she was told. It wasn't often they got the chance to relax together, and it was a lovely warm evening. Chris brought a chilled bottle of wine and two glasses, which he put on the table. Finally, he brought a large bowl of salad and a piping hot lasagne, which smelled delicious.

113

'Made it myself,' he said proudly. He put the food on the table, and Sara expected him to sit down or pour some wine, but he stood next to her, looking nervous. 'Do you think this looks romantic?'

'It does, rather.' Sara smiled. 'Thank you for doing all this. It's lovely.'

'Good, I was hoping you thought that.' Chris pulled up the second chair and sat next to Sara, taking her hand. 'You see, I've been thinking a lot recently. About us, I mean.'

Me too, Sara thought. *Now what? Is he going to tell me to sell the cottage and move in with him? I'm not sure I'm ready for that.*

'We've been going out for a year now.' Chris's voice wobbled slightly. 'I think we could move on to the next level, don't you?'

'Depends what you mean by that.'

Chris shuffled his seat and pressed her hand tightly. 'If you're ready, I am.'

He dropped onto the grass on one knee, let go of Sara's hand and pulled a small box from his pocket.

Sara froze. *Oh no*, she thought, *not that, please don't ask me that.*

Chris opened the box. Inside a gold band with diamonds and sapphires nestled in royal blue velvet.

'Sara Hirst, will you marry me?'

CHAPTER 27

The soapbox derby had been a huge success. Apart from a few minor bumps and grazes, the competitors had all survived. The prizes had been awarded by one of Daisy's maids-in-waiting, while the committee struggled over which of the three should be promoted to Carnival Queen. Adele had expressed a preference for the title to remain unfilled as a tribute to Daisy, while the three other girls took on the remaining duties fairly. She wasn't sure that the others had listened.

Greg, Xander and his two friends had spent much of the afternoon in the marquee drinking beer. When a tall, gangly-looking young detective constable had arrived to invite them to give statements about Friday's dance, they had been too drunk. All four of them had been told that they had to turn up at the police station the following morning at ten. Adele had watched this carry-on from the bar, where she had been buying a cup of coffee. It had made her squirm with embarrassment. The boys were all young and she doubted they understood the importance of what they were supposed to be doing. Greg was another matter. He was supposed to be the adult of the party, not the ringleader.

Henry had gone home as soon as the derby had ended. The Shantymen were singing in Norwich that night, and he'd needed to get ready. Adele had stayed on to keep an eye on the clearing-up operation. By seven o'clock, it had all been done.

The house was empty when she let herself in. Adele was grateful. There were pizzas in the freezer if anyone was hungry when they got back. She put one in the oven for herself before taking a shower. The en-suite looked like a hurricane had blown through. Clothes and towels littered the floor. Greg had vomited inaccurately in the toilet at some point last night. It had dried on the floor and porcelain. Adele cleaned up after him, then stood gratefully under the water, letting it wash more than the dirt from her.

Once she was dressed, she went down to check on her pizza. She had just cut it into slices when a taxi pulled up, and Greg led the boys inside. Jacob and Xander were as bad as each other. They blew noisily into the kitchen, grabbing slices of her pizza from the plate without asking, took beers from the fridge and loped out to the back garden. Greg looked at her and laughed as he did the same, taking the last slice for himself. Only Benji hung back, looking apologetic.

'Was that for you?' he asked. When Adele nodded, he looked around the kitchen. 'Shall I do you another one? Are they in the freezer?'

'That's OK. I'll do some more. Why don't you join your friends?'

Benji hesitated, twisting his hands together. Adele could see he was sober. She unwrapped more pizzas and put them in the oven to cook. 'Orange juice?'

'Oh yes, thank you.' Benji seemed relieved.

'Benji, if you don't like all this drinking, you don't have to do it.'

'I've got races coming up.' He shoved his hands into his trouser pockets to keep them still. 'They don't understand.'

'Well, they should. They're your friends.'

'Are they?' Benji looked straight at Adele. 'I'm not sure. I think perhaps I ought to go home.'

She could hardly blame him. Not only had Xander attacked him, but she had heard the spite in Jacob's voice when the police had turned up. This had something to do with Greg. What might seem like banter to him felt like cruelty to the person on the receiving end, as Adele knew all too well.

'I have to make a statement to the police in the morning,' Benji said, looking out the window as gales of raucous laughter drifted in from the back garden.

'Why don't you give your mum a call this evening. Make sure it's all right with the police when you speak to them, then you can head home.'

'You won't be offended?'

'Me? No. Why should I be?' She glanced outside. 'You might have to choose your moment with Xander.'

Benji smiled. 'Thank you, Adele. You're such a kind mum. I don't know why Xander doesn't appreciate you more.' He went outside tentatively, to be greeted with drunken cheers and ribald comments about his choice of drink.

I do, thought Adele. *Because he follows his father's lead.*

She waited, perched on a kitchen stool until her timer told her to check the pizzas. She had placed two of them on the chopping board when Greg staggered back into the kitchen and over to the fridge. Extracting more tins of beer, he dumped them by the pizzas. Adele ran the cutting wheel across one pizza, pulling apart the slices and arranging them on a plate.

'I want a word with you.' Greg's voice was slurred. Adele didn't look up, waiting for the accusation about Henry that she had been expecting since lunchtime. Perhaps she could distract him with the food.

'What about?' She kept her voice low and even, desperate not to antagonise him further. She began to cut the second pizza.

'The boys have got to talk to the fucking police tomorrow.'

'Yes?' The wheel crunched over the pastry base. Adele didn't say that she already knew. 'So do I.'

'We're all going to say the same thing.'

117

Adele pulled the pizza in half, swivelled it around and cut more slices.

'That we all went to the pub afterwards.' Greg leaned over to grab Adele's hand. She held onto the cutter, pressing it down to keep her hand steady. 'Then we came back here. You are going to tell them the same.'

'Am I?' Adele looked up in surprise. 'Can't I just say I was asleep and didn't hear you come in?'

It was an easier lie to carry off. She might get away with that. Her heart was beating faster, her breath high in her chest. Panic rose from her stomach.

Greg walked around the kitchen island, still gripping her by the wrist. He wrenched her hand upwards and shook it until Adele dropped the cutter. Towering over her, he pulled her towards him so their bodies were clamped tight together. 'You are going to say that we all came in together. Is that clear?'

She looked up at him unwillingly. He grinned at the obvious signs of terror she knew would be visible on her face. Pushing her backwards step by step, she could feel the heat from the open door of the oven behind her. The third pizza, her dinner, was waiting on the bottom shelf. She hadn't even had time to turn the thing off.

'You're going to say that we all came home about one o'clock.' Greg's voice was a low growl. 'That Benji drove us. All of us. Together. We woke you up.'

He had her pinned against the door now. Adele could feel the heat against the back of her legs. She tried to bend her knees a little to stop the metal bars from burning the back of her calves. Greg felt her movement, responding by pushing her harder. A bar burned into her skin and she cried out. Her husband pulled her away from the open door, grabbed her other arm and forced her down to the floor.

They knelt in front of the oven, heat blasting at them. He twisted Adele around to face the black interior. 'Do you understand?'

'Yes, yes.' Adele nodded frantically.

Unsatisfied, Greg pulled one arm and deliberately pushed it against the metal bars of the shelf. Adele screamed, struggling to free herself. Greg released the pressure a little, allowing her arm to rise a fraction above the danger.

'What will you say? Answer me.'

He pressed her arm against the bars again. The pain was unbearable. Adele screamed again.

'You all came home together. Benji drove. You got here at one.'

Greg let go, and Adele slumped to the floor, weeping. As he stood up, she could see another pair of feet standing in the doorway to the utility room.

'Came for the beers,' Xander's voice slurred with too much alcohol. 'Hurry up with that pizza, Mum.'

CHAPTER 28

Chris had gone home after they had eaten the lasagne in a difficult silence. Sara knew she wasn't ready for marriage with anyone, let alone someone who wanted to have his relationship cake and eat it doing some amateur theatricals. She had told Chris that she wanted to think about it.

'It's about this place, isn't it?' He'd pointed at the cottage on his way out. 'You put this place before us.'

Sara had refrained from saying that he could just as easily do less acting, give up his flat and move out to live in Happisburgh, but she hadn't wanted it to sound like an invitation to move in with her. He'd driven off looking hurt, with the ring box stuffed back into his trouser pocket.

Sara tossed and turned in her bed until dawn before giving up the struggle and getting up. She reached the SCU office at the Police HQ in Wymondham before seven, distractedly clearing old paperwork.

'Good Lord!' said Aggie when she found Sara by the filing cabinet. 'I wasn't expecting anyone else this early.'

'Just clearing up,' Sara replied without turning around. Aggie was observant when it came to people and their emotions. 'I'll make the coffee.'

Sara had set up the incident board, bought bacon sandwiches and cleaned the stack of dirty mugs by the time the team gathered at eight. Stifling a yawn, she could feel Aggie watching her.

Edwards kicked things off. 'Where are we with the shoes and handbag?'

'I left them with Forensics.' Sara poured herself a drink, keeping her head down. 'I checked the contents. A purse with some cash in it and Daisy's bank card. Make-up, tissues, mobile.'

'That could be useful.'

'It's with Digital. The battery had run out, so I couldn't try it. They'll let us know about the contents, assuming it's easy to access. Then there was something else. A small bag with tablets in it. Looked like ecstasy to me. Forensics are sending them off for testing.'

'Excellent. And the kid at the restaurant?'

'I think he was telling the truth, sir. No reason not to, and he showed me the damage to the wall.'

Edwards nodded. 'How are we getting on with the CCTV?'

'Still chasing the local council,' said Aggie. 'The amusement arcade and the pub are sending us what they have this morning.'

'Good. Kit Grice says they went to the beach and parted somewhere near the RNLI café. See what the council has along the prom and the main streets.' DI Edwards tapped the photo of Daisy on the incident board. 'Mike, you and Ian can get on with the interviews this morning. I want to know what really happened at the dance on Friday.'

'If they tell the truth,' said Bowen in a sour tone.

'Do your best. Time is moving on, and we haven't got very far. Get statements from everyone you can, including any theatre staff. Track down the security guys as well. They might have seen something. Sara, we're off to see Doctor Taylor.'

The coffee had kicked in by the time Sara and the DI arrived at the mortuary. Dr Taylor led them to the family viewing room, where Sara had said goodbye to her father the year before. Daisy was laid out as discreetly as possible. Her hair had been combed and the dirty make-up removed from her face. She looked young and innocent. The pristine sheet covering her was pulled up under Daisy's chin.

'Daisy's father is coming in soon to do the formal ID,' said Dr Taylor. 'I have the notes in my office, but I thought you might like to see her before we put her into the freezer.'

'There doesn't seem to be a mark on her,' said Sara. 'Will it be long before you release her?'

'There'll be a coroner's inquest, of course. It will be up to them, but I doubt it will happen soon. Especially when there are marks like these.' Dr Taylor twitched the sheet down. There were bruises and red marks on her neck. 'The rest are less obvious. Best come to my office.'

Dr Taylor's room was down a warren of corridors that had no daylight in them. It felt suitably subterranean, given the nature of his work. He produced a thick folder. Turning his PC screen so they could see it, he opened a file of photos.

'I'll start here.' He pointed to an image of the back of Daisy's head. The hair was matted with sand. 'Common beach sand, as far as I can make out. It's present across the back of her scalp and in this head wound.'

'Thrown onto the beach perhaps?' The DI squinted at the screen.

'More complicated than that. Daisy was wearing an evening dress. There was sand on the back of that, not much, but enough to be sure. I suspect we'll find it in her shoes and handbag as well.'

'Underwear?' Sara asked.

'Matching set, in green lace. Sand in those as well. And elsewhere.' Dr Taylor hesitated and glanced at the two detectives. He frowned as he carried on. 'I'm afraid to say that Daisy was raped. This is where it gets complicated.'

'The damage is clear?' asked the DI. Sara was happy for him to lead. She found rape cases the most difficult to deal with. They made her so angry.

Dr Taylor's hand hovered over the computer mouse. 'I have photos of the evidence. Do you want to see it?'

'Not really. We'll take your word for it.'

Sara was grateful for Edward's refusal. It seemed Dr Taylor was too.

'Thank you. It always seems such an invasion of privacy to me, although it is absolutely necessary, of course. The thing is, I found a few grains of sand inside her. Which indicates to me that she had intercourse where she could pick it up, like the beach.'

'DNA samples?'

'I've sent a vaginal sample for analysis,' the doctor said. 'There was also a small number of pubic hairs in her underpants. They should be hers, but you never know, so I've sent them off as well. Belt and braces.'

'Daisy died having sex on the beach?' Sara asked. 'Why were her shoes found all the way uptown? What were those marks in the alley behind the chippie?'

'I'll get to that in a minute.' Dr Taylor brought up pictures of the soles of Daisy's feet. 'She had walked quite a way with no shoes on. Look how dirty her feet are. That could have been before or after, of course. However, I believe that she died in the alley opposite the bus station.'

'What?' Edwards was surprised.

'I can't be sure of the sequence, but there were other traces in her head wound. They look like paint or bits of plaster. My assistant is looking into that now.' Dr Taylor pointed to a younger man, who was working at a large microscope. 'She was plucky, tried to fight her attacker off. There's debris under her fingernails, also gone for analysis. Now, look at the top of her feet.'

He brought up another picture. The tops of Daisy's feet were covered in scratches and bloody scabs.

'She's been dragged with no shoes on and her feet trailing on a rough surface. She must have been alive because the wounds have bled enough for me to be sure of that.'

'Raped on the beach and then moved?'

'Possibly. Or in the alley behind the posh chippie. Look here. There are more scratches on her back.' The doctor flicked up more photos. 'Then there is the damage to her neck that I showed you. Whoever attacked Daisy was violent with her. They slammed her down, held her by the neck while they did what they wanted to do.'

'She was strangled?' Sara's eyes widened as she tried to put the evidence together.

'No, she didn't die of strangulation. I can't find the correct injuries for that. I think that she's been held by the neck, probably by the man's forearm. When she resisted, he probably pinned her down that way. Naturally, this reduces the oxygen supply. It would have been enough to make her pass out, and once she became passive and compliant, I think her attacker loosened his grip.'

Edwards narrowed his eyes as he put the pieces together. 'Daisy is attacked, held down and raped somewhere where she can get both sand and plaster in her back, and her clothes. She passes out. When the attacker has finished with her, she's moved — dragged, say — and dumped in that alley.'

'That would be my best estimation.' Taylor nodded as he held up some report forms from the file. 'I think she was still alive at that point, though unconscious.'

'So how did she die? Exposure?'

'Vomit.' Taylor laid a piece of paper on the desk. It showed several graphs. 'I checked her lungs and stomach. She'd had a bit to drink. There were some chemical traces in her stomach as well. I'm waiting for the test results before I can say what she'd taken.'

'And?'

'Once she had passed out due to lack of oxygen, it would have been hard for her to wake up again. She threw up as she lay on her back in the alley. And inhaled it. She drowned in her own vomit.'

CHAPTER 29

It was a sight Adele had never expected to see. Standing next to Henry in the Carnival Field car park opening, their view and the main access to the parking area were blocked. Dozens of ramshackle caravans, rusty horseboxes and old vehicles were parked in an approximate circle. Horses were tethered on ropes and chains across the remaining grass. Dogs ran freely around the place, emptying rubbish bins and snapping at one another. Children of all ages were playing a makeshift game of football in the centre. Washing flapped on lines that stretched between caravans while women stood in groups smoking and talking. Several men watched Henry and Adele with suspicion.

It reminded Adele of an old-fashioned cowboy movie, with the waggons drawn into a circle in defence. Except that would make her and Henry the attackers. The worst thing was that the camp had been set up near the entrance. The carnival marquee was behind the circle and largely hidden from view. The funfair was marooned at the back of the field. It would be impossible to reach the remaining car parking spaces without going around the encampment. Would anyone want to leave their vehicle there now?

'I don't like Travellers,' said Henry. He stood with his arms folded, his face rigid with anger.

'Just because they don't live like us doesn't make them bad people.' Adele spoke quietly in case anyone from the camp overheard their conversation. The men who were watching them looked aggressive, and she really didn't want any confrontation.

'I know that,' replied Henry. 'But look at 'em. They're trouble, they are. Is the marquee all right?'

The pair walked along the car park fence until they came to a small gap for pedestrians. Crossing the grass, Adele could see that a couple of the men had moved around the caravans to a new position to keep an eye on them. Henry unlaced part of the door to the tent, and they went inside. Everything was as it had been left.

'Well, that's a mercy. Thought them buggers would have nicked all the booze by now.'

'What are we going to do?' Adele was watching through the gap in the canvas. 'We won't be able to do any of our events with all those vehicles parked there.'

The biggest event of the week was the carnival parade. It happened on Wednesday afternoon, and hundreds of people were waiting to take part. There would be dozens of lorries and trailers dressed up and waiting in garages. Teams had been working for weeks at the chance to win the prize for the best-decorated float. Dance troupes, majorettes and marching bands would have routines rehearsed. Clowns, jugglers and stilt walkers were booked. Everyone congregated at Carnival Field. The roads were closed, the pavements roped off, and the parade left at half past two to go right around the town in a circle. It took all afternoon to pass by and return to the field.

Adele's head spun at the idea of trying to reorganize the parade. It would be impossible. Besides, this was why the parking area was called Carnival Field. It had been the meeting place for the parade participants long before it had been turned into the overspill car park.

'How will we manage?' Adele turned to face Henry, who was already on his mobile.

'Calling everyone up here who can make it,' he said. He pulled out a table and a couple of chairs and sat with his back to Adele. 'Can you work the coffee machine?'

'I think so.'

Henry's first call was answered, and he launched into a tirade. Adele went behind the bar to see what she could do. By the time she had worked out how to turn on the electrics and found the bags of coffee for the filter machine, Henry had spoken to several more of the committee. Adele sat with him, waiting for the filter to finish gurgling.

'We'll have enough people for an emergency meeting. Brian says the council have been called in too.'

'Good. We'll think of something between us.' Adele's stomach bubbled, and Henry smiled at her until she folded her arms across her belly.

'What's this?' Henry gently took one of her hands and extended her arm. Two large sticking plasters covered much of the underneath of her forearm. 'What you done?'

'Just an accident.' She pulled her hand away, not looking Henry in the face. 'I was cooking pizzas last night, and I caught myself on the oven shelf.'

The memory of the previous evening made Adele shake with nausea and fear. That was why her stomach was out of order. When she had managed to get off the floor, she had run cold water over the burns on her arm. The pain had been excruciating, as the burns were deep — sufficiently deep that she ought to have gone to the local hospital. Fear of having to explain how she came by the burns had stopped her. Besides, Greg would have been furious, and she couldn't cope with any more of him last night. The burn on her calf was less deep. It also had a plaster over it.

The worst thing had been when Benji had come inside to fill his juice glass. Adele had been sitting on the high kitchen stool trying to open the home first aid kit with the wrong hand. His mouth had opened in shock at the sight of her arm, and he had rushed to help her.

'Don't make a fuss,' she had whispered, although she'd let him unwrap the two large plasters and stick them in place. 'It only makes me feel worse.'

'Mrs Hayward — I mean, Adele.' Keeping his voice low, Benji had stumbled over his words. 'It's none of my business, but this is wrong. Is there nothing you can do about it?'

'It's OK, just an accident. I'll be fine.'

Benji had frowned. 'What happened? Why didn't Xander help you?'

Adele had shaken her head in reply, and Benji had gone to his room and rung his mother. She was working away for a couple of days and had promised to pick him up as soon as she could on Wednesday morning. Adele was too busy with the carnival to take him back to Essex, and she doubted Greg would agree if they asked him.

She found it acutely embarrassing that an eighteen-year-old saw what was going on and cared enough to ask when her own son didn't. Xander seemed to think all this was normal. It appeared that Greg had persuaded her son that this was an acceptable way to treat his mother. Perhaps he told Xander it was Adele's fault and that his mother deserved it. Why not? When he said it to her often enough.

She had spent the night in the other spare bedroom with the door bolted. Not that she had actually got any sleep. She had welcomed Henry's outraged phone call summoning her down to Carnival Field.

Henry gently took her hand in his rough, tanned, working man's palm. 'An accident? Really?'

The kindness in his voice made Adele weep. Feeling betrayed by the tears, she wiped them away with her free hand. 'I really did get burned by the bars in the oven.'

Henry was having none of this. 'Not an accident, though, was it? I don't know what's going on with you, and I know you'll say it's nothing to do with me.' He gripped Adele's hand even tighter when she tried to pull it away. 'No, don't do that. Listen to me.'

'Let go, Henry.' She didn't need this now. Her next task would be to talk to the police and lie to them about Friday night.

'Let me finish. I know I'm a boring old bugger. I knows what I look like, and I ain't no catch. I just wants you to know . . .'

Adele wrenched her hand free and stood up so quickly that the folding chair fell backwards onto the grass. She couldn't cope with anything else. 'Leave me alone. It's none of your bloody business.'

CHAPTER 30

Whatever they found out now, Sara knew they were heading into complex legal territory. If the attacker hadn't actually strangled her, then the charge would be assault and rape, which was bad enough. But if she was still breathing when they had left her, it was manslaughter, not murder. And Sara wanted it to be murder because she felt their callous actions in moving Daisy amounted to the greater charge, and the perpetrator should be punished accordingly.

'This mustn't get out to anyone else,' Edwards insisted as he drove them up to the Cromer Police Station.

'Not even the team?'

'Not at the moment. The report will be out once those test results are back. I don't want any leaks before that.'

'What about her parents?' Sara thought of the devastated couple they had left mourning their only child.

'It's a suspicious death, and they know that already. Someone brutally attacked Daisy. We'll bring them to justice for that.'

Cromer Police Station was a newbuild and fully equipped with a viewing area behind the interview rooms. Noble and Bowen were taking a statement from one of Xander Hayward's friends.

'Benji Wilder,' supplied Sara. 'That's the one they had fallen out with the other day. He doesn't look very happy.'

Bowen asked for a DNA swab, and the young man readily agreed. Once it was completed, Noble thanked Benji and escorted him out. Edwards and Sara headed in to catch up with Bowen.

'How have you got on?' asked Edwards.

'Mixed bag,' Bowen admitted. 'He was the last of the Hayward men. They're all telling the same tale. That one is going home on Wednesday. He's given his home address, so I didn't see any reason why he couldn't leave. Anyway, he's given us a DNA swab. The others haven't.'

'Hayward, father and son, I assume?' Sara grimaced.

'Spot on, and the other friend. Jacob Marsh, he's called. Mr Hayward got very huffy and had obviously warned them to say no before they got here. We can't force them to do it unless we have grounds to caution them, and we don't have enough evidence at the moment.'

Sara wasn't sure if these overprivileged young men annoyed or amused her. 'What tale? You said they were all telling the same tale.'

Bowen looked at his notes. 'They say Mrs Hayward left early because she was busy the next morning. They stayed on with Dad, and they all had a dance with Daisy at some point, even Mr Hayward. Dad bought lots of booze, it would seem. The funfair boys turned up late and took exception to Xander dancing with Daisy and started a fight, which the security men broke up.'

'Do the security men agree on this?'

'As far as it goes. I think one was probably having a smoke outside but wouldn't say so. Anyway, the bar manager decided to shut the evening down, so the Hayward party went on to The Duke on New Street because there was a band on.'

'All of them? Even the father?' Edwards looked sceptical.

'So they say. Benji doesn't drink, but he can drive. They sent him to fetch Dad's car, and he drove them home later on. End of.'

'That all sounds rather neat,' said Sara. 'Hopefully, Aggie can get some CCTV from the pub to confirm it.'

'And Mrs Hayward?' asked Edwards

'She's coming in next. Do you want to speak to her?'

Mrs Hayward was waiting in the reception area when Sara went to check. It was a hot, sunny day, and Mrs Hayward was wearing a floral short-sleeved dress with a lightweight cardigan draped over her shoulders. It slipped to the floor when she sat in the interview room. As she bent to retrieve it, Sara saw her wince. Once she was seated, Mrs Hayward held it on her lap with both hands. That didn't prevent Sara from noticing that she had two large sticking plasters on her right forearm.

'Are you happy to do this, Mrs Hayward?' she asked. 'Have you injured yourself?'

'Oh, it was a silly accident,' she stuttered. 'I caught myself. On the bars of the oven. Last night. You can call me Adele.'

She clamped her lips shut as if she was afraid that she had already said too much. Sara looked at the plasters and wondered how big the burn was when it required so much cover. Edwards thanked Adele for coming in, then leaned back and let Sara lead.

'Adele, can you tell me in your own words what happened on Friday?'

'I don't really know. I went home before the others.'

'Why was that?'

'I'm on the carnival committee. I have to be up early every day to look after various things.'

'Did you see any of the dancing?'

'Daisy opened the ball.' Adele looked down at her fingers, which were twisting the flimsy cardigan. 'She did the first dance with her father. I left soon after that.'

'What time did the rest of your party get home?'

'I'm not exactly sure. I was asleep. Greg disturbed me a bit, but I soon got off again.'

'Can you estimate the time?'

Adele looked worried. Beads of sweat began to pop on her forehead. 'Late. Maybe one? I'm really not sure.'

'Had the boys been drinking?'

'Oh yes, I expect so. Greg bought a round before I left the dance.'

'But the other three didn't disturb you? Only your husband?'

'When he came into the bedroom.' Adele was biting her lip now.

'How had they got home if they were all drinking?'

Adele looked at Sara in a panic. Her eyes darted left and right before settling back on her hands in her lap.

'I'm not sure.' With a glance at her boss, Sara let the question hang. Adele twisted the cardigan again. 'Did they get a taxi? Yes, they must have got a taxi.'

'How had you got to the dance?'

'We took both cars because I knew I would be leaving early.' This answer seemed to come more easily. 'I went home in my car.'

'Where was your husband's car on Saturday morning?'

'It was in the Carnival Field. He brought it back the next morning.'

Sara could tell she was lying from the look on the woman's face. After that, Adele would only say that she couldn't remember any more details. It was a witness interview. There was little else that Sara could do. Edwards wound up and escorted Mrs Hayward out of the room. When he returned, Sara let out a big sigh as Noble and Bowen joined them. The team sat around the interview room table.

'Thoughts?' the DI asked them.

'That didn't add up, did it?' Bowen mused.

'What about the mention of the taxi? Did the others say they'd used a taxi?'

'No, they all said Benji had driven them home in the Porsche.'

'Sara, get hold of Aggie and ask her to speak to the local taxi firms. They'll have a record of bookings and runs.'

Sara nodded. 'Shall I ask for number plate recognition on the Porsche as well? That would give us a time for it being moved.'

'Yes. I think our Mrs Hayward is hiding something.'

'Perhaps she really can't remember,' suggested Bowen.

'Or perhaps she has been told what to say,' said Sara, her tone dark. 'That was some accident with the oven if it needed two bloody great plasters like that. There was another one on the back of her leg.'

'She looked stressed to me,' ventured DC Noble.

'Why?' she asked, wanting to encourage him.

Noble considered his answer carefully. 'She wouldn't look at you much and kept twisting that cardigan. She looked really uncomfortable.'

'Good observation,' said Edwards. 'Sara?'

'I think we should find out a bit more about this family. Especially Greg Hayward. I think there is something here he doesn't want us to know. It's too convenient that all four of those men are giving us exactly the same story. And he's a bully.'

'What makes you say that?'

'Used to getting his own way, then.' Sara thought about her encounter with the estate agent. 'I find him bombastic, to be honest. Thinks the world of his son, that's obvious. And the son was free with his fists until we interrupted that fight. Like father, like son?'

'OK, you dig around on that for a while.' Edwards nodded. 'I agree. He's not very likeable. But that doesn't make him guilty of anything. Bowen?'

'We have some of the theatre staff in here this afternoon.'

'Good.'

There was the sound of shouting in the reception and people running past the interview room door. Several police cars started up with blues and twos and drove off rapidly towards the town. When they went out into the corridor, Sara could see the desk sergeant talking urgently on the phone as a pair of officers raced out pulling on stab-proof vests.

'What on earth is going on now?' Edwards asked in annoyance. 'Just what we needed — more drama!'

CHAPTER 31

Neither Jessie nor Yazza could decide what to do about Ricky Easton. Drinking or taking recreational drugs when the shows were running was forbidden to cast and crew. What you did in your own time after a long day was your own affair, so long as you didn't do it on the premises. Jessie didn't tell Yazza what she had overheard on the cans or about him crushing her fingers. If he was high half the time, then he was hiding it well. In her book, he was a habitual user and was capable of anything, including damaging her hands.

'We have no idea what he's taking,' said Yazza. They were relaxing in the living room after a Monday morning lic-in. 'And we can't just go up and ask him.'

'Hardly.' Jessie had to smile at the idea. 'Or about this bloke I've seen him with.'

'Did you get a good look at him?'

'He was well-built, sort of like a bodybuilder.' Jessie tried to focus on the image in her mind. 'Middle-aged, late forties probably. Same height as Ricky, with a shaven head. Not much neck.'

'You may as well be describing any pusher anywhere. Nothing distinguishing?'

'Tats.' Jessie sat up suddenly. She sounded positive. 'I didn't see them clearly, but there was definitely ink. Snakes? They came up the back of what neck he had and wound up his skull and around his ear.'

'I think you should report him.'

'Who to? The police? I'm not doing that.' Jessie was beginning to panic. 'I don't have any proof, do I?'

'I meant to Larry.' Larry Gibson was the musical director and production manager for the season. Anything to do with the cast or crew was his responsibility.

'I can't. If I say anything, Ricky will say it's because I'm rubbish at my job. That's why he's been on my back all season, building the case for my incompetence.'

'All right,' said Yazza, trying to sound soothing. 'I get it. You'd best keep out of his way for a while. I'll keep an eye on him backstage.'

Jessie's phone rang. The screen told her it was Donal Byrne, the general manager. For one heart-stopping moment, she thought that Ricky had gone ahead and complained about her. That Donal was calling to sack her. With wild eyes, she refused the call. Yazza looked at her in confusion.

'He'll leave a message,' said Jessie. Holding the mobile at arm's length, she waited until the callback number began to ring. Yazza's phone trilled a few seconds later. She took the call and left the room.

Donal's message explained that the police wanted to interview all theatre staff about Friday evening and she should make an appointment. Jessie was so wrapped up in her own problems that she thought he meant the tattooed man and Ricky. Had someone else seen and reported it? Surely, she had been the last person out by that door? Everyone else was already either in the bar at the front or had left.

Yazza looked into the living room. 'We've all got to be interviewed by the police in case we saw anything to do with poor Daisy.' Jessie sank back into the armchair in relief. 'I wrote the number on the pad in the kitchen.'

The man who answered Jessie's call sounded as if he was running an appointment system. 'Would 1.30 p.m. be suitable?'

'That would be fine.'

'When you get to the station, ask for DC Noble. I'll come and find you in reception.'

I'm helping the police with their inquiries, thought Jessie. That was a first.

'Fancy some fresh air?' she asked Yazza when the dancer had showered and dressed. 'We could go up to the Big Sky.'

'Good idea.'

It was a beautiful August day, and the town was busy with pedestrians and traffic. The Big Sky Café was the wood-and-thatch building between the clifftop gardens and Carnival Field. It was Jessie's favourite coffee shop in the summer. Dozens of plastic tables and chairs stood on the green outside, and the view from the clifftop was magnificent. It wouldn't matter if it was busy up there — they could sit on the edge of Carnival Field and admire the view just as easily.

As they headed up towards it, there seemed to be more drivers than usual squabbling over the on-street parking spaces.

'Look at that.' Yazza pointed to a plume of smoke that was rising behind the café. The air was full of the acrid smell of burning. Police sirens rapidly approached, screaming onto the car park on Carnival Field. Even in the bright sunshine of midday, Jessie could see blue flashing lights. There was a lot of shouting too.

The tables outside the café were empty. The staff were standing by the kitchen door at the back of a crowd of people. Everyone was looking into the car park. Neither Yazza nor Jessie could see over their heads. They moved a pair of chairs onto a set of paving slabs where the queue for refreshments usually waited. Climbing up, they had a much better view.

There was a Traveller encampment, right in the middle of the Carnival Field. Dozens of caravans, horseboxes and knackered old vans were parked in a circle. A bonfire had been lit in the middle, which seemed to consist of smashed-up pallets, old tyres and bags of rubbish. It was burning fitfully. The smoke was black and oily and decidedly unpleasant. Some of the watching crowd were coughing. A group of men that Jessie assumed were Travellers stood arguing loudly with half a dozen uniformed police officers. A group of sullen-faced women and children stood inside the circle, watching silently.

'Oooh, I think it's going to kick off,' said Yazza.

A police officer tried to move one of the Traveller men out of the way. It was enough to spark off the fight that had obviously been brewing for some minutes. Jessie wasn't good with watching violence and didn't share Yazza's amusement at what they could see. It made her feel sick, even when the man on the receiving end was Ricky bloody Easton.

Despite the threatening appearance of the Travellers, the police soon seemed to be getting the upper hand. Two men yellow hi-vis vests with *Security* emblazoned on the back and raced from the carnival marquee to help. The Traveller women looked on, shouting abuse without moving any closer.

'Fascists!' Screamed one of them. 'Racists! You're only here because we're Travellers. Bastards!'

This raised a ripple of laughter from the watching crowd. More sirens approached. Another police car swung into the field, closely followed by a fire engine.

'They only want to put the fire out,' yelled a man's voice from the back of the crowd. 'Stupid buggers.'

The rest seemed to agree with this sentiment. The fight seemed to have resolved itself with three Traveller men held on the ground in handcuffs while other officers tried to move the women away from the bonfire. As the firemen unrolled their hoses to douse the oily flames, Yazza climbed down.

'That was fun,' she said. 'It stinks, though. Shall we go somewhere else for coffee?'

'I think we probably should,' agreed Jessie. She dropped to the floor hurriedly. 'Let's go before this lot move on.'

And before the drug dealer with the snake tattoos sees me, she thought. He was standing on the farthest edge of the crowd, laughing with the rest.

CHAPTER 32

When they heard about the Traveller encampment, Sara's reaction couldn't have been more different from Edwards's and Bowen's. Her thoughts were of the carnival and all the organization that had gone into it. Could it be more difficult for them? First, the hideous murder of their Carnival Queen, and now the Carnival Field was occupied by a hostile group, who could stop the parade on Wednesday. Edwards and Bowen laughed. Sara frowned.

Noble looked between the three in bewilderment. 'Going to be a dust-up,' said the sergeant. He sounded glad to be fixed behind his desk. 'They've lit a bonfire.'

'Shall we?' Bowen asked Edwards, who grinned. 'Coming?'

'No,' she said. 'Noble and I will get on with the other interviews after we've had some lunch.'

The pair strode out, leaving Noble with his mouth open.

Sara shrugged. 'Don't tell me you've never done that — gone to join in a fight?'

'When I was in uniform.' Noble looked ashamed to admit it. 'Prince of Wales Road in Norwich on a Saturday night.'

Sara had forgotten that Noble was a local lad. 'They'll only go as spectators. You know how it is.'

139

Noble knew. He asked the desk sergeant, 'Where can we get a decent sandwich?'

As they walked down into the town shops, a fire engine raced past, followed by another police car. Neither of them bothered to acknowledge it. From the main street, they could see black, oily smoke rising above the roofline of the houses.

The First Café was as good as the sergeant had suggested. Sara sent Noble to order food while she bagged an outside table and rang Aggie.

'Couple of jobs for you,' she said when their admin answered. Sara explained about checking with the taxi firms and the number plate request. 'How are you doing with the CCTV?'

'Not bad. The pub has a camera that covers the entrance to its beer garden and looks up New Street. The amusement arcade has one on the front as well. They worry about people breaking in for the cash. I'm waiting for some street views from the council and a café near the church. Is it true you've been invaded?'

'Seems to be. I haven't seen it myself. The boss has gone up to the field with Bowen.'

Aggie snorted with laughter. 'Of course they have. I've looked this lot up. Trevor told me about Lowestoft. It's not going to go down well.'

'In what sense?'

'They seem to be a renegade group, not much liked by any other Traveller families. There's a history of theft, bad behaviour and fighting. The local council had an emergency session this morning, and an eviction order is being sought immediately.'

'Apart from illegally occupying the car park, I'm not sure that will be easy. Could take days.'

'Indeed. I'll let you know when I have anything from the taxi firms or the number plates.'

Trevor? Sara wondered as she ended the call. *First name terms? Weren't Aggie and Bowen an item? Wasn't DS Trevor Jones married?* Relationships, it seemed to her, were far more complicated than murder inquiries.

* * *

The afternoon was hot, and the interview room stuffy, even with the windows open. Sara and Noble settled in to talk to several of the theatre cast and crew. The first to arrive was one of the dancers, followed by an older woman called Jessie Dobson, one of the technical crew.

'I'm the sound engineer,' she explained. Sara felt impressed. If she had thought of anyone doing sound, the automatic image was of one of those long-haired, tattooed men of indeterminate age who pushed big boxes of equipment around. Jessie didn't fit this description on any count. 'I'm usually one of the last out because I have to sort out the performers' mic packs before I can finish.'

'Have you been doing this job long?'

'Since I left drama school.' Jessie looked directly at Sara and smiled. 'Nearly forty years. I trained as a stage manager but took to the mixing early on. It isn't all *Metallica* or Glastonbury, you know. I did West End musicals for years.'

'How have you ended up in Cromer?' Noble sounded as surprised as Sara felt.

'The West End is very pressured. This is much easier. Sort of early retirement. Besides, I fell in love with the town.'

Jessie's gaze slid over Sara's shoulder to the high-level window. Something about the woman's breezy chatter felt studied to Sara. A smokescreen to hide a secret.

'Were you the last to leave on Friday night?' asked Sara.

'By the back door,' said Jessie. 'Pete and I lock up backstage once everyone has gone. He goes out through the auditorium, and I lock the stage door.'

'And what did you see when you got outside?'

Jessie hesitated long enough for Sara to notice. 'The usual. A handful of people night-fishing over the railings.'

'Would you recognise them?'

'Some of them are regulars. Can't say I'd know them by name.'

'There wasn't anyone else that caught your attention?'

'No.' Her face froze in a grimace. 'Why?'

'We just want to find out who was about at that time of night. Did you see Daisy?'

'Oh, no.' The woman seemed relieved. 'She would have been up at the ball still, wouldn't she?'

'What time did you leave?'

'About ten thirty.'

'You went straight home?'

'No, we went for a drink.'

'Where?'

'There's a new café opened that's a cocktail bar at night.' Jessie waved a hand vaguely towards the town. 'Can't say I think it will last long. I went there with the dancers.'

'One of them mentioned the visit.' Noble searched through some papers and producing a signed statement. 'Yzobelle Grady?'

'Yazza. She's my lodger for the season. Has been for three seasons now.'

'Yazza says that you joined them later.' Sara watched Jessie's reaction closely. 'You didn't walk up with them.'

'That's right.' The woman didn't seem worried by this question.

'You walk around at night on your own?' asked Noble.

'Of course.' She glanced at him in amusement. 'This is Cromer. It's hardly dangerous. At least, it hasn't been until now.'

'What route did you take? Did you see anyone at all on the promenade?' Sara leaned forward.

Jessie frowned. 'I went up the zigzags. I didn't see anything or anyone on the prom, apart from the people outside at North Sea Nights.'

'North Sea Nights?'

'Café at the end of the prom has barbeque evenings in the summer. Look, I can't help you. It was late. I wouldn't expect to see anyone, and I didn't. Can I go now?'

'Of course, and thank you for taking the time to come in.'

'Sure. No problem.'

Jessie stood up from her chair as if it were on fire and was out of the door before Noble could reach it.

'She gone?' asked Sara when the DC turned back into the room.

'Yup. So fast it would make your head spin. What was that all about?'

'I'm not sure. But I haven't finished with Ms Dobson yet.'

'You think she saw something?'

'Or someone. Either way, she's hiding it, and I want to know why.'

CHAPTER 33

Monday had so far proved to be a difficult and nerve-racking day for Adele. Before she'd gone to speak to the police, the committee had convened in the marquee. After much debate, they had reluctantly agreed to move that day's children's events down to the pier and cancel that evening's open mic. They'd spent the rest of the morning carrying as much of the booze as they could out to vans that had to park on the main road. The two security guards had agreed to sit in there all evening if anyone who hadn't heard turned up. If the rented fridges, coffee machines and ice cream carts got stolen, it was too bad. They were insured.

She had been so nervous by the time she had got to the Police Station, Adele had become confused. The times Greg wanted her to talk about were simple, but the pain from the burns on her arm and leg had distracted her. The female detective particularly looked as if she didn't believe her, although it was the woman's job to be suspicious.

Something else was nagging Adele about Friday night. She could remember Benji arriving back in Greg's car and going to bed. She could also recall Greg coming back later in a taxi. That's where Adele had got the idea of the rest arriving home that way. Even so, Adele felt sure that Greg had been alone, that she would have heard Xander and Jacob if they'd been with him. The more she thought about it, the more she was sure that her husband had gone out again. Exhausted and half-asleep, Adele couldn't remember the exact time, but Greg's mobile had beeped several times when it was still dark. Then, Greg had got up, dragged on a tracksuit, and driven off in the car. He must have still been drunk, she realised.

It took her nearly fifteen minutes to walk back to the marquee, and when Adele arrived, the field was chaos. Police cars were zooming in from all directions. A fire was burning, and a crowd was watching the free entertainment. There was a scuffle going on between some police officers and Traveller men. As Adele went through the pedestrian cut-through, she saw their security guards running over to join in. Henry was watching the proceedings from the door of the tent.

'That's not going to help,' he murmured when Adele joined him. A fire engine roared in to put out the bonfire in the middle of the camp. 'I'd be angry if they did that to me, let's be honest. How'd you get on?'

'There wasn't much I could tell them,' she said. 'After all, I left early. What's left to do?'

'Nothing for now.' Henry dropped the tent flap. It deadened the noise of the conflict outside, even if it didn't silence it entirely. 'We've moved everything we can. Have to wait for the council. Brian says they're trying for an eviction order. Because of the parade.'

'All our work.' Adele sighed. 'It's going to waste.'

'Not if we can move them on.'

'We could lose the parade and the fireworks.' She sank into one of the chairs, looking dejected. The firework display was due to be installed by professionals on Thursday afternoon at the field's cliff-edge. It was set off from nine in the evening and was one of the week's highlights, being both spectacular and free.

Henry sat next to her. 'We'll do our best. Can't do no more than that. What you doing now?'

'I should go down to the pier, I suppose.' Adele didn't sound very enthusiastic.

'No need. Mary's gone to see to that. You got to go home?'

'I guess not. I saw Greg taking the boys out, I'm not sure where.'

'I landed some lovely crabs this morning. If we go past Leigh's place on the way, they should be ready by now. We could have a decent lunch out of them.' Adele thought of what Greg might do to her if he saw his wife with another man and shook her head. Henry watched her before adding. 'At mine, I mean. No one would see us there.'

'I've never been to your house,' she said.

'I know. It's not far.'

The fight outside had finished, although a couple of police cars remained near the camp. Some of the Traveller women were berating a pair of officers trying to calm the situation. Henry and Adele slipped through the gap in the fence and walked to the town through the crowds. They stopped at the fishmonger's shop on the way to collect two freshly dressed crabs.

'Not far now.' Henry crossed the main road to a side street lined with Victorian fishermen's cottages. He opened the door to one and ushered Adele through to the rear, where there was a square of gardens.

'I never knew this was here,' she said. 'What a lovely secret.'

'No one can see us here, 'cept the neighbours. Jessie on that side—' he waved to the next garden — 'She works at the theatre. Bill, on the other side, works for the council. The rest is holiday rentals.'

He left Adele with a cup of tea to enjoy the peace. The noise of traffic and people in the town hummed beyond the houses. She could see Henry in his kitchen through the open back door, doing something with the crabs and salad and fresh bread. The moment felt precious to Adele. No one knew where she was, and, for once, she didn't have to account for herself to anyone else. When Henry brought out the food, they settled in the sunshine to relax.

'I had no idea you could cook like this,' she said.

'Hardly cooking. Just a salad. I've had to look after myself for years now. Ever since my wife died. I didn't want to live on fish and chips.'

Adele knew that Henry's wife had died of cancer when she was only thirty-three. Emboldened by the privacy and Henry's smile, she asked, 'Do you like living on your own?'

He forked out the cooked crab's cream flesh and loaded it onto the crusty bread as he considered his answer. 'No. I dun't. Got used to it, I suppose. Could you?'

It was a loaded question. She didn't want to ruin the atmosphere by answering truthfully. 'I'm married, Henry. It doesn't apply.'

He was wise enough to let it drop while they finished eating. They talked about the carnival and what they might do if the Travellers wouldn't move on. Henry showed her the traditional pots he was mending, spoke about the sea and its moods. Adele cleared the table and made more tea. It was just as if they were good friends and no more, until Henry gently took Adele's hand and looked at the sticking plasters. 'They could do with changing.'

'Probably,' she agreed. 'I'm right-handed, so it's on the wrong side.'

He brought a first aid kit and put it on the table. The plasters stuck to the fine hairs on Adele's arm. She winced as she pulled them slowly away from the burns.

Henry sucked in a sharp breath. The injuries left by the oven's bar were deep. They cut two narrow strips through the skin and upper flesh to a raw redness beneath. A clear liquid and blood oozed from the wounds.

'Them's proper burns,' he said. 'You should get them seen to. I could go with you up to minor injuries.'

'No, I can't.'

'You can and should. Say you did it on the oven bars. You don't have to tell them the truth.'

'What truth, Henry?' Adele's voice wobbled as she suppressed tears.

'This ain't no accident, is it? Not the first time I seen things. You know it's not.'

Adele gasped in surprise. She had gone to considerable trouble to hide any previous injuries and never discussed her home life or Greg with anyone. The jokes and snide remarks had been going on for years. This tendency to hurt her physically was a relatively new thing. Six months ago, Greg had slapped her hard enough to bruise her cheek. She'd hidden that with make-up. Having got away with it once, more had followed.

'Did your husband do this to you?' asked Henry. He was trying to wipe around the wounds with clean water and cotton wool. Adele pulled her hand away, unable to bear the pain. 'You can tell me. You should tell someone.'

'I can't. Not yet. It's not as simple as everyone seems to think.'

'Never is. I just want you to know this. If you need me, you just calls me. Anytime.'

Adele knew that he meant it. She gritted her teeth as he covered the burns with fresh dressings and stuck them down. He tidied up the rubbish and went inside to the bin, as Adele's mobile rang. It was Greg's number.

'Where the hell are you?' her husband demanded. 'Why aren't you at home?'

Adele stammered something about carnival business.

'Doesn't matter. You need to get down here now.'

'Where?'

'Sidestrand gap. There's been an accident.'

CHAPTER 34

The team gathered in the interview room for an update. Edwards and Bowen had returned to the station in the wake of the three arrested Travellers, plus a stop at a fish and chip restaurant. Sara declined to listen about the outbreak at the Travellers' camp. She didn't feel it had anything to do with their investigation, and she disliked the prejudice it displayed.

'Except that, it shows what these people are like,' said Bowen. 'They'll be charged with assaulting a police officer. Up to six months for that.'

'Or a fine,' replied Sara. 'Which they'll never pay.'

'All the more reason to send them down.'

Sara looked at Edwards, who didn't seem to be listening. 'You're making a lot of assumptions. Not all Travellers are alike.'

'Alike enough for me,' said Bowen. He looked mulish, which Sara took to mean she was challenging one of his "dinosaur thinking" moments. 'Like that lad this morning.'

'Kit Grice?' Edwards was interested now. 'We haven't had time to talk about that.'

Noble brought out his notebook. 'Mr Grice was accompanied by his solicitor. He volunteered information about the movements of the victim and himself after the dance.

They walked along the prom, sat on the beach for a while, where Mr Grice says he proposed marriage. After that, they walked back, and he left Daisy at the bottom of the cliff steps. He seemed really upset about that.'

'It's a good cover,' grumbled Bowen. 'Kill your girl-friend and then cry over it. Seen it all before.'

They all had. Parents, partners, family members, neighbours, all going on television to make appeals and sobbing. Only to be charged with some hideous crime once the evidence against them stacked up. Snatching an unknown victim at random was highly unusual.

'Did you believe him?' Edwards asked Bowen.

He shrugged. 'Not really. All Travellers are liars.' Bowen looked at Sara from under hooded eyes. 'So are boyfriends who are hiding something.'

'Except Kit Grice isn't a Traveller,' said Sara, unable to stop her anger from bursting out. 'He's a Show Man. There is a difference. He's a businessman, part of a family who have lived in Norwich for generations.'

The DI sighed. 'Jeez, Mike. Will you two stop winding each other up?'

Bowen laughed and pointed a finger at Sara. 'Gotcha! See, you are teaching me something. I'm not such a dinosaur as I used to be.'

'All right.' Sara smiled briefly. 'You still didn't believe him?'

'No. Basically, Grice came in and gave us a prepared statement. Then he wouldn't say any more. That seems wrong to me.'

'What about the other interviews with the theatre staff?' the DI said, moving the conversation on.

'They seem to be backing one another up, more or less, apart from that sound operator, Jessie Dobson. I think she saw something unusual and doesn't want to say.'

They interviewed more of the theatre staff as the afternoon wore on, without gaining any further helpful information. Noble and Bowen headed home when the team broke up for the evening. Sara and Edwards didn't. As they left, a group of people were getting loud with the unfortunate desk sergeant in reception.

'I'm from Traveller Support,' a man was saying. 'Those men are my legal clients, and I demand to see them.'

With a grunt, Edwards bypassed them and went out into the warm evening. 'One more job to do. It will be quicker to walk.'

It was nearly teatime. The town was still busy, and the traffic was backed up on the one-way system. Edwards seemed to know Cromer well. They cut through the terraces of little hotels and side streets until they came out opposite the Carnival Field. The Traveller camp was still there, except the vehicles had been moved closer to one another, and the spaces between filled with a barricade of junk. They turned into the side road that led to the Shaws' house.

It was Daisy's mother who let them in. 'You'd better go into the sitting room.' She sounded exhausted.

Fred Shaw sat on the sofa, looking shell-shocked. The family liaison officer sat next to him, watching carefully but not attempting to offer unwanted comfort. 'I'll leave, sir,' she said. 'If you'd prefer.'

'Mrs Shaw?' asked Sara.

Karen slumped into an armchair. 'The day can't get any worse. Let her stay.'

'Stella took me to the hospital,' said Fred. He indicated the FLO. His voice was low, the tone distant. 'To see Daisy.'

'I'm so sorry, Mr Shaw.' Sara thought of the viewing room and the dignity with which the mortuary staff tried to deal with bereaved families. It was still the hardest thing any parent ever had to do. 'Thank you for going.'

'Someone had to.' Fred's voice was reduced to a whisper. 'My little girl. My beautiful girl.'

'Have you found him yet?' Karen demanded. The anger in her voice was barely suppressed. It made her shrill, and Sara couldn't blame her. 'It's been days.'

'We're still making inquiries,' said the DI gruffly. Karen snorted with derision. 'There is one thing we need to ask.'

'What now? Just arrest someone, for God's sake.'

'We're sorry, Mrs Shaw,' said Sara. It sounded trite. 'We're still putting together Daisy's movements after she left the tent.'

'Did she have a boyfriend?' Edwards suddenly asked without preamble.

Fred frowned. 'Not a regular one. She had a few dates, but I couldn't tell you exactly who with. Apart from that singer at the pier. She went for a drink with him once or twice.'

'Not someone she might have been seeing on and off for several months?'

'No, I'm sure she would have told us.'

'Someone she might have been considering marrying?'

'Daisy didn't have a regular boyfriend,' snapped Karen. 'What are you implying?'

'We think Daisy left the dance with a young man. A visitor for the carnival.'

'What sort of visitor?' asked Fred. He sounded confused. 'A holidaymaker? Or that singer? Or one of the funfair people?'

Edwards and Sara both waited for Fred to carry on. Karen beat him to it.

'My Daisy was a good girl,' she shouted. She launched herself out of the armchair in a fury. 'She wouldn't have left with a stranger. Especially not a bloody Traveller. How dare you? You make it sound like it was her own fault.'

CHAPTER 35

There were police cars, an ambulance and a crowd. Greg was waiting for Adele at the top of the Sidestrand slipway, leading her past the onlookers and down to the sand. An inflatable RNLI inshore lifeboat bobbed a few feet from the shore. One of the crew sat at the steering wheel, though the engine wasn't running. Two more crew members were hauling a jet ski onto the beach. One side of it was damaged. A second jet ski was already parked on a bank of shingle. A smaller group of people, including Xander and Jacob, stood talking to a police officer, who was turning his body towards them, his hand on a bodycam. Adele presumed he was recording the interview.

Not far from the tideline, the two paramedics and another of the lifeboat crew knelt on the sand. As she looked at the group in wide-eyed fear, Adele felt a cold sweat breaking out all over her body. The RNLI woman had Benji's head in her lap while the paramedics worked on different parts of him. Benji's eyes were unfocused, his breath rasping. His wet suit was torn, the zip to the chest pulled low to reveal the bruises already forming there.

Suddenly he half sat up, wracked with coughing, until he spat something out. He subsided exhaustedly back onto the woman's lap. The paramedic spoke to him briefly before carrying on gently wrapping Benji's left leg in an emergency splint. The second paramedic hurried off to the ambulance.

'What on earth happened?'

Greg shuffled from foot to foot, watching the people working on his son's friend.

'Greg?'

'I borrowed a second jet ski,' he said. 'So two of the boys could go out at once.'

'Racing, as it were?'

Greg nodded, his eyes still fixed on the injured Benji. 'Xander and Benji went out. I told them not to go too far. "Don't go out too deep," I said. But they chased each other.'

'Chased?' the query slipped out of Adele's mouth in surprise.

'Racing, like you said.' Greg threw an angry glance at Adele. 'We couldn't see it properly — they went out too far. They collided with each other.'

Adele felt a prickle of suspicion run down her spine.

'Benji lost control of his ski and fell off,' Greg continued. 'The ski must have hit him as he went down. Xander was a hero. Did a super-quick turn to get back and pull Benji from the water.'

It all sounded so plausible. Adele didn't believe a word of it. Unconsciously she put a protective hand over the plaster on her arm. 'Have you contacted his mother?'

Greg shook his head. 'The officer took Benji's mobile and did it. She's on her way.'

Although they had been keeping their voices low, Benji turned his head in their direction. He reached out towards Adele and called, 'Mum?'

Greg grabbed his wife's arm. 'You're not his mother.'

'I know.' She looked pointedly at Greg's hand, and he released his grip. 'Have you even told him his mum is coming?'

When Greg shook his head, Adele went over and knelt at the prone boy's side. 'Benji? It's Adele. Your mum is on her way. Shall I stay with you until she comes?'

'Please,' he said, gazing at her.

'Where is his mother coming from?' asked the paramedic.

'Colchester.'

'Then tell her to go to Norwich hospital. We're taking our young friend here to A & E. He'll need X-rays on that leg and his collar bone.'

'Can you come with me?' asked Benji, his voice a whisper.

'Of course. I'll just get your phone.'

The second paramedic had returned with a stretcher. Adele hurried away to explain the situation to the police officer and Xander.

'Can you ask your dad to park up my car? I'll just get my handbag.'

'Of course, Mum.' Xander nodded. He was trembling, and his face looked drawn. 'I'm sorry about Benji. I didn't do a very good job, did I?'

'What?'

'You told me to look after my friends,' mumbled Xander. 'I let Benji down.'

Adele patted his arm. 'Accidents can happen.' She would have offered him a hug, but he never wanted them from her these days. Too grown-up for such things. Xander flinched and turned away.

Whether it was the shock or the fact that people in authority were watching, Greg was helpful. 'Call me when you're free. I'll come down to pick you up.'

Adele thanked him, even though she thought he would almost certainly have been drinking. She had her purse with her and could withdraw enough money for a taxi when she needed to.

With the help of the lifeboat crew, Benji was carried from the beach and put in the back of the ambulance. Adele strapped into the seat next to him while the crew prepared themselves. One sat on the radio requesting triage, while the other fired up the engine and drove them under sirens up the twisty lane that went to the coast road. It wasn't until they reached the Norwich road near Cromer that the driver could get up some decent speed.

'How you doing?' Adele asked Benji. She was holding his hand lightly, hoping it would reassure him. The young man tried to look over his shoulder at the paramedic, strapped into a more forward seat. The man was still on the radio, and it was quite noisy inside the vehicle.

Adele moved closer. 'It's all right, I don't think they can hear us. Are you OK?'

'Does Mr Hayward hurt you often?' Benji's voice was weak. Adele strained to hear him. He squeezed Adele's hand more firmly than she expected. 'Does he?'

'Sometimes. He doesn't mean it. His anger gets out of control.'

'No excuses,' breathed Benji. 'That's where Xander gets it from.'

'Xander?'

'You don't know? About school?'

'School?' Adele hadn't been expecting anything about school. 'What about it?'

'When he got sent home for a fortnight, at Easter?'

'He had a rugby injury.'

Benji smiled weakly. 'Lost his temper with a younger boy. You ask him. Today it was my turn.'

'What?'

'When we went out on the jet ski, I told Xander I was going home in the morning.'

Adele's blood froze in her veins. That would not have played well. 'How did he take it?'

'Called me gay. Said I was weak. Challenged me to race him.'

Benji coughed suddenly. The paramedic put down the radio and came over to check him. In seconds, he had fitted an oxygen tube to Benji's face, two little prongs up his nostrils to aid his breathing.

'No more talking now,' he said, checking Benji's vital signs on the machine he was hooked up to. The ambulance hurried on. They were near to the Norwich bypass now and were making good time. The paramedic sat back in his chair, recording the results on a form on a clipboard.

Benji squeezed Adele's hand again and pulled her close to him so only she could hear. 'Xander rammed me,' he whispered. 'On purpose. Then he turned his circle and came back to finish me.'

CHAPTER 36

Adele sat with Benji in Accident and Emergency until his mother arrived. The poor woman was frantic with worry as the doctor explained about the two fractures and the water in his lungs. There was also a nasty gash to his scalp, with cuts and bruises to his chest and hands. Benji smiled weakly at his mum as they discussed what would happen next.

Adele slipped out of the cubicle and wandered about the reception area until she found a cashpoint. There were taxis on a rank outside waiting for customers.

'I'm off home,' she explained when she went back to say goodbye. 'I can't tell you how sorry I am. Benji has my number if you need to ask anything.'

'He tells me you weren't there,' said Benji's mother. She looked pointedly at Adele's arm where the dressing Henry had put on no longer looked at all fresh.

'I'm on the carnival committee. I was busy with some problems we're having.'

'You'll get a text from me soon.'

Adele went outside to delight a taxi driver with a long trip. Halfway to Cromer, Adele's mobile buzzed.

Benji has told me all about it. You are lucky I won't be reporting this to the police. He doesn't want me to. He won't be going near your family again. And if you want some advice, you should get away from them too.

As if she didn't already know that.

It was after midnight when she reached home and locked herself in the spare bedroom. She couldn't cope with Greg or the boys tonight. They arrived home after her, falling up the stairs with drunken laughter, before going to bed. None of them seemed to miss her.

When Adele woke up the next morning, there were so many things flying around her head that she didn't know which one to worry about first. Working swiftly through her chores, she tried to decide which was the most important. Pausing in the hall to listen up the stairs for signs of life, she slipped into Greg's study, hands trembling with fear. Searching through the desk drawers, she found a file labelled *Langton Hall*. Adele paused to listen again. It was still all quiet upstairs.

Leafing rapidly past the invoices and invites to fund-raisers, she found a letter she had hoped might be there. She folded it up until it was small enough to be hidden in her hand and returned the folder to the drawer, hoping that it didn't look as if it had been disturbed.

She left breakfast muffins on the island worktop, then grabbed her bag. Stuffing the letter in an inside pocket, Adele got into her car and drove down to the Gangway. As she pulled into one of the spaces overlooking the beach, she realised that she hadn't drawn a full breath since first standing in the hallway and wound down the car window to let in the sea air. The tide was high, and Henry's tiny inshore fishing boat was a small speck out at sea, beyond the reach of her mobile signal. Only now did Adele unfold the letter and read it.

In respect of our recent meeting, I regret to inform you that your son, Alexander Hayward, has been accused of inappropriate behaviour at school. We have investigated the matter thoroughly. Unfortunately, it seems that Alexander was involved in two separate incidents.

Naturally, we have spoken to your son at length about the inappropriateness of his language and behaviour. Given the seriousness of the complaints, we are suspending Alexander from school until Easter. We are also removing his privileges when he returns for the Summer Term. He will no longer be allowed to play sport on behalf of the school. Nor are we willing to support his trials for the Norfolk rugby squad.

Adele sat in the car and watched. First, one boat came up to the beach, then another. The men offloaded large plastic buckets filled with crabs and lobsters, which they carried up to the landing area. Henry's boat approached the shore, engine running hard. It cut out at the last minute, and the little boat ran up the shingle out of the water. He skippered the boat alone, but the fishermen all knew and helped one another. They carried his catch to the concrete sea wall while Henry tied up to the metal buoy buried in the sand. Finally, Adele joined him by the buckets.

'Good morning,' said Henry. He was dropping paper slips into each one to show whom they belonged to. The buyer from the local seafood company was weighing each tub and offering prices. Adele waited until Henry had dealt with the man.

'I need to talk to you,' she said. The little café at the end of the promenade was open, and she pointed to it. 'And I need a coffee.'

Henry went inside to order while Adele waited at an outside table. The wind whipped around the corner of the building, making her shiver despite the sunshine. Pulling up her cardigan sleeve, she gently peeled away the corner of the dressing on her arm. The wounds still looked raw, and blood was crusted around the edges. Henry made her jump when he put two mugs and plates on the table.

'How be it?' he asked.

Adele showed him.

'Still think you should go to the hospital.'

'Perhaps you are right.'

Henry looked at her in surprise. 'Do you want me to take you up there?'

'Yes, please. If you don't mind.' Adele pulled down the sleeve then sipped her coffee. Henry was rarely a talkative man. He watched in silence as she nibbled at the pastry until it was gone.

'Something's changed,' he said.

She pulled the letter out and passed it to him. Once he had read it, she explained about the jet ski accident the previous day.

'Greg has been hiding this school thing from you?'

'They both have. I don't believe anything Greg told me about yesterday.'

'Do you believe this other boy?'

Adele folded the letter and put it into her handbag. 'I do. I just don't know what to do about it. Especially this week.'

'We've got problems, right enough.'

'The council?'

'Working on it.'

'This other stuff will have to wait until next week,' said Adele firmly.

'I still want to take you to the hospital.'

'I'm ready when you are.'

They headed back to Adele's little car.

'What will you tell them? They're bound to ask how this happened.'

'The truth. That my husband did it on purpose, to force me to tell lies to the police. I want an official record of it.'

CHAPTER 37

Aggie's baking was the talk of Norfolk Police HQ. This morning, she had brought two tins containing a Victoria sponge and a coffee and walnut cake.

'I thought you could take one with you up to Cromer,' she said. 'After we've had the briefing. Just waiting for our visitor.'

'Let's start with the taxis. Aggie?' said Edwards.

'There are only two firms in Cromer,' she said. She opened a notepad. 'County Cabs has an office near the petrol station. I spoke to the manager, and he was on duty Friday night. He remembered a drunk man coming in late and demanding a taxi. Mostly it's pre-booked runs at that time of night.'

'Greg Hayward? Or one of the boys?'

'Description made it sound like Mr Hayward. The manager is trying to get hold of the driver for more details.'

'So, they didn't all go home with Benji in the car. How about the number plates?'

'ANPR are emailing me a video of movements from 10 p.m. on Friday night until 9 a.m. on Saturday. There's a camera at the traffic lights on the Norwich Road junction. That's the road out to where the Haywards live.'

'Excellent work,' said Edwards.

Aggie smiled. 'There's good news from the techs as well.' She handed a printout to Bowen. 'They got into Daisy's phone. Here's the list. Only two numbers are showing in the same time frame. Daisy's mum rang and left messages over thirty times, poor woman.'

'And the other?'

'Kit Grice,' said Bowen. He compared the list to the statements from the previous day to check the number. 'Asking where she was and if he'd offended her.'

'Good morning. Is this a good time to join you?' Their visitor was the pathologist, Dr Taylor. Sara realised she might have guessed — coffee and walnut was his favourite type of cake.

'I thought it would be simpler if I came and explained where we had got to,' he said. 'Mmm, this is as lovely as ever, Ms Hewett.'

'Call me Aggie,' she said with a faint blush. Bowen frowned at the exchange. With a smile, Sara wondered if the DC was becoming jealous.

'What have you got for us, Stephen?' asked the DI.

'The shoes and handbag haven't added much,' the pathologist admitted. 'The tablets are ecstasy. No surprise there. There was beach sand among the food waste on the bag.'

'The marks on the wall of the posh chippie?'

'They look like scratch marks, don't they?' The doctor pulled up a photo on his laptop, and they gathered round to look. 'I said there was debris under our victim's fingernails — some of that debris matches the paint and plaster that has been scratched from the wall.'

'You think she was attacked here and not on the beach?' Sara asked.

'Daisy has beach sand in her clothing and hair. She had also been in this alley and got that sample under her nails. Unfortunately, there is also sand at this site. When the wind blows, there will be traces of sand everywhere in the town.'

'Balance of probability?' The DI looked at Taylor.

'I think she was attacked here. You remember I did a belt and braces set of tests on DNA samples from her body and clothes? Well, the two samples don't match.'

'Not from the same person?'

'No.' Doctor Taylor pulled up some reports from his email. 'The internal sample is not from the same person as the pubic hairs that we found in the underpants. The sample of skin from under Daisy's nails matches the sample from her vagina. That would make sense if she was being attacked. She tried to fight back and scratched the attacker before he pinned her down sufficiently long by the throat for her to pass out. What doesn't make sense is the second foreign DNA. I've sent the results over to you to see if there are any matches on the database.'

'Sara, run it now,' said the DI. She moved to her computer and fed in the data while keeping an ear on the rest of the conversation. 'Are you saying that Daisy had sex with two people that night?'

'Depends exactly when she changed her underwear. The hair could have been there from earlier in the day. Or it could have been from the evening. The internal sample isn't mixed up with this other one, however. It was a straight result.'

'Meaning?'

'It looks as if Daisy had consensual sex with someone who wore protection. Presumably a condom. Then was attacked and raped later by a second man.'

'By someone not wearing protection?'

'Yes.'

'Anything else?' asked Edwards.

'The contents of her stomach were surprising. I thought it would show ecstasy, given the tablets in the bag.'

'It wasn't?'

'Something I see less often these days. Ketamine.'

Sara swung round on her chair in surprise. 'That hasn't been popular for a long time.'

'It's still used for medical reasons and by vets, of course, and it's still easy to obtain illegally. Daisy would have felt disassociated once it had taken effect. Awake, but not really aware and happy too. It can also induce vomiting.'

The DI sat down next to the pathologist. 'Daisy died because she inhaled vomit.'

'Yes. Because she was lying on her back and unconscious. It wouldn't clear from her mouth and throat before she inhaled it.'

'And she vomited because she had taken or been given ketamine?'

'She had been drinking,' said Dr Taylor. He considered for a moment, then sighed. 'The level of alcohol in her blood was moderate. Enough for it to be traceable, but in my opinion, not high enough to make her vomit.'

'So, if someone fed her the drug that made her vomit, that would be classed as murder and not manslaughter?' asked Sara.

'I think the CPS would say yes. A good defence lawyer would try to argue it was the booze and therefore her own fault.'

DI Edwards groaned. 'We need to find out who gave her the drug, as well as who attacked her, and why they moved the body all the way from the posh chippie to that alley.'

Sara's computer pinged. She swung round to check the screen and clicked on the results. 'Sir! There's a match.'

The rest of the team gathered around her chair. One of the samples had no match. The other had.

'Well, look at that,' said Bowen with a smirk. 'Kit bloody Grice. Once a Traveller, always a Traveller.'

'Mike? Shut up,' snapped Edwards. 'Why is he on the system?'

Sara checked their local database. 'Involved in a fight last winter, on Prince of Wales Road in Norwich. Charged and got some community service hours. A swab was done to check blood samples on the victim's shirt.'

'Young Mr Grice is not as innocent as he makes out.' Edwards raised an eyebrow in Bowen's direction. 'Let's get him back into the station for another chat. You and me this time, Sara, and under caution.'

CHAPTER 38

Tuesday was a full two-show day, so Jessie headed down to the theatre to run her pre-show checks. The interview with the police had not gone well. She was sure that she hadn't seen Daisy that evening. What she had seen was something she didn't want to talk about to anyone — especially given what had happened since.

There was a strange atmosphere in the town as she walked towards the pier. Café owners stood in their door-ways, scanning up and down the street. Several shops had *Closed for lunch* signs up, which was bizarre in the height of the season. In the craft shop, she could see two staff picking up broken items from the floor. One was blowing her nose.

As she reached The Duke, Jessie heard shouting. Several male voices were raised further down the street. Then the sound of feet pounding and more yelling, as a group of four young men ran at full speed across the road in front of her. They were all carrying bottles of alcohol, the supermarket security tags still in place. Further down the street, a security guard and a shopworker were giving chase at a cautious jog.

As the youths passed the pub, one skidded to a halt, turned and screamed obscenities at the two chasers. Then he raised one of the bottles of booze over his head and launched it up the cobbled street. It twisted in the air and landed with a loud crash in front of the supermarket worker, who skidded to avoid it. He barrelled towards a family on the pavement, whose father grabbed the man to prevent him from careering into his wife and children. People up and down the street began to scream. Parents picked up toddlers and old people shrank against the buildings or pushed into open shop doorways.

The youngsters ran on up the hill towards Carnival Field. They barged past holidaymakers, trampled on children's toes, and one jumped over a pushchair with a screaming child strapped in it. No one tried to stop them. A small crowd issued from The Duke to see what was going on.

Jessie stood watching with her mouth open and her heart racing. The sudden threat of violence jarred uncomfortably with the warm, sunny afternoon. It wasn't the sort of thing anyone expected to see in the town at any time, let alone the high season.

'Where are the police when you need them?' one of The Duke's customers asked.

'What's going on?' Jessie asked the drinker.

'Gangs of those little buggers have been wandering around town all morning.' He waved after the disappearing young men. 'Nicking stuff and breaking things. There are only a few coppers. Not enough to control them.'

'Why haven't they sent for backup?'

'God knows.'

The security guard was on his radio, while the supermarket worker apologised to the man and his family. Hovering on the edge of the Duke crowd, Jessie watched as the young man ran back towards the store. The danger seemed to have passed, and people began to move.

'They say that they've been threatening people too,' said the drinker. He waved his plastic pint glass in general disapprobation. 'It'll be those pikeys up on the car park.'

Two police officers jogged down the street from the church end, halting by the security guard. The pair looked harassed. One began a heated discussion with the guard, while the other talked hurriedly on their radio.

'We need more people,' Jessie heard the officer say. 'Sir, we need them now.'

'Shouldn't be allowed.' The drinker emptied his glass, then unsteadily pulled out his mobile. 'I'm gonna tweet the hell out of this.'

Jessie didn't have much to do with social media. She had a Facebook account where she sometimes heard from old friends she had worked with in the West End, but that was it. Maybe the man's tweets might bring some help.

The supermarket worker came back with a dustpan and brush and started collecting the broken glass. The family man was berating the police officer, whose radio crackled into life. He listened, then grabbed his partner's arm. A few seconds later, they were running in the opposite direction.

Cromer isn't that big a place, thought Jessie. *What's going on?*

Feeling rattled, she headed down to the prom. There were families on the beach, a handful of paddleboarders out on the sea, but the place was quieter than Jessie would have expected for a hot August day. The pier was usually jammed with people at lunchtime. Today there was only a handful, and the carnival's children's events had few takers.

Donal was standing with his arms folded, watching through the box office and gift shop window. Jessie stepped round a customer in the doorway and greeted him.

'You look like you're on guard.' She tried to keep her tone light.

'Have you seen them?'

'Unfortunately, yes. Up in the town. Looked like they'd been stealing booze from the supermarket.'

'Little sods have been in here twice this morning.' Donal waved around at the gift shop. 'In here, for God's sake. It's souvenirs, what do they want those for? I had to follow them to make sure they didn't pinch anything.'

Jessie glanced around the shop at the tea towels, knick-knacks and children's buckets and spades. 'Is there cash behind the box office?'

Donal glanced at her. 'Not much these days. Most people pay with cards. There's the till.'

'Good job you were here,' said Jessie. The manager was tall and well-built. His presence was intimidating if he wanted it to be. 'Are they just shoplifting?'

'Partly. Some of it is just plain badness if you ask me. I've been talking to some of the other business owners. It started this morning after the council served them an eviction order.'

'They have to leave Carnival Field?'

'First thing tomorrow. This is revenge, I suppose. The shops are closing early. The restaurants and pubs too. They're driving the customers away.'

'I'd better get on,' said Jessie. 'See you later.'

Donal raised a hand in acknowledgement as Jessie left to hurry down the boardwalk. She wanted to get the mic packs done before any of the performers arrived, and she had just spotted Ricky Easton heading down the prom deep in conversation with Larry, the musical director. What the singer might have been saying sent chills through her.

CHAPTER 39

The team headed to Cromer. Bowen and Noble to catch up with the staff they hadn't spoken to at the theatre, Sara and Edwards to talk with Kit Grice. The traffic was heavy, both in and out of the town as Edwards drove them up to Carnival Field.

'Sir, if you don't mind my opinion, I think it would be provocative to caution Kit at this juncture. Would it better to just have a quiet chat?'

'You know it can't be used in evidence if we do.' The DI glanced at her as he parked the car on the road outside the field.

'Yes, sir. I know he is a person of interest. But there is by no means enough to charge him yet. We will get into prejudice territory if we go in too heavy.'

Edwards glanced at her. 'All right. You lead, and let's see where it gets us. Have you noticed anything else?'

'Sir?'

'I've just been able to find a parking space without any bother. That shouldn't be possible in August. Why aren't there more people here today?'

They found the pedestrian gap in the car park fence that let them into the rear of the field. The Travellers' caravans and vehicles had been pulled even closer together. The handful of horses staked out on the grass yesterday were now tethered at the edge of the circle. Adult voices were being raised inside, and children ran about screaming. Several older Travellers stood watching out of various gaps as if they were keeping guard. It looked like a demolition site, with piles of rubbish everywhere. There was a bonfire of burning pallets sending smoke into the sky.

The carnival marquee stood unused, the white canvas doors tied shut. There was no sign of life inside it. The funfair stood forlornly behind that. None of the stalls or rides were open, their lights were switched off, and the overnight boards were still in place. Kit and his parents were standing near the waltzers, talking to a man Sara felt she recognised. As they approached, Mrs Grice rolled her eyes.

Will Grice made the introductions. 'This is Lewis Black. He's the legal advisor to the Traveller community.' Grice gestured to the circle of caravans. 'Not to my family, as you already know.'

Black shook hands with both the DI and Sara. He had been in reception yesterday, demanding to speak to the arrested men.

'I don't like to be prejudiced,' continued Grice, with the sort of statement that often preceded some kind of -ism in Sara's experience. 'That sort of behaviour isn't doing any of us any good. It was a waste of time opening last night — no one came. Well, would you walk past that?'

Black winced. 'They served the eviction notice this morning. It's all gone a bit Pete Tong since then.'

How typical of the council, thought Sara. *Move them on. Make them someone else's problem. Just like they did in Lowestoft two days ago. Is it any wonder they feel the way they do?*

'What do you mean by that?' she asked.

'Some of the youngsters have taken it badly. They've gone off into town, and the reports aren't good. I've suggested to one of your senior officers that releasing the three men you have in custody might help.'

'Why?' Edwards sounded offended.

'One of them is an elder in the group. He might be able to rein in the youngsters.' Black smiled in a placatory way.

Will Grice frowned angrily at him. 'I don't understand why your lot do this to themselves. Look at that! Is it any wonder other people don't want you here?'

'Including you, Mr Grice?' asked Black.

'Damn right. You've lost me a good day's business. And people like this—' he indicated Sara and Edwards — 'think we're all one. They think we're like that.' He turned and stomped off towards his living van. Black watched him go, his face carefully neutral.

Mrs Grice turned to Sara. 'What did you want? Or have you come to enjoy the show?'

'We wanted a quiet word with Kit.'

Kit nodded to his mother, and they followed his father to the living vans. He sat on a chair from a set of plastic garden furniture that stood by the van's door. Sara and Edwards joined him while his mother went inside. Through the open door, Sara could see her putting on the kettle and speaking to her husband.

'You've found it then?' Kit asked. His father leaned casually in the doorway, making it clear he was listening to everything that was being said. 'My conviction isn't spent yet, is it?'

'Not yet,' said Sara. 'You have some community service hours left to do.'

'Only three. They said I could do them when we get back for the winter, as I'd turned up for all the others. It was just a stupid fight. Sort of thing that happens every weekend on Prince of Wales Road.'

He was right, and that's why he had been given a community service order. When Sara had checked the records, his opponent in the fight had also been given the same. The next bit was going to be more difficult. 'We need you to tell us exactly what happened between you and Daisy on Friday night after you left the tent.'

Kit considered his options, gazing past Sara to the Travellers' circle. She waited, hoping that her boss would do the same. Finally, Kit looked straight at her. 'We walked down to the prom, just the two of us. There was some sort of event going on down near the lifeboat museum, so it wasn't very private. We were just talking, to begin with. I was building up the courage to propose.'

Mrs Grice pushed past her husband in the door and, with a heavy hand, placed three mugs on the plastic table. Milky tea slopped onto the surface. 'Sugar?'

DI Edwards nodded, and Mrs Grice retreated back inside. It was Kit's father who dropped a sugar bowl beside the mugs, then sat next to his son.

'And then?' prompted Sara.

'We walked along the path in front of the beach huts until it ran out. After that, we walked along the beach past the first groyne. Daisy couldn't climb over it easily because of her dress. So, we stopped and sat there for a while.'

'Sat?' Edwards asked. He lifted his mug to sip at the contents. 'We have the forensic results now.'

Kit blushed a little, glancing sideways at his father.

'We're all grown-ups here,' said Mr Grice.

'All right, I asked her to marry me, and we made love.'

'How did she react to your question?' Sara took the lead back.

'She said she wanted to think about it. I understood why. This life might look glamorous, but it isn't easy. Daisy knows how hard it is for the people involved in the shows at the pier, and then there's the prejudice to deal with.'

'Did she seem happy that you'd asked her?'

'I think so. She seemed really spaced out, like she couldn't quite concentrate. She wasn't behaving like she usually did when we went out.'

'How long have you been going out?' Sara thought of Mrs Shaw's flat denial of any boyfriend.

'A year,' said Kit. 'Friday night was our first anniversary. We met during the carnival. Then we saw each other a lot over the winter.'

'And that's when you ended up in the fight?' Sara asked.

Kit nodded. 'Some bloke was coming on to her in the nightclub and wouldn't hear no, and I wasn't having that.'

'You don't like anyone who talks to your girlfriend, do you?' Edwards said. 'You punch one guy in Norwich, and get into a fight with another one here.'

'I'm protective, I suppose.'

'Daisy's parents tell us that they knew nothing about any boyfriend.' Edwards was beginning to push Kit. 'How is that?'

'I never met them. We usually went out in Norwich, not up here. Daisy never invited me to meet them, though I would have liked to.'

'What about your own family? They don't seem to know anything about this either.'

'We knew Kit was seeing someone,' broke in Mr Grice. 'Once we were back out on the road, I assumed it had finished. That's usually what happens if the girl isn't from our background. I didn't want to upset Kit.'

'It wasn't too hard, Dad. We managed to see each other now and then — some of the fairs are local bookings. Daisy understood because she was busy on the pier in the spring and summer. After we got here on Thursday, we talked again and realised how much we'd missed each other. That's when I decided to propose. Make or break, I guess.'

'Did you buy a ring?' Edwards asked.

'No. I thought if Daisy said yes, we could choose one together.'

'Did you propose before or after you "made love"?'

Sara could hear the inverted commas Edwards put around "made love". The Grices heard it too.

'Before.' Kit was on his guard now.

'Did you wear protection when you had sex?' The change of tone was unmistakable.

'Yes, I did. I wouldn't do that to Daisy. I mean, try to get her pregnant on purpose or anything. I loved her.'

'You didn't get angry with her when she couldn't decide?'

'Absolutely not.'

'You didn't follow her afterwards?'

'No, I've told you that. This wouldn't have happened if I'd walked her home. Daisy asked me to let her go on her own, so she could think.'

Cheering erupted from the Traveller camp behind them. Everyone turned to see what was going on. A group of four youths ran from the clifftop gardens and pushed into the circle, laughing and shouting. They brandished bottles of booze.

A siren whooped in and out as two police cars turned into the field. Lewis Black walked forward to greet them. The three Travellers who had been arrested got out of the vehicles, grinning and shaking Black's hand. One punched the air in a triumphant salute, which raised a cheer in reply from inside the circle. While they were all distracted, DI Edwards suddenly turned back to Kit.

'Kit Grice, did you force Daisy into sex when she wouldn't give you an answer?'

CHAPTER 40

Jessie managed to unlock the dressing rooms and change the batteries in the mic packs in double time. Running up the auditorium steps, she got to the soundbox just before the staff door behind her opened. Ricky and the musical director, Larry, came in chatting as if they were the best of friends. She glanced over the edge of the wooden wall down into the well where the entrance and the fire exit met.

'I'll have a word with her.' Larry's voice was neutral — it was hard to tell what he might be thinking. Jessie bit her lip, stepping back where the pair couldn't see her.

'If you could,' said Ricky. He sounded grateful, but Jessie knew he never was. 'Her poor work is affecting my performance.'

'Rest assured, it doesn't show to the audience.'

They appeared in the side aisle, walking towards the pass door.

Jessie grabbed the plastic cover on the sound desk and pulled it up. She screamed.

The two men turned to look at her as the staff door behind Jessie opened again.

'Are you all right, miss?' A young man called up.

No, she wasn't. With a shaking hand, she pointed to the sound desk. 'I can't . . .'

'Jessie?' called Larry from the front of the theatre. Behind him, Ricky turned to go through the pass door, a smug smile on his face. Jessie watched him, wide-eyed.

Two men loomed into her eyeline, crossing through the short row of seats in front of her. Jessie knew she ought to recognise the younger one. He reached the open half-door to her workstation and looked where she was pointing. It was one of the detectives who had interviewed Jessie yesterday. She didn't know the other man.

'That's not very nice, is it? Do you want me to move it?'

Above the faders, where the digital displays usually danced, lay a dead rat. Its head was arched back, and blood had seeped from the wound in its neck onto the desk. It looked as if its throat had been cut. The blood may have run through the fader slots, Jessie realised.

Larry reached them and looked at the offending rodent. 'Bollocks,' he said. 'Let's hope it hasn't damaged the board. Chuck it out, will you?'

'Hang on,' said Jessie, with a croak in her voice. Most people here knew that she had a morbid fear of mice and rats. Being practical was a good way of staving off the shock. She pulled her mobile from her bag and snapped a picture of the corpse. 'If it's ruined the board, we'll need to claim on the insurance.'

'Fire up the system,' said Larry. 'Let's see what we've still got.'

The young detective pulled an evidence bag from his jacket pocket and gathered up the dead rat with it. 'Is there a bin I should use?'

'Yeah, chuck it over the side for the seagulls,' said Larry as he went back down the auditorium steps. Jessie waited until he had gone through the pass door before slumping down onto her high-rise stool.

'Are you all right?' asked the detective again. He had rolled the bag up so that the contents were hidden. 'I'm DC Noble. We met yesterday at the station. This is DC Bowen.'

'I remember. It's just that I hate rats. My God, if it was alive, it could have jumped out at me.'

'Unlikely. Its head was nearly off,' he said. Jessie retched. 'Sorry, miss. I just mean that it looks like it was caught in an old-fashioned snap trap. Most people don't use them now.'

'You mean it didn't crawl under the cover and die?'

'I doubt it.'

There was no doubt in Jessie's mind who would have put it there. The rat looked too large to have been caught by a mousetrap. The throat must have been deliberately slashed.

'Looks like a nasty practical joke to me,' said DC Noble. 'I'll get rid of the evidence.' He headed outside with the bag.

'Miss Dobson?' asked Bowen.

Jessie nodded.

'There are one or two people from here that we weren't able to contact yesterday. Could you take us backstage and introduce us to them?'

Jessie took an anti-bac wipe from a pack under the desk and cleaned the congealed rodent blood. 'Let me see if the desk is working first. Then I'll get Larry for you. He's in charge.'

There was a set order in which Jessie had to fire up the racks and stacks at the beginning of each day. Some of the power came from the lighting box in the balcony, and Jessie went upstairs. Voices carried up there easily, as the acoustics were designed to do. The staff door swished open as DC Noble came back in, having disposed of the corpse.

'That was a nasty trick,' he said, joining his partner.

'Rather gives the lie to what the boss was saying, doesn't it?'

'What?'

'He said that the manager claimed it was like a big happy family. The boss thought it might be difficult to get them to say anything about one another.'

'Closed shop?'

Jessie clattered quickly down the balcony stairs. Holding her breath, she fired up the soundboard and waited while it ran its computer checks. Section after section of programming responded as her fingers danced through the stored scenes and voice levels. Naturally, she had a backup of the show, but it would take ages to reset the machine, and the replacement was an old analogue desk that lived in a cupboard backstage gathering dust. Thank God it all seemed to be there. She could have cried with happiness.

'It isn't damaged then?' asked DC Noble.

Jessie smiled. 'It all seems good. I don't understand why anyone would do that. It could have ruined the show.'

'Expensive bit of kit?'

'Twenty-five grand.'

DC Bowen whistled. 'I'd no idea.'

The curtains on the stage drew back, and Larry appeared from prompt corner. 'Is it working?'

'Yes, thank goodness. Can we run some music through just to be sure?'

'Righto.' Larry came down the stairs, which connected the stage to the auditorium. His piano and computer lived in the orchestra pit to one side of the stage. He fired everything up, then put house music into the speaker system. Everything sounded fine.

'Let me introduce you.' Jessie took the two officers down to Larry and explained what they wanted.

'We'd like to speak to you,' DC Bowen said. 'Then your two singers. We couldn't find either of them yesterday.'

'I was at home,' explained Larry. 'In Doncaster. I always go back at the weekends. So does Hallie. She has a young family in London. Ricky should have been around, though.'

'He was,' said Jessie. 'At least I saw him on Sunday when we went for our full English breakfast.'

'I know he's in already. Why don't you start with him?'

'Is it all right to go backstage?' asked DC Noble.

'Sure. So long as you are out by five to two. Jessie, take these two back, will you?' Larry headed through the pass door.

'Why such a specific time?' Noble asked.

'Show starts at half past. Everyone has to be in place at twenty-five past. That thirty minutes before a show is sacrosanct to any company. It's called "the half". No one is allowed backstage after that call, so the performers can get ready in peace.'

'You didn't see Mr Easton on Monday?' asked Bowen.

'No. I'm not his keeper.'

'Do you think he went out for the day? We asked your manager, Donal Byrne, to contact you all about interviews.'

'I'm sure he tried,' said Jessie. 'He got hold of Yazza and me. I'm sure he would have rung everyone. It's this way.'

The corridor and dressing rooms were far from glamorous. Although they got the occasional coat of paint, the wooden walls dated back to the 1950s, and the carpet was dirty and worn. Ricky's dressing room was halfway along the back. Jessie knocked and waited.

'Come,' called an imperious voice.

The door opened inwards, blocking Ricky's view of the corridor. It also meant that anyone in the corridor couldn't see the occupant changing.

Ricky grinned at her as she walked in. 'Enjoy your little present?'

'You put the damn thing there?' Jessie was furious but not surprised. Another piece of sabotage. One that could be construed as a failure on her part if the desk had been broken and she couldn't programme the spare in time for the show.

'I didn't say that. Looks like a piece of karma to me. A warning from the gods.'

'About what?'

'Don't lose your head and talk out of turn. Nobody likes a rat.' Ricky grinned at her.

'No, they don't, do they?' Jessie smiled back, which made him look uncertain. Then she stood back and invited the two detectives in.

'These two police officers would like a word with you,' she said. The colour drained from Ricky's face. 'I don't know what for.'

As she pulled the door shut, Jessie caught a glimpse of Ricky in the large make-up mirror. He was trying to look nonchalant but succeeding in looking horrified. It was Jessie's turn to smile smugly.

CHAPTER 41

It took Sara some time to calm down the Grice family. DI Edwards had gone to speak to the officers who were returning the Traveller men to their camp. Kit was deeply distressed, and Sara believed it was genuine. She thought about Chris going home with the engagement ring he had offered her. The proposal had been unexpected to her, just as Kit's had been to Daisy.

You don't always get the answer you expect, she thought.

The ring Chris had bought wasn't to her taste, and she wouldn't be able to wear it at work as the stones were set too high. If Sara accepted him, it might have to be changed anyway. Choosing a ring together sounded thoughtful, not a sign that Kit was somehow covering his tracks about the evening.

'If you could come down to the station this afternoon, with your solicitor,' she said to the Grices, 'we can take a formal statement about what you've told us this morning. It has really helped fill in a lot of details.'

Mercifully, Kit agreed. Sara went to join her boss.

'There are several lots of them,' Sergeant Matthews was saying to Edwards. 'No end of complaints. Shoplifting and displays trashed. Supermarkets, cafés and restaurants all having stock stolen, especially booze. The pubs are sending staff home and closing for the evening. The traders have had enough.'

'We saw one group arrive here.' Edwards pointed to the Traveller caravans. 'The rest are still out there?'

'At least a dozen of them. Running up and down the place, frightening the tourists. I've only got five spare officers to deal with it all. Not helped by a stupid tweet from HQ.'

'Tweet?' Sara knew the force had various social media accounts but never paid them that much attention.

'Someone complained on Twitter that riots were going on up here. An exaggeration, of course. Whoever sits behind their computer and does this stuff replied that they'd had no such reports and it was a minor incident.'

'I bet that went down well.'

'Lead balloon.' The sergeant snorted. 'Complaints all over the place from local traders, councillors and residents. It worked in the end, thankfully. There are several more teams on the way from other stations as we speak. We've got to stay here until they arrive.'

Edwards looked thoughtful as they went back to their car. 'The sooner they move this lot on, the better.'

'It would be good to at least get them off the Carnival Field before the parade tomorrow,' said Sara. Her mobile rang. It was Aggie. 'Got anything?'

'Three things,' said their admin. Sara put the phone on speaker and gestured for the DI to listen. 'I've spoken to the taxi driver from County Cabs. He gave me the address where he took the fare. It was the Haywards' house. There was only one passenger, late forties and very drunk. He remembers him because he was worried the man would throw up in the back seat.'

'Got to be Greg Hayward,' said Sara. 'Go on, Aggie.'

'Well, I don't know if this is of interest, but there's an incident logged about a jet ski accident yesterday afternoon. Involving Xander Hayward and his friend Benji Wilder. Wilder ended up in hospital.'

Edwards's eyes narrowed. 'Accident?'

'That's what they're saying.'

'Any luck with the number plates?'

'Still waiting.'

'So, what was the third thing?' asked Sara.

'You forgot the cake. Mike will complain.' Aggie rang off.

'What do you make of that?' Edwards opened the car and climbed in.

'Sounds all wrong,' said Sara. 'We don't believe in coincidences, do we, sir? I think those young men have had a big falling-out. It wouldn't hurt to find out what's at the bottom of it all.'

'They never explained why they were fighting on Sunday at the soapbox race.'

'No, sir. You may not have heard what one of them said after we broke it up. The other visitor, Jacob, was really angry with Benji. Said something like, "See what you've done now, runner boy, the police are involved." Words to that effect, anyway.'

'I never liked the fact that they all had a story off pat about Friday night.'

'And to be honest, sir, I'm worried about Mrs Hayward. I'd like to offer some help, even if she tells me to mind my own business.'

Edwards scowled. 'Have you got their address?'

Sara nodded.

'Good. Time for a word with that Hayward boy, without his father knowing in advance.'

CHAPTER 42

The wait at Cromer Hospital's Minor Injuries Unit had been brief. Adele didn't ask Henry to go with her when a nurse ushered her into a curtained-off cubicle.

The nurse pulled off the old dressing. Adele winced.

'When did this happen?' she asked.

Checking that there was no one in the adjacent cubicle, Adele began to explain. The nurse cleaned the two wounds and re-dressed Adele's arm. At first, Adele wondered if the woman was listening or if she was wasting her time. Once the fresh dressing was in place, the nurse advised how to look after the wounds. Finally, she looked directly at Adele. 'How long has all this been going on?' she asked kindly.

'Years,' said Adele. 'When it started, it was just things he said. The violence began a few months ago. It was getting slowly worse, until these last few weeks. Now it's almost all the time.'

The nurse nodded. 'That's often the way of it. Do you intend to go back? Go home to this man?'

'I don't have any choice. I've nowhere else to go.'

'Hang on there a minute.' She went out of the cubicle. Adele slumped back against her chair in exhaustion. It had taken a lot of courage to talk to Henry, and now this stranger.

At least both of them seemed to believe her. She doubted it would make any difference to Greg's behaviour. He showed every sign of enjoying his cruelty. As she gazed at the jaunty pattern on the cubicle's curtains, Adele realised it was herself who had changed. Sunday's injuries and Benji's acknowledgement of what was going on had been the final straw.

The nurse returned with a couple of leaflets and a form on a clipboard. 'There are places you can go, although it's not always easy to get in. This group might also be of help.'

Adele looked at the information for a woman's refuge and victim support. There was a number for emergency help and contacts for counselling. She didn't feel that her situation was an emergency — there would be women in far more danger than her. She stuffed the leaflets into her handbag.

'Are you going to report him to the police?' The nurse scribbled on the form. Adele shook her head. 'I think you should. I would advise you not to wait until he does something else, but it's up to you. Take this.'

She handed a copy to Adele. The nurse had written a comment on the bottom of the form. *The patient says she is a victim of domestic violence, flag DB.*

Adele folded the paper and pushed it into her handbag with the leaflets.

'This will be logged on your hospital record,' the nurse said. 'It takes a few days to get through the system. Please be careful.'

Adele drove Henry back into town, then went home. Greg's car was missing, she realised gratefully. Xander and Jacob were sitting in the kitchen, looking the worse for wear and drinking coffee.

'Been up long?' she asked, trying to keep her tone neutral. She put her handbag by the sink and gathered the dirty pots.

'No.' Xander rubbed his forehead. 'We got any painkillers?'

Adele produced a packet from a kitchen cabinet, and Xander swallowed a couple. 'Did you get injured yesterday?'

'Oh, at last, she asks me,' sneered Xander. 'Having spent all night at the hospital with someone else's son.'

'Someone had to go with him.' She loaded the dishwasher. 'What happened to you after I had to leave?'

'We celebrated,' said Jacob with a laugh. 'Old Xander here is a hero, saved runner boy's life.'

Xander laughed too. The pair high-fived each other. 'You should be proud of me, Mum.'

'I am. Where has Dad gone?'

'Taking the other jet ski back. The one Benji broke. Where have you been?'

'Carnival stuff.'

'Always more important than your family.'

'During carnival week? Just for once, yes, it is.'

Xander looked at her in surprise. Adele always apologised when challenged like that.

The front doorbell rang. Neither of the teenagers moved, so she went to answer it. Two detectives held up warrant cards. She recognised them — the woman was DS Hirst, and the man was her boss, DI Edwards. Hirst looked calm enough, but Edwards looked impatiently past Adele into the house.

'Can we have a word with your son, if he's about?' Hirst asked.

'I don't see why not,' she said and led them through to the kitchen. The pair introduced themselves again and asked if there was somewhere private they could talk.

'There's my husband's study.'

'That would be great,' said Hirst. 'It would be best if you came with us. Xander may be eighteen, but we do like a parent to be present.'

Xander walked with a swagger across the hall, taking himself round to his father's leather executive chair on the far side of the desk. The officers sat on the other side, while Adele was left to stand. It looked as if Xander was interviewing them, not the other way around. He swung the chair gently from side to side as if he hadn't a care in the world. 'Well?'

'You had a difficult time yesterday at the beach,' said the DI.

'Yeah, Benji's an idiot. He was lucky I was there to save him.'

Adele compressed her lips to stop herself from speaking out.

'Can you tell us what happened?'

Xander grinned. 'Don't have to. It will all be in the papers later on.'

'What?' Adele couldn't stop herself blurting out. 'What papers?'

'Dad got on to the press, told them what a hero I am. It's going to be in the *Evening News*.'

The DI glanced at Adele. His face looked grim.

'About Friday,' began DS Hirst.

'I'm not saying anything else about that unless Dad is here,' snapped Xander. 'I've said all I'm going to say.'

'We really could do with a DNA sample from you.' Hirst persisted. 'To eliminate you from our inquiries.'

'Yeah, right. You'll use it to fit me up. Not gonna help you with that one.'

'Alexander,' said Edwards. His patience was clearly wearing thin. 'A girl has been raped, murdered and dumped. You were one of the last people to be seen with her.'

'It was that damn Traveller from the funfair,' Xander snapped. He had turned pale. 'She left with him, worthless piece of shit.'

Adele wasn't sure if Xander meant Daisy or the man from the funfair.

'Did you see her again after that?'

'No, I didn't.' Her son knotted his fingers together and picked at a scab on the back of one hand. It started to bleed.

'We need a more detailed talk with you,' said Edwards. 'At the station. Under caution, if necessary.'

Greg's car pulled into the drive, and Xander heard it. He stood up, looking relieved. 'That's my dad. He'll send you packing. You got nothing on me.'

CHAPTER 43

Greg Hayward had not been pleased to see them. When they asked again for DNA swabs, he refused on behalf of the entire family. DI Edwards told him that they could apply for an enforcement warrant and was briskly told to get on with it.

'I can arrest your son under suspicion,' DI Edwards said.

'Of what?' Hayward barked. 'We've all told you where he was. Lots of witnesses. This is harassment.'

As they were escorted out of the study, Sara smiled at Mrs Hayward and asked if she would mind giving her a glass of water.

'Of course not,' she said. Her husband grunted his displeasure in the background before ordering his son from his desk chair.

Sara went into the kitchen. Xander's friend had made himself scarce. Mrs Hayward reached down a glass from a cupboard and filled it.

'Thank you.' Sara gulped down the water in a couple of swift swallows. There was a handbag on the worktop next to the sink. Feeling in her pocket, Sara gripped the business card she had written on before they arrived. 'Is it all right to leave the glass here?'

'Anywhere,' said Mrs Hayward. Sara made sure that the woman was watching as she placed the card under the glass next to the handbag. The two women looked at each other for a moment and Sara went to the front door. Glancing over her shoulder, she was pleased to see that Mrs Hayward was reading the back of the card.

In case you need help was the message she had left. She heard the door to the dishwasher being pulled down.

'That went well,' said Edwards. 'I'm not having that.'

'Sir?'

'Get on to Aggie and get some DNA enforcement warrants sorted out,' he replied. 'Or I'm going to find something to charge that young bugger with and bring him in.'

'What about Benji Wilder? If they've fallen out, it might be easier to get the truth from him.'

'Get Aggie to track him down and do some background checks on him and his family.'

Aggie was working on the list of number plates when Sara rang her. 'I've found Hayward's Porsche,' she said. 'It leaves the town at 11.45 p.m. I'm working through the rest.'

Sara gave Aggie the new set of requests.

'I'll check with the hospital to see if he's been discharged,' said Aggie and signed off.

'Thoughts?' Edwards asked.

'I think there are a lot of people here who are keeping secrets. From one another and from us.'

'Such as?'

'I don't think this jet ski accident was an accident, for a start.' Sara tried to form a list in her head. 'The statements from Greg Hayward and the other three we know are incorrect. They didn't all go to the pub and go back in the car. The car left town at 11.45 p.m. and Hayward got a taxi later.'

'We think,' countered Edwards. 'We ought to get a formal identification to be sure.'

'OK,' said Sara. 'Then there's the theatre people. Jessie Dobson is hiding something, I'm sure. Fred Shaw said that

Daisy had been on dates with Ricky Easton, the singer. But she obviously reconnected with Kit Grice. Was Easton angry about that? And where did she get the ecstasy from? That seems out of character with everything we've been told about her so far.'

The next call only confirmed Sara's suspicions. Bowen rang from the pier to update them. 'We've been thrown out for now,' he said grumpily. 'The matinée started, so we spoke to the bar staff who were on that night. No one saw anything. Something is going on, though.' He told them about the dead rat and Jessie Dobson's reaction. 'It was a nasty trick — she was terrified of the thing. Not to mention the fact that it could have ruined this expensive bit of kit.'

'Best not to get involved,' said Edwards.

'I know. It just seemed odd. I wasn't happy with one of the cast interviews either.'

'Which one?'

'The singer, Ricky Easton. His answers were evasive, and my gut tells me he's hiding something.'

'Well, there's enough of your gut to go around,' laughed Edwards.

'Thanks, boss.' Bowen didn't sound offended. 'There is one person in the cast that we still need to speak to after the show, so we'll stay on here.'

They were almost back in Norwich when Aggie rang back. 'Benji Wilder has been sent home from the hospital. His mother insisted, apparently.'

'Where's home?'

'Colchester. I've got the details.'

'His family?' asked Sara.

'His father died about ten years ago. You're going to love his mum, though.' Aggie sounded excited. 'Bethany Wilder.'

'Should we know her?'

'Only by reputation. Mrs Wilder is a criminal barrister. She works for the Crown Prosecution Service, mostly in Essex.'

Edwards let out a low whistle. 'We'd better be on our toes with that interview. Aggie, please can you make an appointment with them both for tomorrow morning. I think we need a trip to Colchester.'

'I'd like some more background on two of the theatre people if you have time,' said Sara. 'Ricky Easton, the singer and Jessie Dobson, the sound engineer. Social media footprint, reviews of performances, whatever you can think of.'

Edwards added, 'Call everyone in at eight tomorrow morning. We need to start getting some answers soon.'

Sara collected her car from headquarters and began the hour-long drive home. If the case was about secrets, she had one of her own. She hadn't spoken to Chris since Sunday and still didn't know what to say to him. Surely, if she loved him enough, the answer would have been simple. Perhaps it would help to talk about it, and there was only one person she trusted with something as important as this.

As she queued at a roundabout, Sara hit a number on her mobile phone. It was quickly answered.

'Mum? I really need your advice about something.'

CHAPTER 44

There was enough time between the matinée and evening shows for Jessie and Yazza to go back to the cottage for a meal on weekdays. They walked up the zigzag ramps together, keeping their distance from Ricky, who had walked ahead of them. Without a backwards glance, he went into The Duke on the corner.

'He'll get into so much trouble if Larry finds out,' said Yazza. 'Do you think he put the rat there?'

'I'm sure of it, though I can't prove it. The worst is that if he had damaged the board, I would have been in a real fix.'

'It's just spite.'

'I know.' Jessie sighed. She looked around. 'Isn't it odd? All of the shops and restaurants are shut. It's way too quiet.'

The local news told them why, as their headline story was about the gangs rampaging around the town, causing mayhem. The police were declining to comment about an "ongoing situation". One of the pub landlords complained loudly that they'd had to shut up for the night during carnival and lose trade during the busiest week of the year.

'Typical of them to be behind the actual news,' said Jessie. 'It's like a morgue out there.'

It didn't seem any busier when they walked back for the evening show. The small supermarket in the centre of town was still open, though it appeared to be alone. The Duke was dark, its doors locked, and a hastily scribbled note saying *Closed, back tomorrow* had been stuck in the window. The prom was also deserted, as was the boardwalk. Only the box office and bar were still lit up and open for business. They didn't have any customers, despite the show being sold out that night.

Jessie did her mic pack inspection in the dressing rooms before taking a drink to her work area. She didn't put the cover on the desk between shows. It seemed untouched as she ran her usual checks.

She sat on her high stool to sip her coffee while the dancers warmed up on stage. One by one, the performers and front of house staff returned from their breaks. Each time the staff door opened, the sound of expectant audience members in the bar grew louder. It was one of those cherished moments that kept Jessie sitting where she was, working as part of this team. The well-oiled machine of the show began to whirr as she went backstage, and the house was opened.

She went back to her workstation at the appointed time, checked the mic lines, then waited with her cans on.

'We need to have a chat before you leave tonight,' said Pete, the stage manager, as they waited for clearance from Front of House.

'Oh?' A shiver ran down Jessie's back.

'Yeah, can you pop down to the office afterwards?' asked Larry. Pete and Larry shared the tech office next to the wardrobe room. 'I've got the files ready.'

Larry wasn't big on paperwork. Files usually meant music. She felt a flush of relief. 'You mean about the float in the parade.'

'I put them on my old MacBook,' Larry continued. 'If that gets damaged, it won't matter. I'm going to collect the lorry first thing. We need a plan for getting it fixed up.'

'We have clearance,' said Pete. 'Standby.'

'Standing by,' said Jessie.

'Standing by,' said Larry.

'Standing by,' said Artie up on the follow-spot.

And the show began.

After a while, Jessie heard the occasional rumble of wheels being dragged across the boardwalk outside. It was one of the theatre's peculiarities that it was fixed onto the boards of the pier and suspended above the North Sea. There was little in the way of noise exclusion. When the night fishermen arrived with their gear in draggable boxes, the small wheels created a peculiar, if familiar, rumble that Jessie could hear from her perch. It never seemed to worry the audience, who were further away from the wooden walls and deep inside the soundscape that the carefully placed speaker system created.

They were about forty minutes into the first half when Jessie heard something she wasn't expecting. At first, it was distant shouting, which got rapidly closer. Then there were multiple heavy footsteps running at speed. It was hard to tell how many people there were. The footsteps raced past outside, around the back of the theatre and back down the pier. Obscenities were yelled by the fishermen as the feet hammered away.

Eyes accustomed to the dark, Jessie looked over to Larry in the pit. He shrugged his hands theatrically, then pulled on his cans. Jessie fired up the next scene, a musical number for Hallie that she liked to concentrate on to keep the balance sweet. In the middle of the song, the signal light on her head-set began to flash. It must be an emergency. Once the show was up, they only used the system this way if something was wrong. She dragged the headphones on.

'We've just had a phone call from the police,' said Larry. 'They've told us to lock up the venue and not allow anyone out at the interval.'

'What's happening?'

'Apparently, we're the only bar still open in the town. This gang that's been causing problems all day are heading our way.'

'That's mad,' said Pete. 'If they nick something here, the police will just be waiting for them at the entrance. It's not like they can get off the pier any other way.'

'It might not be about stealing anything,' said Jessie. 'It might just be about causing a nuisance.'

'Either way,' said Larry, 'no one's to go outside at the interval, not even for a smoke. Get Ricky to make an announcement at the interval before you put the house lights up.'

She could hear more pounding feet and shouting outside. There was a crash from the bar area. Sirens howled in the distance.

'They're already here,' said Jessie.

CHAPTER 45

A convoy of police vehicles had arrived at Carnival Field at six in the morning. There were officers from all over the county, many in riot gear. The Traveller camp residents were up to greet them with abuse and the occasional missile. They made as much noise as they could, slamming doors and calling to animals. The police stood watching, looking threatening in their black helmets and stab-proof vests. The only people who seemed to be speaking to one another were a senior police officer, the Travellers' legal man, and one Traveller. Nonetheless, by seven o'clock, the caravans and horseboxes had been hitched up. The horses were loaded, the families and pets got into their vans and cars, and the procession set off, led by a police van. Several more police vehicles followed in the rear.

Henry and Adele stood at the door of the marquee. The Travellers blew their horns and shouted through open vehicle windows, disturbing the residents in the houses opposite. Many of them were watching from front gardens and behind curtains. There was even a camera crew from the local news. It disturbed the funfair families too. As the convoy pulled out, Will Grice joined Adele by the marquee.

'Where are they taking them?' he asked.

'King's Lynn way, I think,' replied Henry. 'As far as the Fens perhaps.'

'Away from here, thank God.' Will Grice surveyed Carnival Field. 'What a mess. How are you going to manage?'

'The council are sending refuse trucks in half an hour. They've promised to get the place cleaned before ten, when the first floats are due.'

'We can give them a hand,' offered Mr Grice. 'The sooner it's cleared, the better it is for all of us.'

The clear-up began on time. Half a dozen small lorries with open backs and wire sides arrived. The operatives began to heave bags of rubbish, pallets and heavy junk into them. Several of the funfair men walked over to help.

Henry pulled out his mobile. 'Let's get this tent reloaded,' he said to whomever answered his call.

Ten minutes later, Brian Medler pulled up in a white van. More of the committee arrived to unload drinks and coffee machines. It took an hour before the tent was back to working order. The caterer set up his hot plates, and soon the scent of fresh bacon and sausages began to waft out of the door. Henry and Adele sat at a separate table from the others, enjoying their celebratory hot sandwiches.

'How are you?' he asked, looking at her arms.

'It's healing,' Adele assured him. She pulled a leaflet for the woman's refuge in Norwich from her handbag. 'The nurse gave me this. It seems it's the nearest place I can go.'

Henry took the leaflet and read it thoroughly. 'There's nowhere in Cromer?'

'No. Besides, it would be too close. If I try to leave, Greg will follow me. I'm sure of that. His ego wouldn't allow me to get away.'

'You can come to me.' Henry gripped Adele's hand fiercely. 'As a friend. I don't expect more. Just pack a bag and come.'

Adele smiled with gratitude. 'You're so kind. I'll think about it. I can't do anything until this is all over, or even before Xander goes to university.'

'I don't understand.' Henry frowned and released her hand. 'Why do you need to wait so long?'

'He didn't used to get violent.' Adele shook her head. 'It's just these last few months. He's been drinking a lot, out with the boys. I don't know why he started doing that, but he's still my husband, and we loved each other in the beginning. This could all pass.'

Henry gave her an old-fashioned look. 'It might not, an' all. You're in real danger.'

'Greg will cut me off without a penny.' Adele pushed the refuge leaflet into her bag. 'I need to plan if I'm to get away without him punishing me. I need to work out how I'm going to live.'

Henry dropped the remnants of his sandwich on the paper plate. 'We'd best get on.'

As the last of the refuse trucks left the field, Henry put up the barrier at the gate, and Adele joined him. He had a list of entrants, and Adele had a box of numbers printed on large cards for the parade vehicles to display. As the lorries arrived, they were booked in and waved into a parking space.

A sense of excitement hovered in the growing crowd. The tent became busy with teams buying breakfast. The funfair workers took down the stall coverings, flicked on the lights, and opened for business. Spectators began to wander in. The biggest day of the carnival week was starting just as it should, despite all the problems they had faced.

'I've forgotten my handbag.' Adele handed the numbers to Henry and jogged back to the marquee. The table they'd used was occupied. She looked round in panic before heading to the bar, where Brian was working the coffee machines. 'I don't suppose you've seen my handbag?'

'Yeah, you left it on the table.' Brian nodded. 'So busy, you forgot, eh?'

He reached under the counter and pulled out the bag. Adele accepted it gratefully and went to zip it shut. To her horror, some of the contents were missing. She rummaged for a moment, pulling items out onto the bar.

'Everything all right?'

'My purse is here.' She tapped it with a trembling hand. 'And my mobile.'

'I should think so, too,' smiled Brian. 'It was your son who brought it over. Said he'd been looking for you.'

'Why didn't he bring it to me himself?'

'Told me he couldn't see you, and he was going off with his dad for the day.'

'I was on the gate. How could he have missed me?'

'Came in the pedestrian entrance? Does it matter? Did he take anything?' Brian looked confused. 'I know a lady's bag is private, but he's your son.'

Adele pulled at the popper on the side of the purse. The two twenty-pound notes she'd had in there were gone. No doubt Xander had helped himself. Flipping open the credit card section, Adele felt with shaking fingers in the small compartment at the back. With relief, she pulled out the business card the detective woman had so pointedly left for her.

'No, it's all OK. Thank you for looking after it.'

Brian nodded happily and served the next customer. Adele went back to help Henry, with the handbag over her shoulder and a sinking heart. The missing items were of a much greater value than the money. Xander had obviously looked in her bag and taken two other things. One was the report from the hospital. The second was the letter from his school.

CHAPTER 46

The team gathered for the morning meeting. Bowen was still feeling grumpy about Ricky Easton and was running the background checks on him.

'He's hiding something,' he insisted. 'He may be involved in some way. I reckon he put that rat on the sound desk, and why would he do that? He's a nasty piece of work.'

'Did you finish the ANPR video?' Edwards asked Aggie.

'No, sir.' She looked frustrated. 'I did the DNA warrants.'

'Has all the CCTV footage come in?'

Aggie nodded. The DI turned to Noble. 'You and Aggie see if you can do a complete timeline from the CCTV. I want to be able to watch the couple before they have sex and after they split up. Then look at what happens at the pier entrance after the show on Friday evening. Let's see if this Easton bloke is telling us the truth. If you get time, finish the number plate trawl.'

Aggie held up warrant requests. 'These, sir?'

'Mike can take them to the duty judge on my behalf this morning.'

The appointment to interview Benji had been booked for lunchtime, and Sara and Edwards were soon hurtling down the A140. Her boss chose to drive, leaving Sara with leisure to gaze out of the window and think. The chat with her mother the previous evening had solved one thing. Tegan and Javed were coming to visit on Friday for the week. At least she hadn't wasted her money on hiring the holiday cottage.

'Penny for them?' asked Edwards as they swung east onto the A14.

'Something personal, sir.' Sara shrugged. 'Sorry, I should be concentrating on the interview.'

'That's OK.' Edwards pulled into the fast lane and hit the accelerator. 'You know you can always talk to me, don't you? Especially if it's about work issues.'

'Work is fine, thanks.'

Sara no longer felt so isolated as an officer of mixed heritage on the force. She had been invited by ACC Miller to help implement a policy to encourage and recruit under-represented ethnicities. So far, DC Adebayo had joined the drugs team after Christmas and was making a name for himself as a thoroughly tough cookie. A British-Vietnamese uniform officer had joined Traffic in the spring. Apart from the occasional bit of joshing, usually with DC Bowen, Sara thought that attitudes were improving.

'It's my home life that's a bit of an issue.'

Edwards nodded. Sara knew he was curious about how she was settling into her father's cottage. 'We won't be there for an hour if you need to make any calls.'

'I made them last night, thanks. My mum and her partner are coming down for a week to visit me. She was still unsure about staying in Dad's cottage, so I booked the holiday home next door.'

'Doesn't that look exactly the same?'

'Not quite, but near enough.'

'Her visit worries you?'

'No, it's not that.'

'Then what is it?' Edwards glanced at her, his forehead wrinkled. 'Not thinking of going back to the Met?'

Sara smiled. 'No, sir. It's my boyfriend that's the problem.'

'Ah.' She knew that this was territory that DI Edwards was far less comfortable with. 'Chris, isn't it?'

'That's right. The problem is that Chris proposed on Sunday.'

There was a long silence.

'I'd be sorry to lose you.'

'Lose me? What makes you say that? Married women are allowed to work in the police these days, you know.'

'No, no,' stuttered Edwards. 'Not like that. I just mean, you know, having babies and all that. You might want to leave to look after them. Besides, you don't seem the type.'

'Bloody hell, boss! There is such a thing as maternity leave. And what do you mean "not the type"?'

'I thought you were a career woman.' Edwards was turning bright red.

Sara sighed and decided to let him off the hook. So much for attitudes changing. 'I *am* a career woman. I'm happy on my own, and I love living in that cottage. That's the problem.' Besides, the middle of a major investigation was not the best time to be reviewing her feelings about marriage. She didn't want to be seen as not being dedicated to her job. Perhaps she had already said too much and put Edwards on the spot.

Caught out being human again, she thought. She pulled a wry face.

Edwards changed the subject. 'When we get to the Wilder's house, I'll lead the interview. His mother will expect me to.'

Edwards's mobile trilled and cut in through the system.

'Sir? You need to know what we've found.' It was DC Noble. 'I've been going through all the CCTV with Aggie, and we've got a full timeline.'

'Good, go on.'

'We first see them coming down the prom. If the times are accurate on the cameras, it was about 11.45 p.m. They go off, past the beach huts. That's where the cameras stop. We don't see them again for nearly an hour when they walk back. They separate outside the RNLI café. Grice watches her climb the steps up the cliff to the town, and then he goes back along the prom.'

'Fits with Kit's statements,' said Sara.

'So far.' Edwards grumbled. 'Any more?'

'Yes, sir,' said Noble. 'We pick Daisy up as she walks behind the church, where the taxi rank is. She sits on the wall for a while, her head in her hands.'

'That could be the ketamine or the booze, making her feel dizzy,' suggested Sara.

'Then she takes off her shoes.'

'They were rather high heels. Her feet were probably hurting.' That was Aggie in the background.

'She carries them in her hand with her bag. She looks rather unsteady, like she's drunk. Daisy goes down the cobbled street at the back of the Hotel De Paris. It leads to The Duke.'

'Was the pub still open?'

'Looks like it was starting to close. They tend to have licence extensions during carnival week. Quite a lot of punters outside drinking and smoking. Anyway, she has a bit of banter with some guys outside the pub and walks towards the posh chippie. Then we have to switch to the view outside the games arcade. It's got to about 12.45 a.m.'

'Is someone following her from the pub then?' Edwards asked excitedly.

'Daisy gets to the alley that cuts behind the posh chippie, where it looks like someone is waiting for her. The angle isn't great, and it happens so fast, we've had to keep going over it. An arm reaches out as Daisy gets to the end of the alley and drags her into the dark.'

'Fucking hell! Someone was waiting for her?'

'Looks like it.'

'Could Kit Grice have gone back that way?'

'It would have been a long way round, and he'd need to have sprinted all the way down the clifftop gardens or back along the prom. The prom camera has him at the far end at the same time, near that set of cliffside steps that go up to Carnival Field. I suspect that's where he was heading.'

'What about New Street?'

'There are no cameras trained down that cut-through.'

'And that's not all,' Aggie cut in again. 'Ian's such a clever guy with these things. Go on, tell them what you saw.'

'They were followed.'

'What? Where?'

'First time is when they go out to the beach. There's a figure in a dark tracksuit with the hood up. It follows them past the beach hut.'

'Dog walker or insomniac?'

'I doubt it, sir. Assuming it's the same person later, once Grice and Daisy split up, a man in a dark hoodie climbs the stairs after her. I can't see him when she sits down at the church. He must be in a doorway or something. After she has wandered off with her shoes in her hand, he reappears and goes after her.'

'He follows her past the pub?' asked Sara.

'No.' Noble sounded anxious to explain. 'Where the road splits near the supermarket, he turns and goes towards the front of Hotel De Paris. No CCTV cover there. But whoever it was would have had enough time to go along the walkway in front of the bed and breakfast places on the clifftop there and reach the alley before Daisy did. I think the man followed them from the beach.'

'Where Daisy and Kit had sex?' asked Sara.

'Exactly. He may have watched them on the beach and then followed Daisy.'

'Goddammit,' snarled Edwards. 'So, it could be some random voyeur and nutcase. That's all we need.'

'Or maybe it's someone we've already interviewed,' said Sara. 'Like one of the Hayward party. Or the singer from the pier.'

CHAPTER 47

It was a beautiful sunny morning. As Jessie walked down to the theatre, there was no sign of the incursion from the previous evening. The crew and a couple of the performers made their way to the theatre at eight. The day looked as if it was going to be perfect for the parade.

Larry wouldn't let anyone else drive the lorry. He was already parked at the entrance, the flat back of the hired lorry swept clean. They had decided to take part of the set from one of the big production numbers, *Annie Get Your Gun*, and fix it to the lorry. With the help of Paul Chapman, the comedian, Jessie ferried down boxes of sound equipment, two huge speakers and cabling. Larry's laptop was the last item to be loaded. It took most of the morning to ensure the set was safe and the sound working.

Jessie went up to Carnival Field in the lorry with Larry. It wasn't a comfortable moment for her to be alone with him. She was primed with excuses against Ricky's accusations, which Yazza had relayed last night. But Larry was too busy concentrating on driving to talk about backstage feuds.

The field was heaving with floats and participants. The public were allowed to come into the marquee and funfair but were not supposed to be walking between the floats. Any

205

space between the participants was there for dance troupes and marching majorettes to gather and practise if they wished to. Several pier staff were already there, wearing cowboy-style fancy dress and handing out flyers for the winter season. Doing publicity for the venue was a constant activity.

A crowd of onlookers were also gathered by the Big Sky Café, which was doing a roaring trade. Apart from a few burnt patches on the grass, there was little sign that the Travellers' camp had been there last night.

After furnishing Larry and herself with refreshments, Jessie climbed onto the back of the lorry to retest the sound system. She plugged in the laptop, which had travelled in the cab up to the field. It buzzed into life, full of static and far from clear. Gritting her teeth, she set about checking all the cables and connections, replacing where necessary from the crate of spares.

'Need anything?' asked Larry.

She shook her head. 'Just checking it through.' Finally, she found a connector that had shaken loose. She seated it firmly, strapped it to the bed of the truck with gaffer tape and stretched up. 'That better?'

'It's fine, well done.' Larry turned to talk to one of the publicity ladies, who was wearing a skimpy cowgirl's outfit.

Jessie had ensured that two small pieces of scenery had been fixed to the back of the cab, forming a little boxed-off area. The laptop and mixer sat here in a small flight case that had been locked down. She had a low stool to sit on as the parade took ages to wind around the town. It was a secret cave where she could work without being seen, just as she liked it. She flicked on the house music to add their own bit of cheerful noise to the cacophony created by the others. Her coffee was cold when she got back to it, as was her bacon roll. She sat in the cab to finish them anyway. It was going to be a long day.

The dancers and performers began to arrive in dribs and drabs. They were all wearing their *Annie Get Your Gun* costumes. Paul Chapman was sporting a child's gun in a belt that was far too small for him. Jessie suspected it might be a water pistol, as he had a large bottle of water stuffed in his waistcoat. Hallie was wearing her Annie Oakley costume.

She came round to where Jessie was sitting. 'You didn't dress up then?'

Jessie smiled. She was wearing her usual black backstage clothes. 'No one is going to see me. At least I hope not.'

'You should get in the spirit of things.' Hallie handed her a cowboy hat. 'Just in case. Come on, Jessie, have some fun for once.'

She pulled on the hat. *Was that how they saw her? Someone who was no fun?*

The parade was due to kick off at half past two. At two, Larry went round to check who was there, just as he would have done at the theatre. There were two absentees — Linda, the smallest of the dancers, and Ricky Easton.

'Climb up on the back and see if you can spot them anywhere,' Larry suggested.

It was sunny and hot. Jessie was grateful for the hat now that she was scanning the crowds. It shaded her eyes, which sometimes struggled on a bright day after nearly forty years of working in the dark. Starting at the road, which the police were busy closing to allow the parade out, she turned slowly, checking the marquee, funfair and the row of chemical toilets on the cliff-edge. Her turn was almost complete when she got to the onlookers at the Big Sky Café. Their lorry was parked close enough to the café to give her an excellent view.

Her skin prickled with anxiety. Jessie had spotted two people she knew. The first was the dealer with his muscle-bound body and his tattoos. There was no mistaking his build and stance. Behind the man, trying to look inconspicuous, hovered Ricky in his cowboy outfit. As he walked past the dealer, the man rapidly handed him something.

Ricky walked on through the crowd. One or two people recognised him from the show, and he was delayed by speaking to them. Everyone in the show was expected to interact with customers — it was part of their contract. Reaching the edge of the parking area, Ricky ducked under the tape that was, in theory at least, holding back the public.

For a moment, Jessie lost him among a group surrounding one of the other floats. When he emerged, she watched as the young dancer, Linda, joined him. Ricky handed something over, and Linda pecked him on the cheek. *Now what's going on*, Jessie wondered. Had Ricky transferred his attentions to Linda already, or was he dealing in the drugs himself?

'Have you caught the sun already?' Hallie's voice made Jessie jump.

'I don't know, have I?'

'You look really red. I've got some sunscreen if you need it.'

'Might not be a bad idea.' Jessie dropped down from the back of the float. Turning to Larry, she said, 'I think I can see them coming.'

Larry nodded. 'Are you happy with what you are doing?' he said to the dancers. 'Don't forget that you're going to have to repeat it endlessly, and you will get tired.'

She followed Hallie to the cab, where Larry kept everyone's personal stuff for safekeeping. It didn't do to leave things at the field.

'Gosh, the back of your neck is bad,' said Hallie, plastering cream on the sunburn. 'You don't get out much, do you?'

'Not in daylight.' Jessie tried to sound jovial. 'You know all the crew are vampires, don't you?'

Hallie laughed.

'You'd know all about that.' Ricky's voice cut across their conversation. 'You'd suck the lifeblood out of anyone.'

CHAPTER 48

The Wilders' house was a chicly restored thatched cottage in a village about ten miles from Colchester. It stood in a traditional garden with manicured lawns, where expensive wooden garden furniture sat under shady canvas umbrellas. Somehow, she had been expecting a newbuild on an exclusive estate, similar to the one where the Haywards lived.

Mrs Wilder was waiting for them. She had appeared on the gravel drive before Edwards had turned off the car engine. Immaculately dressed in smart-casual summer clothes, her hair cut short and fashionably spiked, Benji's mother was no more than five foot tall. Sara's image of a tall, aggressive, bewigged barrister vanished before she got out of the car. She didn't doubt there was steel in Mrs Wilder's character too.

They were led around the house to the back garden, where Benji lay on a lounger. The injuries he had sustained two days before were obvious in livid bruising, a cast on his leg and one arm in a sling to support his broken collar bone. A jug of iced tea stood on the table with four glasses. There were several printed sheets, the top one said *North Norfolk News*. Mrs Wilder offered them a drink, then pointed to a handheld recorder.

'For your information, I am going to record this conversation.' Her voice was cold, her words chosen carefully. 'You may wish to do the same.'

Edwards nodded to Sara, who produced her mobile and turned on the recorder function. When it was running, she looked up at Mrs Wilder.

'You're ready?'

Sara nodded. What followed sounded as much like an official interview as it was possible to unofficially be.

'First of all, I would like to make it clear for the recording who is present.' They all stated their names. 'My son is giving this witness interview on my advice. If he chooses not to answer a question, he is under no obligation to do so. If he wishes to seek my opinion before answering a question, the recording devices will be paused. Are we all agreed?'

Sara felt Edwards bristle at the officious tone and answered before he could. 'That's fine by us, Mrs Wilder. If anything is said here which requires an official statement, arrangements will be made.'

'Agreed.'

Edwards turned his attention to Benji. The young man looked tired. There were dark circles under his eyes. Sleeping with injuries like that wouldn't be easy.

'How are you recovering?' In her head, Sara awarded him a small round of applause. His tone was almost fatherly. 'Those are severe injuries.'

'It will take weeks to mend,' said Benji. 'Really buggers thing up for me.'

'I'm sure they must be painful. In what way does it make things so difficult?'

'I was due to run at the Essex County Championships next week.' Benji looked angrily at his leg. 'I won't be running for months. If ever again.'

Mrs Wilder smiled encouragingly. 'I'm sure you will make a full recovery. Benji is upset because he is being watched by the national squad. The championships were a trial for being coached at the centre of excellence when he goes to university.'

'Which one?'

'Cambridge, King's College.'

'I studied at Girton,' offered Mrs Wilder.

'And what are you reading?' asked Edwards.

'Law,' said Benji. 'Like Mum. I want to be a barrister.'

No wonder they were being so careful, Sara realised. Having any kind of criminal record would be deeply unhelpful with that ambition.

'How do you know Xander and Jacob?'

'We were friends at school.' Benji briefly told them about his time at Langton Hall. 'This was going to be our last summer together in any case. Jacob and Xander are going to Oxford.'

'You have your exam results? These are confirmed places?'

Benji nodded.

'Why did you go to visit Xander?'

'Mum has to work away a lot. I don't mind being here on my own, but I thought it would be nice to spend a few days with them before we went our separate ways.'

'It didn't turn out so nice?'

'No.'

'Benji, what happened on Monday evening?'

The young man turned to his mother. She nodded, picking up the printed sheets and holding them up. 'Certainly not this.'

Mrs Wilder had obviously printed out an article from the Cromer-based newspaper's website. It said, *Hero saves friend after jet ski accident.* A picture of Xander with a broad grin was embedded in the text, along with a smaller one of Greg Hayward patting Xander on the shoulder in congratulation.

Sara took the pages and read the report. 'That's fulsome stuff,' she said, handing it to Edwards. Benji grimaced. 'It says that you lost control of your jet ski and turned it over, getting trapped underneath. According to this, Xander drove in close, pulled you out of the sea and carried you back to the beach on his own machine.'

'I'm sure that's exactly what the reporter was told,' said Mrs Wilder.

'You don't believe it?' asked Edwards. He put the pages back on the table.

'No, I don't. I believe my son's account.'

Edwards turned back to the young man, who was lying back in the lounger, eyes closed. 'Are you all right to go on?'

'Yes,' said Benji faintly. 'I didn't want to go out in the first place. Greg had borrowed a second jet ski from a mate so we could get more water time. I was happy for Xander and Jacob to use them. Stay on the beach.'

'So why did you go out?'

Benji hesitated. He looked at his mother again, who moved to sit on the lounger next to him. She took his hand.

Edwards nodded at Sara to take over.

'You'd better start from the beginning,' she said gently. 'Had your trip turned out as you planned? You'd fallen out by Sunday when we saw you at the soapbox derby and broke up that fight.'

'What fight?' Mrs Wilder sounded surprised. 'Benji?'

'It started long before that.' Benji sat up, with great difficulty. 'Before we left school.'

All three adults remained silent, giving the young man time to think.

'We've been mates for years. We shared a common room once we were in the sixth form. Jacob and Xander played rugby. I was always a runner. Cross country in the winter, track in the summer. We shared an ambition to get to national level if we could. That's why we got on.'

'And that changed?'

'Not the ambition part,' said Benji. 'It was Xander who changed. Slowly at first, I didn't notice much. Then he got accused of bullying a younger player. He was drinking by then, as well. It was like he had become this dark version of himself.'

'When was this?' asked Edwards.

'Before Christmas. I wasn't eighteen, so I didn't join in.'

They were going to have to take that one at face value.

'When I did try drinking on my birthday, I hated it. They got me so drunk I couldn't remember anything that happened. I was sick all over my bed, and they left me to lie in it until the next morning. It horrified me. I've never touched a drop since then. That was when they began to despise me.'

'You don't want to repeat the experience?'

'No. I want to run for England.'

Sara nodded. 'So that was when you first fell out?'

'Yeah. Then there was Lyra at school. I liked her.'

'Can you tell us about that?'

'No. I don't want to.' Benji was becoming agitated.

'You should ask the school,' said Mrs Wilder.

'Why did you go to visit Xander?' asked Edwards. 'If you felt like that about him?'

'I thought we might make it up. That it would be good to start uni with no bad feelings about my old friends.'

'How were you received?'

'It felt like they were making a fool of me. Even Greg, Xander's dad, seemed to be in on the joke. They kept trying to force drink on me from the moment they picked me up at the station. Telling me I was a wimp or a lightweight. I kept saying I had my trials coming up, so I didn't want to get shitfaced. They just laughed at me.'

'Why were you fighting on Sunday?' Sara asked.

'I wasn't. Xander attacked me. They started drinking before lunch. Greg kept giving them beers, topped up from a vodka bottle. Then we went down to watch the racing. I thought that would be fun, and Adele would be there. I felt sorry for her.'

'Mrs Hayward?'

Mrs Wilder frowned and shook her head. Benji changed tack. 'Greg went to get a round in at the beer tent. Jacob kept pestering me to get drunk. Xander started slapping me on the

213

shoulder, saying I was no friend of his. That I hadn't been there for him when he'd needed me.'

'When he'd needed you to do what?' Edwards was managing to keep his tone neutral. Sara was impressed with his self-control.

Benji's voice began to break. 'They wanted me to lie about something.'

'Lie about what?' Edwards leaned forward. 'Benji, this could be really important. What lie?'

'They wanted me to tell you that we had all come home together on Friday night.'

'Which you did in your statement on Monday?'

Benji nodded miserably. 'It wasn't true. After the dance at the marquee, they all went off to the pub. Greg gave me his car keys and told me to make myself useful. Said I should drive his car home because I hadn't had a drink.'

'And did you?'

Benji looked down at the grass. 'Yes.'

'Who was at home when you got there?'

'Only Adele, I think. I could hear her in the bedroom.'

'When did the others come back?'

'I don't know. I was asleep.'

Sara thought he was being evasive but didn't want to interfere when Edwards was getting so much out of the youngster.

'And the jet ski accident?'

'It was no accident,' snapped Mrs Wilder. 'Xander rammed his jet ski into Benji's deliberately. The impact threw Benji over the far side, and it broke his leg. You check the machines — you'll see the damage.'

'Did it overturn?'

'No,' said Benji. 'That's quite hard to do unless you hit a wave at the wrong speed and angle.'

'And then?' Edwards encouraged Benji to carry on.

'I was floundering. I couldn't swim because of my leg. It was so painful. Xander circled and came at me from the other side. Drove straight at me again. I thought he was trying to crush my head against the side of the ski. I ducked under the water to escape.'

'He caught his collar bone as he surfaced,' Mrs Wilder added. 'That's how it got broken.'

Benji continued. He was shaking at the memory. 'Xander came back again, pulled up alongside me. He held out his hand, and I reached for it because I thought he was helping me.'

'He wasn't?'

'No. He grabbed my hair and held my face down in the water. I was drowning.'

Even Edwards was silenced by this. Mrs Wilder rubbed Benji's back to comfort him while Sara looked at the young man in horror.

'I was in such a panic. I tried to pull Xander into the water. Then suddenly someone else was there.'

'How?'

'Another man, on a jet ski. He was yelling, I think. Xander grabbed me, pulled me half out of the water. The next thing I knew, I was on the beach. This paramedic was doing something as I coughed up all this water.'

'Benji, why didn't you report this?' Sara asked.

'He was in no fit state to do so,' said Mrs Wilder.

'Not at first,' agreed Sara. 'After you got to the hospital?'

'I think we've finished now.' Mrs Wilder stood up. 'You got what you came for, haven't you? We have no intention of asking you to press charges against Xander. What would be the point?'

'He tried to kill your son,' Edwards snapped.

Mrs Wilder's expression froze. 'Neither Benjamin nor I wish to get embroiled in some court case that is essentially his word against someone else's. You, of all people, know how difficult that sort of prosecution can be. That family has done enough damage to my son. I won't let him get dragged through the court, being branded a liar.'

Sara knew that Mrs Wilder was probably right. Her experience working for the CPS would have provided plenty of examples.

'You don't want to press charges?' Edwards confirmed.

'No, we don't. I hope that answers all your questions, Detective Inspector. Because we've finished helping the police with their inquiries on this or any other matter concerning Xander or Greg Hayward.'

They were escorted off the premises by the small firebrand that was Mrs Wilder, QC. Edwards turned onto the main road, heading back to the A12 and, eventually, Norwich.

'I still think he's hiding something,' said Sara. 'I think he knows what time people came back, for a start. If we believe what Benji is telling us. God, what a mess.'

'We certainly need to talk to that family again. Shall we go now?'

'No point, sir.' Sara glanced at the clock in the car. 'It's carnival parade day. The town will be shut down.'

'First thing tomorrow then. And if you still fancy Easton for it, let's get that singer in too.'

'And another thing, sir,' said Sara thoughtfully. 'Who is this Lyra? Someone at the school? Why did Mrs Wilder stop him from talking about her?'

CHAPTER 49

There was so much for the committee to do on parade day that Adele had no time to think about what had happened to the missing letters. It was nearly six o'clock when the last remnants of the parade wound their way back to Carnival Field. There was a buffet laid on in the marquee, prizes to be handed out, local councillors to be congratulated, even though the organization of the day had nothing to do with them. It had grown dark by the time the day was winding down, and the lorries had, for the most part, left the field outside empty. Spectators roamed through the town, buying drink or food from the relieved traders, grateful to have so many customers after yesterday. It felt like the celebration it was meant to be. Adele said her goodbyes to the rest of the committee, including Henry.

He escorted her to her car. 'Are you going to be all right?'
'Yes, I think so.'
'You should change that dressing. It's dirty after such a long day.'

Henry was right again. The dressing looked grubby, and after the short drive home, Adele got out the first aid kit. She had been grateful to see that Greg's car was absent. Not so happy to hear Jacob and Xander upstairs playing a wild computer game that seemed to involve a lot of machine-gun fire and shouting. All that was left in the kit were a couple of plasters. They would have to do.

Xander ran in his heavy-footed way downstairs. 'What are you doing here?'

'What do you mean?'

Xander opened the fridge and extracted two tins of beer. 'I thought you were leaving us.' He sounded angry. 'Good job if you did.'

Adele was so shocked she stood with her mouth open, watching her son as he pulled the tab on the tin and noisily slurped the contents. 'Did you take those letters from my handbag?'

'Damn right I did.' Xander slammed the tin on the island work surface. He dug in his pocket and pulled out two crumpled pieces of paper. 'Where did you get this from?'

'The hospital, obviously.' Adele couldn't keep the sarcasm out of the reply. 'Like it says on the top.'

'Accusing dad of hurting you? How the hell could you say that? You don't deserve what he does for you.'

'You think I deserve this?' Adele ripped the dressing from her arm. The two burns still showed the under layer of skin and were seeping blood. 'That he has the right to do this to me?'

'It was an accident,' snarled Xander. 'You caught yourself. How dare you blame him!'

'An accident? Is that what your father told you?'

'Why should I believe you and not Dad?'

'Because, Alexander, you stood in the doorway and watched him do it.'

Xander shook his head furiously. 'He was helping you. I couldn't see it anyway.'

There are none so blind as those who won't see, thought Adele in horror. Greg had given Xander his side of the story, and Xander wanted to believe his father, not his mother.

'This isn't the first time that he's hurt me,' said Adele. Her voice was almost a whisper.

'I don't believe you. Dad says that you're accident-prone. That's where the marks come from.'

'You've seen the marks?' Adele felt her temper give. She was tired. Exhausted by the hard work of such a tough carnival week. 'The black eye that I had to cover with make-up? The bruises on my legs where he trapped me against the wall? No, you wouldn't have seen those. He made sure they would be under my clothes. The scratches on my face where he tried to gouge out my eye at Easter? More make-up for that one. You haven't heard or seen any of this?'

'And if I have,' shouted Xander, 'you deserved it. Always out at that damn committee. Never here for us.'

'Xander, no one deserves to be beaten up by their husband. Grow up. Talk sense.'

'You're the one who needs to grow up.' Xander sounded like the petulant schoolboy he still was. Not the adult he wanted to be. 'Stealing things from Dad's study. Making unfounded accusations to destroy his reputation.'

'Stealing things?'

Xander waved the second piece of paper. It was the letter from the school. 'You had no right to take this.'

'I had every right,' screamed Adele. 'I'm your mother. You two should never have kept such a thing from me. What happened? What did you do?'

'Mind your own business.'

'It is my business.'

'You're pathetic, criticising me.' Xander slammed his fist down on the half-finished tin of beer, crumpling it and spraying the contents across the kitchen. 'She led me on. He called me names.'

Adele stared at him, all the anger draining out of her. 'What are you talking about? Xander, what happened?'

'Rubbish. The little shit said I was crap. Waggling her arse, flashing her tits. What a whore. And him! Little shit couldn't even carry the ball. I taught him.'

Adele watched at her son in amazement.

'They're all just like you.' Xander was breathing heavily. 'Always fucking lying.'

'Xander?' Adele held out her arms to him.

He stepped back out of her reach. 'You're a liar. You're planning to leave Dad and me.' He began to cry and wrapped his arms around himself as if he were trying to give himself a hug. 'Were you even going to tell us? Or were you just going to piss off and vanish?' He brandished the papers. 'Well, I'm going to tell him as soon as he comes home. You're not going to get away with this.'

'I wasn't going to leave without talking to you both,' said Adele with a calmness she didn't feel. 'But you must see that I can't go on like this. Whatever your dad is telling you, the truth is that he hurts me. Physically. Often. And it's getting worse. Xander, please give me the letters. If he knows about this, he might kill me.'

She held out her hand. Xander looked at her and laughed. 'It would serve you fucking well right.'

He swung his hand round swiftly, deliberately hitting Adele on the still-raw burn marks. With a scream, she spun away, and Xander fled from the room.

CHAPTER 50

Thursday's morning orders started at Aggie's computer screen. They watched the CCTV timeline that Noble and Aggie had put together. They agreed it was a male figure, but the raised hoodie obscured his facial features. Aggie and Noble had also spent time checking the prom footage and put together a timeline of the people leaving after the theatre show ended.

'You might find these useful if you're talking to the theatre staff.' Aggie gave Sara a series of printed screenshots from the camera, which she showed to the team before adding them to her file of statements.

'Now, that is interesting.' Sara held one up. 'First sighting of our stalker?'

'That's what we think,' confirmed Noble.

DC Bowen had run social media checks on the theatre company.

'Ricky Easton has a sizeable social media presence,' he explained. 'From his agent to a personal website. He's played in the West End and on big tours, all of it in musicals.' Bowen glanced at Aggie with a smile. Sara reckoned Bowen wasn't much of a theatregoer, but perhaps Aggie was. 'Seems to have made the jump to lead roles about twenty years ago.

Interestingly, he hasn't worked much recently. This job at Cromer is the biggest he seems to have had in three years.'

'And Jessie Dobson?' asked DI Edwards.

'Only has a Facebook account, and she doesn't post much on it. Perhaps she doesn't need to do it to get work like the singer does. It says that she moved to Cromer ten years ago, and there's no reason to doubt the entry.'

'Number plates?'

'That's interesting too,' said Noble. 'Hayward's Porsche comes back to town just before three. You can't see who's driving it.'

'If it's Hayward, he would still have been drunk,' said Sara. 'What time did he get that cab?'

Aggie checked her notes. 'Just after one o'clock.'

'Only two hours earlier? And so drunk the driver thought he might vomit in the back seat.'

'Then it leaves again.' Noble continued. 'About fifteen minutes later. Back up the hill towards their house.'

'OK,' said Edwards. 'Who's in the frame then?'

Sara stood at the incident board and began to write. 'Daisy gets pulled into the alley at about 12.45 a.m. Kit Grice is at the far end of the prom at exactly the same time, so I guess that rules him out. Benji Wilder had driven the car home and gone to bed. Or so he says.'

'We don't have reason to doubt that,' said Edwards. 'Leave them off. Who's left?'

'Xander and Jacob were at the pub with Greg.' Sara wrote all their names on the board. 'They all gave one another alibis. But Benji has confirmed they didn't go home with him as they claimed. Could Benji have been driving the car later on?'

'It's possible. We need to talk to them again, don't we?'

'What about Ricky Easton?' asked Bowen. 'I still think he's up to something. What's with this friction between him and Jessie Dobson?'

'I've been going through the statements from other people at the theatre,' said Sara. 'Easton has been, at best, economical with the truth. The timings in his statement don't agree with at least two others.'

'Let's keep him up there too,' said the DI. 'If only to keep Mike's gut happy.'

Bowen patted his cake-and-beer belly with a grin.

Sara pointed to the last of Aggie's photos. 'This man in the hoodie could be anybody with a dark tracksuit, so it doesn't rule him out.'

'Oh, and on the CCTV, we saw Ricky Easton going into the pub. At least we think it was him.' Noble looked to Aggie, who nodded in confirmation.

'About eleven,' she said.

'OK. Let's talk to Easton again.'

'What about this jet ski thing?' asked Noble. 'Will you try and push the Wilders to get a prosecution?'

'Not yet,' said Edwards. 'Aggie, are those DNA warrants signed off?'

'On your desk, boss.'

'Get another one to search their house. I want to examine the jet ski, which I think is in their garage. The damage will be telling. Let's see if we can get Greg Hayward to tell us who the other one belonged to. If we pile on the pressure, something may pop.'

'What about this accusation at the school, sir? Against Xander.'

'We should follow that up. Aggie, can you contact them and see who will talk to us? Ask about a girl called Lyra. They may all be on holiday, of course.'

Noble stayed in the office with Aggie, tasked with getting the search warrant signed as soon as possible. The other three set off for Cromer. Sara rang Donal Byrne, the pier manager, from the car, and got the address for Ricky Easton's digs. He was staying in a flat over one of the shops in the high street.

They parked in the tiny supermarket car park behind the shops. They accessed the flat by a set of metal steps outside the building, which ran up from the car park to a door with a big *Private* sign. Edwards stayed in the car. Bowen rang and knocked several times before they heard footsteps. The door opened a few inches, and the bleary-eyed face of Ricky Easton looked at them without comprehension. He was wearing a scruffy tracksuit and a pair of old trainers with their laces knotted beyond undoing. The top was a sweatshirt with a hood. The clothes and shoes were black. It looked as if they had just got him out of bed.

'Hello again, Mr Easton,' said Bowen in his best formal tone. 'Mind if we come in for a minute?'

Easton looked as if he wanted to object, glancing over Bowen's shoulder at Sara, with her warrant card held up. He opened the door and let them in.

'Nice place you've got here,' said Bowen. Sara looked around the untidy living room. The smell of dirty clothes and unwashed pots hung in the air.

'It's just digs,' said Ricky. 'They're neither grand nor unpleasant. You get used to it.'

'We want you to come to the station for a chat.'

'I've nothing else to tell you.' Easton slumped into an armchair without offering either of them a seat. 'I didn't see Daisy on Friday.'

'We have new evidence we'd like to discuss.'

'Do I have to?'

'Let me put it this way,' said Sara. 'You can come with us as a witness to give a statement. Or we could arrest and caution you on suspicion of withholding evidence during a murder inquiry. Your choice.'

Easton stood up. 'All right. I'll come, but I don't have much time. We've got a show this afternoon at one.'

'Isn't it two thirty?' asked Sara.

Easton shook his head. 'Not today — it's firework night. We start earlier.'

'The sooner we get to the station, the quicker we'll be finished, sir,' said Bowen.

When they opened the flat door, DI Edwards was lounging halfway up the metal stairs. 'Thank you for your cooperation.'

Sara nearly laughed. The station was only a few minutes away, and they soon had Easton in the interview room, with a cup of tea plonked in front of him.

'Mr Easton, we would like to go over your movements on Friday night,' Edwards began.

'For the record, I left the theatre after the show. It would have been about half past ten. I walked down the pier, up the zigzag ramps and back to my flat.'

'You were supposed to be going to the ball at the carnival marquee, weren't you?'

'Who says?'

Sara checked the statements in her folder. 'Paul Chapman. You were supposed to be going with Mr Chapman and Hallie Powell.'

'The show overran. We decided not to go. The dance would have been over.'

'It seems the other two did, in fact, make the effort. They only stayed for about fifteen minutes, as things were winding down.'

'Waste of time,' sneered Easton. 'They keep making us do this publicity stuff. None of it makes any difference.'

'Mr Chapman further states that he was expecting you to join them. They looked for you backstage and in the theatre bar without success. They decided to go on without you.'

'I thought they'd gone home, all right? So that's what I did as well.'

'And you say this was at about ten thirty?'

'Yes.'

'I have a problem with that,' said Edwards. 'You see, we have the CCTV footage from that evening. The camera that overlooks the pier entrance and another on New Street.'

Sara watched as Ricky Easton turned white.

'I had my staff go through it carefully,' Edwards continued. 'We see the audience leave. Most of them are walking up the ramps. A few taxis come down to the prom for the older folks. A few minutes after that, we can see Miss Powell and Mr Chapman get into a taxi, presumably to go up to the ball. The rest of the cast leaves in a group. Here's where it gets interesting.'

Sara laid down the series of printed images that Aggie had given her. 'This individual leaves in a hurry.'

The man was short and stocky. He looked as if he was a bodybuilder with overdeveloped muscles. His head was bald or shaved.

'He gets some way along the prom before a taxi picks him up. Do you know this man?'

Sara watched as Easton examined the picture, which she knew wasn't very clear. Easton shook his head without looking up. She thought he looked nervous as she pointed to the next picture. 'This seems to be Jessie Dobson, the show's sound engineer.'

'Looks like her,' agreed Easton. He seemed more relaxed with this one.

'She tells us that she is often one of the last to leave as she locks up.'

'Hadn't noticed.'

Sara thought this was odd. Surely, the performers knew how long they had to get stuff from their dressing rooms before Dobson and the stage manager locked up. She moved on to another picture. 'Is this you?'

Easton nodded. 'Yeah, I guess so.'

'The camera shows a time recording of ten fifty. Later than you said. Why the discrepancy?'

'No idea. The camera could be wrong.'

'We understand that the show finished at ten fifteen. Most of the cast have left by ten thirty. Dobson leaves about ten minutes after that and joins the dancers at the cocktail bar. Where were you between ten thirty and ten fifty, Mr Easton?'

'In the theatre.'

'No one saw you.'

'Not my problem.'

He was right — it was theirs. Sara tapped the picture of Easton leaving the pier. 'Why are you holding something to your face?'

'It's just a tissue. I caught myself on a bit of scenery in the last number. It was still bleeding.'

'Where did you go after that?'

'Home. To my digs.'

'Are you sure?'

Easton ground his teeth. 'All right. I went to The Duke.'

'How long did you stay there?'

'Can't remember.'

'We'll check that with the CCTV footage.'

'Feel free.'

Sara indicated another photo showing Daisy and Kit strolling hand in hand on the prom. 'Are you sure that you didn't see Daisy and this man on the prom that evening?'

Easton looked at the picture and sighed. 'Poor girl. That's what you get for going out with a Traveller, I suppose.'

Sara looked at Edwards in surprise. The DI leaned forward. 'How do you know that?'

'She told me,' said Easton. 'We went for a drink one evening, early in the season, and she told me that she was taken. She was waiting for the funfair to come back, so she would see him again.'

'Carry on, DS Hirst,' said Edwards.

Sara put out the last picture. It showed someone in a dark tracksuit with a hooded top turning at the bottom of the zigzag ramps and following the young couple. Easton looked at it and gasped. The tracksuit looked exactly like the one he was wearing now. The hood was raised, the face obscured. The figure was clearly male and about Easton's height and build. One hand was raised to his face, holding something white against the cheek area.

CHAPTER 51

Jessie and Pete were at work much earlier than usual on Thursday morning to piece the borrowed equipment back in their places before the show. It was also fireworks day, and the two shows ran earlier than the usual timings.

Jessie wired the foldbacks into their positions at the front of the stage, then turned on the power. She approached the sound desk with no other thought in her head except that time would run short if she didn't get on with it. Because she was busy, it didn't occur to her that Ricky would have had time to leave another surprise for her. But he had.

At first, she almost missed it. It was the corner of a small plastic bag peeping out from underneath the body of the desk. It was the glimpse of the stark white contents that caught her eye. She stood, holding the desk cover neatly folded in her arms, debating what to do. Jessie had never taken drugs in her life, much to the amusement of her former husband, who had regularly used coke to keep his energy levels up during technical weeks on shows. As a consequence, she recognised this little offering. Ricky had planted drugs in her workspace and was undoubtedly going to report her to Larry when he came in. This was it — the showdown had arrived. He obviously hadn't counted on Jessie being in early and spotting the bag.

Making her decision, she put the cover away and pulled out her mobile. She snapped a picture of the bag in situ, then took a tissue from the pack she kept among her work stuff. Holding the packet by as small a piece of the corner as she could manage, Jessie drew it out. She wrapped it in the tissue, hid it in the cupboard and went on with her start-up routine. After finishing her checks, she knocked on the tech office door. Jessie could hear two voices.

'Come in,' called Larry. Both he and Pete were sat at their desks.

'Can I have a word?' she asked nervously. She sat in the spare chair, and the two men swivelled round to look at her. Jessie could feel herself trembling. 'It's about Ricky Easton.'

'Ah, yes,' said Larry. 'I wanted to speak to you about him. How do you think you get on with him?'

'I think it's more a case of how he gets on with me,' she replied. Pete watched her impassively. 'There are some things you need to know.'

Briefly, Jessie explained about their affair all those years ago. How Ricky had used her and caused her divorce. 'To be fair, my marriage was on the rocks anyway. I know I'm not entirely free from blame. I was flattered and fell for his nonsense. Malcolm was looking for a way to swap me for a younger model. I gave him the perfect excuse.'

'You haven't seen Ricky since?'

'Not until he walked down the pier at the meet-and-greet. I made sure I never worked on a tour he was cast in when I was specialising in that. When I came up here, it felt such a long way from all my old jobs that I felt safe again. It didn't occur to me to check.'

'Why didn't you say something?' Larry asked.

Jessie could hardly answer that she didn't feel that she trusted him enough, hadn't known who's side he would take. 'At first, he didn't say anything. Then he started being rude about my work.'

'We noticed,' said Pete. Jessie looked at him in surprise.

Larry cleared his throat. 'We know that your work has been as good as always. It did seem that Ricky had it in for you. We didn't know why, of course.'

'I thought it was because he wasn't up to the job,' said Pete. 'He moans about everything backstage. Set changes, props not being there, costumes. You're not alone. He won't be asked back again.'

This was the most damning thing either of them could say against a performer. Most singers and comics got a second summer season if the first went well. The audience loved being able to recognise them, and it made life easier for the rest of the team.

Jessie took a deep breath. 'I'm afraid that's not all.'

Pete and Larry looked at each other knowingly. 'You think he put the rat on the soundboard,' Larry said.

'Yes, I do. But I have no proof. And there's more.'

Larry encouraged her to go on.

'When we were locking up last Friday, I heard what sounded like a fight around the back by the lifeboat entrance. I wasn't sure what to do, so I had a look.'

'That could have been dangerous.' Pete sounded concerned. 'You should have called me.'

'I was going to if it was necessary. Anyway, it was Ricky with some bloke. The man had him up against the wall. When I shouted at them, he moved off. Ricky told me not to say anything.' Jessie touched the scratch mark on her cheek. 'On Sunday, I caught Ricky and him in the street behind the pub. Ricky seemed to be buying something from him. Then up at the Carnival Field yesterday when we were setting up, I'm sure he was giving Ricky something then, as well.'

'Any idea what?'

'Drugs.'

The bald statement hung in the air, sucking the energy out of the room.

'That's a big accusation,' said Larry.

'I know. Can you come up to the soundbox with me?'

They followed Jessie out of the pass door and up the auditorium steps. She pulled the little plastic bag from its hiding place. She opened the tissue with cautious fingers and held the contents out on the palm of her hand. This was the moment when she would find out if her bosses believed her or not.

'I don't do drugs. You know I don't.'

The two men nodded.

Jessie pointed under the sound desk. 'It was there. I think it was planted by Ricky. But again, I can't prove it. I think he was going to report me and try to get me sacked.'

None of them voiced the reply that hovered between them, that Jessie was trying to get Ricky sacked. She still hadn't mentioned to anyone about the conversation she had overheard on the cans all those days ago. Nor did she say that she had seen Ricky passing something to Linda, the dancer.

The staff door swished open, and Yazza strode in, followed by Hallie. The pair were chatting with animation about the fireworks that evening. Jessie folded the tissue over the bag.

'Where is Ricky, by the way?' asked Larry. 'He's usually here before the half. What's keeping him?'

CHAPTER 52

When the clock reached half past twelve, Ricky Easton began to get agitated. 'I've got a performance in a few minutes. I'm already late, and now I have to run all the way down there.'

'Perhaps we should take Mr Easton to his place of employment,' suggested Bowen, who had been watching from the observation room, where the team had gathered to discuss Easton's statement.

'All right,' agreed Edwards. 'We need to see if we can find him leaving the pub on the CCTV before moving him up the list of suspects. I'll call Aggie to get that organized.'

Bowen and Sara escorted the breathless singer to their car. Bowen put the blue lights on to force his way through the summer traffic to the posh chippie, turning the car down the access ramp to the prom and along the seafront to the pier entrance.

'Perhaps you should take him in,' Bowen said. 'Explain why he's late. I'll park up.'

Ricky scurried along the boardwalk, dodging between the families enjoying the sunshine. Sara hurried to keep up with him. He headed around the side of the theatre to a small red door at the rear of the building. Sara followed him into a tiny room with a kitchen area and a couple of sofas.

'Ricky!' shouted a man's voice. 'Where the hell have you been? Why are you so damn late?'

A short, middle-aged man wearing black trousers, a black shirt and a bow tie hurried up. He was clearly furious. Ricky pointed over his shoulder to Sara. 'You'd better ask her.' Then he fled through a door, which Sara assumed must lead to his dressing room.

'Who are you?' demanded the man.

Sara flipped her warrant card. 'Detective Sergeant Hirst. Mr Easton has been helping us with our inquiries. He advised us he was late for work, so we gave him a lift.'

The man's attitude suddenly changed. He smiled placatingly and held out his hand. 'Larry Gibson. I'm the musical director and production manager. I'm sure we're all glad to help our local police force.'

Sara shook the outstretched hand. 'We may need to interview Mr Easton again after the show.'

'Of course,' replied Larry. 'He'll be right here.'

Sara's mobile rang. The screen showed it was Bowen.

'I just need to speak to my colleague.'

She turned away to answer the phone as Jessie Dobson pushed past her and out through the kitchenette area. Larry shouted something up to the stage side, bringing another staff member to the corridor in reply.

'I've lost you,' said Bowen. 'Where are you?'

'Backstage at the theatre.'

'On my way.'

There was a tap on her arm. Larry stood there with a smile. 'I thought you might like to see the show if you have to wait. And your colleague too.' Larry waved as Bowen ambled in through the back door. 'Pete will arrange for the stewards to find you a couple of seats.'

Sara was unsure if this would constitute a bribe. Bowen, on the other hand, accepted rapidly and with enthusiasm. They were escorted to a side bench in the auditorium where the stewards perched. Sara began to dial Edwards on her mobile until a steward tutted and shook her head.

No mobiles in here, rang out a message in the auditorium. *No videos, no flash photography. Enjoy yourselves and join in as much as you like.*

As Larry came into the auditorium from backstage via a staff door, the lights went down. He got a round of applause as he sat at a keyboard behind a bank of computers. Music began, the curtains swung open, and a set of scantily clad dancing girls began a routine. No wonder Bowen had been so keen to watch, she realised, watching the high kicks.

As her eyes became used to the dark, Sara scanned the auditorium. It was full. Where the seats rose up a series of levels to her left, she could see Jessie Dobson standing behind some equipment. She was focused on the stage, monitoring the performers as they came on and off. Occasionally, she glanced to her right, where a tall stack of equipment was draped in cabling and almost obscured her from Sara's view. Just once, Jessie glanced at the benches where the stewards were sitting. Her face froze when she spotted Sara, apparently disturbed to see the two detectives sitting there. For a moment, Jessie couldn't tear her gaze away until a change in the music dragged her attention sharply back to the performance.

The show was all very jolly, but it felt like a waste of time to Sara. She needed to speak to the DI. Tapping Bowen on the arm, she whispered, 'You stay here if you want. I'm going to speak to the boss.'

Bowen nodded happily. Sara stood up, as did the steward sat next to her. The woman flicked on a torch and led Sara out of the auditorium to the bar. The sunlight came as a shock, even after such a short time in the semi-darkness. Blinking at the change, Sara wandered out onto the boardwalk. The DI answered immediately. Sara explained their delay.

'Leave Bowen there,' said Edwards. 'He'll be in his element.'

'Certainly looks like he is, sir.'

'Get up to the main street, and I'll pick you up. Noble is here, and he has the search warrant for the Haywards' house.'

Sara weaved her way down the boardwalk to the entrance. Here the pier narrowed between the box office on one side and the restaurant on the other. The building also contained a set of public toilets. There was a queue for the ladies, as there always seemed to be, which stretched past the office. The gents was free-flowing, men moving in and out with casual unconcern, including a man that Sara recognised.

Short and stocky, well-muscled and bald, the man who had left the pier not long before Ricky Easton on Friday night sauntered out of the toilets and nearly walked into Sara as she struggled past a family with two buggies. Now that she was this close, Sara saw that he was covered in tattoos. From beneath his summer shirt up the back of his neck and down his arms, snakes writhed and twisted.

CHAPTER 53

Xander had stamped out of the kitchen and taken the letters with him. After dressing her arm, Adele locked herself in the spare bedroom and waited in fear, straining every sense to listen. Once Xander showed them to her husband, she was terrified of what his reaction would be.

Greg didn't return until after midnight. She heard him stumble on the stairs and go into Xander's room, where the noisy computer game was still in full swing. It sounded as if Greg joined in with the game, as his voice joined the other two shrieking and shouting at the screen. It finally went quiet at about three o'clock, and Adele was able to fall into a doze. Greg had not tried to speak to her.

By seven, she was awake again. The house was quiet. Adele managed to get dressed and get out without disturbing anyone. Henry didn't question her arrival on the prom when he brought his boat in with that morning's catch. Instead, they bought breakfast at the café on the corner, which they both ate outside. Adele was surprised she could eat at all or feel pleasure in the warmth of the sun on her back. Without the need for explanation, she and Henry pottered about the town, ensuring that the day's events were ready. The crowds were returning, and everyone was doing a brisk trade.

They eventually arrived at Carnival Field, where another committee member was looking after the professional firework company setting up that evening's display. They had roped off an area on the edge of the cliff, leaving the rest of the car park free. It was busy with families unloading and heading to the beach. Adele admired the fireworks crew from a distance. It wasn't something she would have liked to do for a living.

The marquee was also busy when they went to get a drink. Today it was housing a small craft fair. About fifteen stalls had been set up around the sides of the tent, where customers browsed while waiting for refreshments. Henry managed to acquire a table for them, and they sat to drink their coffees.

'I promised myself I wouldn't ask,' said Henry.

'How I am?'

'I need to know, Adele.' Henry looked at the table in embarrassment. 'I'm that worried about you.'

'I'm not sure it can wait until Xander goes to university,' she admitted.

'Have he said anything to you?' Henry's Norfolk accent thickened when he was agitated.

'Not yet. I think they were so drunk last night, so absorbed in that stupid game, that Xander forgot.'

'This is too dangerous,' he insisted. 'You should move out. Just go. I'll help you.'

'I need to do it in an orderly way. What about my clothes? I have no money, except a few pounds in the house-keeping account that Greg gives me.'

'Please,' begged Henry. 'Why don't you ring that refuge?'

'It will be full. They always are. With people in more danger than me. I'll deal with it after the carnival is over.'

'Promise?'

'Adele Hayward!' A voice roared across the crowd. Adele's head shot up, her eyes wide. Henry stood as Greg spotted them and pushed his way through the crowd towards their table. He looked furious.

'I'll look after you,' murmured Henry, as Adele cringed back in her chair.

'You,' snapped Greg, pointing at Adele. There was no disguising the menace in his voice. The couple at a neighbouring table stood and moved away. 'I want a word with you.'

'I think you should leave your wife alone.' Henry kept his tone calm and his voice low.

'Mind your own fucking business.' Greg looked at Henry. The fisherman was a head shorter than he was. Greg curled his mouth in derision. 'She's my wife, not your bloody girlfriend. Butt out.'

'Please, Greg, don't make a scene.' The paper coffee cup trembled in her hand. 'Give me a minute, and I'll meet you in the car park.'

'No more minutes. Get up and get out there now.'

Greg leaned across the table and grabbed the cup. He threw it sideways, the hot coffee swung up in an arc, hitting Adele in the face and spattering Henry as it went. She screamed in surprise, reaching up to brush the scalding liquid from her skin. The tent fell silent. For a moment, no one moved or spoke. In two steps, Greg was around the table. He grabbed Adele's arms to pull her out of her seat and tried to drag his protesting wife towards the entrance.

'Enough,' roared Henry. He reached for Greg, catching the arm nearest to him. Another man lunged forward from a nearby table and grabbed Greg's other arm. Adele leaned back, her feet skidding on the grass, pulling in the opposite direction.

Brian Medler ran from behind the bar, shouting for the security guards. He rushed past Adele and hauled at Greg's shirt. Children in the tent began to cry. Greg let go of Adele, making her stagger backwards and fall on the floor. A woman screamed. Another rushed over to Adele and helped her up. She guided the sobbing Adele out of the line of fire.

The pile of men was grunting with the effort of trying to control Greg. One of the security guards hurtled into the fray, grabbed the arm Henry was holding and twisted it up Greg's back. The Good Samaritan holding the other arm let go. Greg swung around to face him, pulled back his fist and planted it smartly on the stranger's jaw. He reeled backwards as his wife shouted for help.

'Leave me alone, you interfering bastard,' screamed Greg. He twisted again, trying to reach the security guard. The second security man arrived, captured the flailing arm and twisted it up Greg's back with the other. Gripping Greg's neck firmly, he forced Greg to bend over.

'Stop struggling, sir,' he said.

Greg swore obscenely and tried to turn around or escape.

'It's no good. Out you go. Before we call the police.'

The two guards shoved Adele's husband out of the marquee. She thought that his shouts of outrage would be heard all over the town. Henry rushed to Adele, who was being tended to by the onlooker. He knelt next to the chair, where Adele sat with her head in her hands.

'He's gone,' he murmured. 'You're safe now.'

'Are you all right?' The Good Samaritan and his wife had joined them.

Adele nodded without looking up.

'You were kind to help,' said Henry. 'Shall we get the first aider for you?'

'I don't think so.' The man rubbed his jaw. 'It smarts, but I don't think he broke it.'

'Shall we call the police? Do you want to get him charged?' Henry sounded almost hopeful.

The man looked down at Adele. 'No, that's OK. I don't want to make things worse.'

'At least let us treat you to a drink,' said Brian Medler, leading them away to the bar.

'I'm so proud of you,' said the wife. 'Stepping in like that. Poor woman.'

The shouting outside stopped. Everyone heard a large car engine roar into life and the skidding of tyres on the dry grass.

The crowd began to chatter again. Some of them left the marquee, others resumed checking out the stalls or sat back at their tables. They had plenty to gossip about now, Adele realised. She couldn't bring herself to move her hands. She felt too ashamed.

'You can't go back there again,' said Henry. 'I won't let you.'

CHAPTER 54

Sara found Edwards and Noble waiting for her outside the church. Two more police vehicles were parked with them. She climbed into the back seat, and the convoy headed for the Haywards' house.

There was little sign of life. Edwards knocked politely, then not so calmly and finally hammered on the door before shouting through the letterbox. Sara stood back on the empty drive, convinced she could hear a radio playing. Between the garage and the house, a small passage led to a tall wooden gate. As she reached it, the radio sound grew louder. She knocked. It caused a curse and a crash from behind the gate.

'What the fuck?' asked a voice.

'Police,' called Sara. 'We're looking for Greg Hayward.'

'Dad's out.'

'Could you answer the front door? Save me shouting?'

'I suppose so.'

Sara joined the DI and Noble as the front door opened. Xander stood with bare feet in baggy shorts and a brightly coloured vest. He seemed to be emulating the surfer look, without much success.

'Are your mother or father in?' Edwards asked.

Xander looked confused. 'No, they're both out. At Carnival Field.'

Edwards stood with the warrants flapping in his hand, unsure what to do next.

'If you want them, you should go there,' said Xander. It seemed that he had no intention of inviting them in.

The problem was solved by the roar of an engine as Greg Hayward pulled onto the drive. There was something about cars like that which instinctively wound Sara up. Their owners always had an inflated sense of their own worth, predicated on the value of their toys, and were usually male.

Dick extensions, she thought, watching Hayward swagger over to them. She knew it was her own kind of prejudice, borne out of the fact that they were the favoured cars of major drug dealers.

The man walked up to Edwards, ignoring Sara and Noble. With a glance at the police cars in the street, he grinned arrogantly. 'What do you want this time?'

'A couple of things,' said Edwards. He squared his shoulders. 'We'll start with those DNA swabs.'

'I've told you before. You can't have them. This is harassment.'

'And I've explained that it is necessary to our murder inquiry. Why are you so reluctant to let us have a sample?'

'It's an infringement of our human rights.' Hayward looked to be enjoying goading the DI.

'It's a shame that you feel like that.' Edwards held up the request warrants. 'We'll start with you and the two boys. This is the paperwork, if you want to check it. Though I can assure you that it's all in order.'

'I'm going to call my solicitor,' snapped Hayward. In the doorway, Xander was watching keenly. He had turned the radio off, and Jacob hovered in the hallway.

'Feel free, sir.' Edwards smiled. 'In the meantime, I'm going to have to ask you all to vacate the premises so that we can carry out our search.' He held up the house search warrant.

Hayward spluttered angrily as the other officers got out of their cars and stood ready on the pavement. 'You have no right, no grounds.'

'Alexander?' Edwards glanced past the youth. 'And Jacob? Put some shoes on, and we will take you down to the station to collect these samples.'

'We're going nowhere with you,' shouted Hayward. He was beginning to rock from foot to foot in frustration. 'Don't move, you two.'

'Dad, you're making it worse,' whined Xander. 'You're so embarrassing sometimes.' He indicated to his friend, and the pair pulled on some trainers before coming out of the house.

Hayward grabbed his son as he passed. 'Don't do this,' he shouted. 'They can't make you.'

'I think you'll find we can, Mr Hayward,' said Edwards. 'Please stand aside.'

'Let go of me, Dad.' Xander pulled away from his father's grip, swatting at the hands that held him.

'Xander! Don't say anything!' Hayward lunged at DI Edwards. 'You can't do this.'

'I can and I will.'

Hayward now made a grab for Jacob as he passed. The youth walked with his head down, looking at the ground, his eyes narrowed. He paused when Hayward snatched at him. Then he looked at the hand on his arm, transferred his gaze to Hayward and held it there.

Suddenly the man let go and turned on DI Edwards. 'I'm going to phone my legal team.' He tried to push his way into the house. Two of the uniformed officers strode up and grabbed an arm each.

'We can arrange that at the station,' said Edwards. 'The swabs won't take long.'

'Meanwhile, you'll be tearing my house apart for no good reason.'

'Every good reason. Where do you keep the jet ski?'

The fight seemed to leach out of Hayward. He looked over at Xander, who turned his back and gazed off into the distance. 'In the garage.'

'If you let us have the keys, there will be no need for us to force our way in,' said Sara. 'Much less damage that way.'

Hayward shook off one of the uniforms' grip and pulled a set of keys from his trouser pockets. He threw them at Sara's head. Without a thought, she leaned to one side and deftly caught the bunch in her right hand. Hayward's mouth dropped open.

'Used to be a ballgirl at Wimbledon,' she said. Noble sniggered, turning it into a cough.

'Take them down to the station for now,' instructed Edwards.

The uniformed officers loaded the two boys into one of the cars, Hayward into the other, and drove away.

The three detectives pulled on nitrile gloves and opened the garage door. The bright red jet ski was strapped onto its purpose-built trailer, its nose towards the door. They didn't even have to go into the garage to see what they were looking for. The nose of the jet ski was damaged. The red body paint had deep gouges, the black underside grey scuff marks. The fender had a big crack in it.

The machine was bigger than Sara had envisaged. There were two seats. The handlebars rose proud of the front body, and the nose was pointed. It looked like an aggressive bit of kit. 'Bet this is difficult to handle,' she said. 'Looks heavy.'

'Like a motorbike on water.' Noble sounded envious. 'Bet it goes like a bomb.'

'Probably,' said Edwards. 'Worth getting Forensics in to check that paintwork.'

'Even if Mrs Wilder won't press charges?'

'It's our lever,' said Edwards. 'You saw how he reacted when we mentioned it. Call them in.'

'Yes, sir.'

'Let's have a look inside.'

Sara followed Edwards through the front door.

'Were you really a ballgirl at Wimbledon?'

'Yes, sir. Did it for two years, though never on Centre Court. What are we looking for?'

'I don't know until I find it,' he said with a wink.

They split up in the hallway, Edwards starting with the study and Sara heading upstairs. The house was a mess, which surprised her. Adele Hayward was a careful housewife, and when they had visited before, the place had been immaculate. Perhaps she was too busy with the carnival this week. The first bedroom room reeked of teenage boys — a combination of dirty socks, half-eaten food and spilled booze on the carpet.

The master bedroom was also untidy. Dirty clothes were scattered all over the place, most of it men's things. The en-suite bathroom needed a clean, and towels were dumped in the bottom of the shower like in a hotel. It wasn't until she reached one of the spare bedrooms, that Sara realised Adele Hayward must be sleeping in here. The bed was unmade, women's clothes spilled out of a laundry basket, and toiletries lay in a jumble next to the bed as if dumped in a hurry.

Edwards called her downstairs. She joined him in the study.

'What do you make of this?' He pointed to the desk. There was a letter, which had been crumpled up but was now smoothed out. 'Found this in the waste bin.'

Sara read it and looked at her boss. 'I think we need to find out what was going on at that school, don't we? I wonder if Aggie managed to get through to them.'

'Then there's this.' Edwards had been trying to sort out a flimsier piece of paper, which had been torn into pieces. Sara stood next to him and tried to help. The heading was easy, with its NHS logo and the details of Cromer Hospital on the top. It seemed to be a form. 'Someone went to the minor injuries unit.'

Sara found a piece with a signature and examined it. 'That looks like Adele Hayward's signature to me.'

Searching through the scraps carefully, she found the adjacent section.

'Sir?' Sara pointed to the comment box.

The patient says she is a victim of domestic violence, flag DB.

CHAPTER 55

A long afternoon had turned into a fine evening. Sara and the team had taken DNA samples from Greg Hayward and the two boys. They commandeered a police car to take the samples to Forensics at Wymondham, marking it urgent. Then Edwards and Sara had cautioned the father for obstruction and interviewed him about the jet ski incident. He had told them who he had borrowed the second machine from but stuck doggedly to the story about Xander being the hero of the hour. Bowen had left the theatre at the interval, when Edwards had summoned him back to the station.

'I was enjoying that,' he grumbled. 'Aren't we interested in the singer anymore then?'

'I am,' said Sara. 'The boss is more interested in this lot. He's right to be. I still think Ricky Easton is lying to us, and I'd like to know why.'

Bowen agreed. He and Noble were sent out to speak to the owner of the second jet ski. Sara was despatched up to the hospital to find confirmation of Adele Hayward's visit. Edwards had to allow the three suspects to leave after that, but as a forensic team had moved into their house, they were not allowed to go back there yet.

'Hayward said he didn't care,' said Edwards later, when the team was sitting around the interview room table, catching up at the end of the day. 'Said they were all going down the pub anyway. Let's catch up and call it a day. Sara?'

Sara produced a photocopy of the report from Mrs Haywards's visit. 'The nurse who saw her was on duty this afternoon. Said that she was rather worried about her and gave her some leaflets about the women's refuge. We should ask Hayward about that injury directly.'

'It's difficult, as you know,' said Edwards. 'We can get all the evidence of assault together, and then the wife can refuse to have the husband prosecuted.'

Sara sighed. 'Do we have any idea where Mrs Hayward is? There was no sign of her at the house.'

'Not sure. Probably at the Carnival Field with the rest of the committee, if she's any sense. Mike?'

'Very interesting conversation with Dave Summers, the owner of jet ski number two. It would appear that he's gone off Greg Hayward recently. They were good friends for years, he said, but not anymore. Said he was surprised when he rang and asked to borrow the jet ski.'

'Mr Summers showed us the machine.' Noble pulled out his mobile and opened the picture gallery. Sara and Edwards studied the photos of the ski. 'You can see that it has damage on one side. When we asked the owner where this came from, he said it had happened when it was out with Hayward.'

'And,' said Bowen triumphantly, 'he agreed that it was consistent with his ski being rammed by another one. Mr Summers is more than happy to make a statement about it.'

'Did they apologise to Mr Summers?'

'Profusely.' Bowen's smile grew broader. 'Apparently, Hayward offered to pay for the damage. And guess what he said then?'

Edwards looked up. Bowen nudged Noble. 'Go on, you tell him.'

Noble checked his notebook. '"We used to be such good mates, but he hasn't spoken to me since before Christmas.

I don't know what I'm supposed to have done. And I don't hold out much hope of ever getting that. All the local estate agents know that Hayward has no money.'"

'I thought he sold high-end expensive country manors as retreats to pop stars and the like,' said Sara. 'Surely that's very lucrative? Bloody Porsche in the drive, for God's sake.'

'Exactly.'

'While that's very interesting,' said Edwards, 'I don't see how that makes any difference to our search for Daisy's killer. I want those DNA results as soon as possible.'

Sara rang Aggie and put her mobile on the desk, with the speaker on. 'How did you get on at the school?'

'Took a while,' admitted Aggie. 'It's the school holidays. However, the headmaster lives onsite all year round. I managed to get him to talk to me in the end, although only in outline.'

For a giddy moment, Sara wondered if Aggie had bribed the man with the promise of cake.

'I told him that you would go and take his statement personally, boss,' she said to Edwards. 'I hope you didn't mind. I think it might have a real bearing on the case. He seemed to feel that anyone of a rank lower than yours couldn't be trusted to deal with the matter sensitively.'

'Sensitively?' Sara snorted. Edwards shot her a warning look. 'Sorry. Go on, Aggie.'

'Apparently, Xander had a good reputation until about a year ago. He was top-notch at rugby, might even be good enough to turn professional and was up for some major trials. Then he changed. Became arrogant. He bullied a younger player to the point where the lad quit rugby.'

'What about this girl?'

'He was even more cagey about that. He said the girl was called Lyra Nash. He wouldn't give me her home address.'

'Bugger that. Let me have the number, and I'll soon sort him out.'

'No need, sir. I looked them up. Found them on the electoral register. Lyra's old enough to vote next time, so

I'm pretty sure it's them. I can send you their address and landline number.'

'Excellent. Great work, Aggie. Make an appointment for me with the headmaster on Monday, will you?'

Edwards's mobile pinged with Aggie's text. Sara dialled the number.

A motherly voice answered. Sara explained who she was and that she was ringing about Langton Hall.

'Oh, thank God.' The woman began to sob. 'Is someone finally prepared to listen to my daughter?'

CHAPTER 56

At the end of the meeting, Edwards and Noble went home. Sara said that she might stay for the fireworks, and Bowen wanted to watch them as well. They wandered past the food stalls and pubs before queuing for fish and chips at the posh chippie. Their evening was purely social, something that Sara had never experienced with Bowen before. The pair sat on the prom wall eating their meal and watching the crowds wander past.

'Was the show good?' Sara asked.

Bowen nodded. 'Excellent. An old-fashioned variety show, exactly what you would expect at the end of the pier. I used to bring my mum before she passed away, five years ago.'

'I'm sorry to hear that.' Familiar words, but Sara meant them. 'What do you make of the singer?'

'He's got a great voice.' He pulled off a piece of battered fish and ate it before continuing. 'Good dancer as well. You remember when I looked him up?'

'Yes. Good career until three years ago.'

'I did a bit more digging this afternoon.' Bowen shovelled more fish into his mouth and chewed. 'There's a fan website about West End shows, with loads of old articles on it. I found one that mentioned Ricky Easton being replaced in *Wicked* following an injury about three years ago.'

'He hasn't worked since?'

'Not according to his agent's website. Then I looked up dancers' injuries. It's not uncommon for them to get problems. It's what they do afterwards that causes concern.'

'Oh?'

'They lose fitness if they're injured, and when they return, the days are long and hard. Apparently, the most common assistance they take is . . .' Bowen paused for effect.

'Go on,' said Sara.

'Da-da-dah!'

She grinned. 'Well?'

'Methamphetamine.'

Sara nearly choked on her chips. 'Crystal meth?'

'Allows you to work all day and night, gives you a buzz of energy, and, of course, decreases your appetite.'

Sara thought how slim all the performers were, especially the dancers. It made sense.

'I rang your mate in the Met,' said Bowen. DS Mead of the Metropolitan Police Force had been part of an investigation the previous Christmas. The Norfolk case had overlapped with the Met's priority hunt for a drugs overlord. He and Sara still kept in touch. 'He says it's a big seller into dance companies and the casts of musicals.'

Sara blew out her lips in frustration. 'Is that what this is about? Nothing to do with Daisy at all?'

Bowen shrugged. He scrunched up the wrapping papers and pushed them into the carrier bag the chippie had given them. Sara added hers.

* * *

There was only a short break between the matinée and evening shows. Jessie and Yazza sat outside the theatre café to eat the food they had brought with them. Yazza was curious about the detectives who had brought back Ricky. 'What happened to them?' she asked.

Jessie shrugged. 'The woman left almost immediately. The man left at the interval. Perhaps Ricky wasn't as important as they thought.'

It had occurred to Jessie that the bag of powder had been left under the sound desk as double protection. Ricky could use it to accuse her of possession with either the theatre management or the police. Larry hadn't wanted to take it, nor had Pete. She couldn't blame them. In the end, they had put it in an envelope, signed over the seal, dated it and got the house manager to put it in the office safe.

The second show was also sold out. It finished at nine, and the excited audience streamed out to take up positions on the pier among the already-large crowd. It was one of the best places in the town to watch the firework display. Even the cast and crew looked forward to it. Uniformed coppers wandered about in pairs among the crowds.

Jessie did her turn-off without waiting for the performers to finish getting changed. If they forgot to turn off their mic packs this evening, she didn't care. She'd replace the batteries tomorrow in any case. She collected a large glass of wine and joined Yazza and the other performers outside the fire exit watching the skies. Ricky was noticeable by his absence.

At half past nine, the first explosion peppered the moonlit sky with colour. It was spectacular. Starbursts of colour, rockets and fountains of white lights filled the sky. The air filled with noise and the smell of cordite, even though the launch site was some distance away. The display was noisy, even at this distance, and the crowd were loud in their appreciation, cheering and whooping at each new explosion. Conversation would be impossible for the next ten or fifteen minutes.

Jessie stood on the edge of the group, sipping her wine quickly. It was making her feel rather light-headed. Perhaps she hadn't had enough to eat that day. Or maybe she was just drinking too fast. Bravado arrived with the effect of the wine on her balance. She'd had enough of that bloody Ricky Easton.

She scanned the crowd that filled the boardwalk between the side of the theatre and railings on the pier's edge. The singer was still missing.

Bet he's meeting that dealer of his, Jessie thought. *Hard to spot in this bloody crowd.*

But not on the far side, where the night fishermen would be staring sullenly over the side of the pier, wishing that the crowds would bugger off and leave them to their hobby. You couldn't see much of the fireworks from there, as the building hid all but the highest explosions from view.

She gulped down another large mouthful of wine. 'Just going round the other side,' she yelled into Yazza's ear. Her friend looked at her and shrugged. Jessie grinned. 'Gonna catch the bastard at it.'

She staggered a little as she walked past the people gathered in front of the lifeboat station. Turning the corner by the stage door at the rear of the theatre, Jessie paused to look at the fishermen. There were only a couple of them. They had left their kit against the outside wall of the theatre and walked to the end of the bar to watch the display. The boardwalk was empty. Jessie felt disappointed. She was just in the mood to have it out with Ricky. She slugged the last of her wine.

With a sudden crash, two figures stumbled out of the darkness of the theatre fire exit. Jessie jumped. Ricky was being driven backwards by the dealer. The tattooed man had one hand round Ricky's throat. With the other, he gripped Ricky by the wrist and scrunched up his arm onto his chest, pinning it between the pair. Ricky's feet barely touched the boards as the angry dealer headed for the rails.

For a moment, Jessie stood with her mouth open, not knowing what to do. The wine glass slipped from her fingers and smashed on the boards. The sound was masked by the noise from the display. She flattened herself against the stage door, hoping the shadows would hide her.

The pair thumped into the rails. Ricky's back bent over the top bar. He cried out as his ribs and back crushed against the unforgiving iron. The dealer smashed into Ricky, his weight pushing the singer harder against the barrier. The man was raging incomprehensible abuse.

'No one will know it was me,' Ricky cried out. 'Or you.'

This seemed to be the final straw for the dealer. He let go of Ricky, took a step back and, before Ricky could right himself, punched him hard in the face. The singer toppled backwards over the railings into the sea.

Time suspended for Jessie, as it often seems to do during an accident. The noise of the crowd and the fireworks vanished. Even the dealer didn't move. There was a splash as Ricky hit the water.

Jessie screamed. The dealer looked in her direction, but she didn't care. She ran towards the lifeboat station, and towards the people watching the fireworks. 'Man overboard,' she shouted at the top of her lungs.

A man standing at the back of the crowd with a child balanced on his shoulders turned to look at Jessie. She struggled to pull a lifebelt from its holder next to the lifeboat station gate.

'What?' yelled the man.

'Man overboard,' Jessie screamed. She pointed wildly to the far side of the theatre. 'Just gone over.'

The man suddenly understood what she was saying. He pulled down the protesting child and handed it over to its mum. He helped Jessie unfasten the lifebelt, and the pair ran back to where she had last seen Ricky. It was inky black beneath the pier structure as they leaned over the rails.

'Can't see a bloody thing,' the man said. 'Get help.'

Jessie ran through the open fire exit doors as the man yelled over the side, 'Anyone there? Lifebelt coming down. Hello? Hello?'

Bursting through the staff door, Jessie hurtled into Charlotte, the house manager.

'Call the coastguard,' she stuttered. 'Ricky's just gone over the railings. Our fucking singer just fell in the sea.'

* * *

The whole carnival committee was at the marquee to watch the firework display. All that remained after this was a folk evening in the tent on Friday and the closing ball on Saturday night. Henry would need to be at both, and Adele would be expected to attend as a committee member. The immediate problem was where she should go at the end of the day. She had made no attempt to visit her home during the day, not even to collect some clothes. Adele knew she was putting off the inevitable confrontation.

'Leave it for tonight,' urged Henry. 'Stay at mine. You can use the spare bedroom.'

'What about clean clothes?'

'We can ask Jessie, my neighbour. She could lend you something.'

They went to say goodbye to the committee members. Brian and his assistant were leaning on the bar when his bleeper went off. Henry's lit up a few seconds later.

'I'm sorry,' he said to Adele. 'It's a shout. I have to go.'

'I'll take you both down.' She grabbed her car keys.

The three tumbled into Adele's tiny vehicle, and she drove at speed across the grass to the entrance. A police car with its lights and sirens blazing raced past on the main road. Adele pulled deftly out into the slipstream and tailgated it down to the corner. Another car had joined behind them, and the three vehicles hurtled down the ramps, the police car scattering pedestrians who were still watching the fireworks.

The convoy reached the pier entrance. Henry and Brian dashed away down the pier towards the lifeboat station. The place was always lit up at night so that inshore boats could see the pier's length. Now it was like a beacon, calling in the volunteer crew for a night-time rescue. The car following parked next to Adele and the driver ran after Henry without bothering to lock his car. It beeped shut as the man's key fob went out of range.

Adele sat for a moment, her heart pounding with excitement. She'd never done anything like that in her life. As her breathing eased, she climbed out and walked towards the pier.

* * *

So absorbed were the pair of detectives that they almost missed the main event. It wasn't until the lifeboat house lit up and a siren sounded that Sara looked around the crowd. Other people had also noticed, and heads turned this way and that seeking the new source of interest. The boardwalk on one side of the theatre was nearly empty. In the dim light, Sara could see a man leaning over the railings shouting and waving. As another set of fireworks distracted the crowd, Sara looked into the theatre bar. Jessie Dobson was there, jabbering and crying. Another woman followed, talking agitatedly into her mobile. Sara nudged Bowen and pointed.

'What the fuck?' He bounced up from the railing where he had been lounging. 'I'll go find out.'

He forced his way through to the bar door. Someone was roughly pushing the other way through the crowd from the dark side of the theatre. It was the tattooed man from the photos. He halted by the first rubbish bin, pulling some items from his pockets and throwing them away — lots of small things that twinkled in the lights from the bar.

A police car, closely followed by a couple of ordinary vehicles, hurried along the prom. Men jumped out of the cars and weaved their way agitatedly through the crowd towards the lifeboat station. Sara had to stand back to let them through. One of the hurrying men reached a blockade formed by a large family with a double buggy and at least three generations of adults.

'Sorry, sorry. I need to get to the station,' the man said. One adult snatched up a wandering toddler to clear the path, but the lifeboat volunteer had already stepped the other way. He cannoned into the tattooed man, who cursed as the rushing man apologised and ran on. He turned to shout abuse after the runner, and at that moment, saw Sara.

She launched herself off the railing and ran towards the man. 'Stop! Police!'

Now the crowd parted like magic, leaving the tattooed man exposed. He ran. Sara was gathering speed, trying to fumble her warrant card from her jacket pocket as she went. Not everyone heard her calls as the man pushed his way through. Luckily two people did. One of the pairs of uniformed officers were standing near the pier entrance. It only took a fraction of a second for them to assess the situation, and they rushed in to tackle him.

The first officer received a punch to the face for his efforts. He reeled back a couple of paces, but his partner rugby-tackled the man to the floor. More officers arrived and cuffed him. Sara held out her warrant card.

'Why did you want him, ma'am?' asked one.

'Get him locked up. Assaulting a police officer will do for now. I'll let you know more later. You come with me.'

Sara pointed to the two officers who were standing by the box office doors. One had his helmet in his hand and was holding his face with the other. Blood was seeping through his fingers. The second accepted a packet of tissues from a bystander, which he handed to his partner. They followed Sara as she marched back down the pier to the rubbish bin.

'Stay there,' she said. 'Until I can get someone to deal with it. No one is to add anything else to the bag, and don't let the bag get taken away.'

She turned towards the theatre bar, wondering how Bowen was getting on. Lengthening her stride, she reached the double doors as there was a rumble and a splash. The lifeboat was at sea already.

Inside the bar, Bowen was trying to make sense of the hysterical Jessie Dobson's words. Sara turned to the other woman and asked what was going on.

'I'm Charlotte, the house manager.' She was clutching her mobile in a shaking hand. 'Jessie says that someone pushed our singer, Ricky Easton, over the side of the pier.'

'Hence the lifeboat call?'

'Yes.'

Jessie Dobson reached out a hand to Sara. 'There's a man. He was trying to help me. He threw a lifebelt in for Ricky.'

'Show me,' demanded Sara. Jessie rocked out of her seat and led the two detectives through the staff door into the auditorium.

The fire exit doors on one side were wide open. They could see a man by the railings, leaning over the side and shouting. As they joined him, a smaller inflatable lifeboat approached the light spill from the pier. It began to comb up and down, its strong searchlight crisscrossing the water.

In the auditorium, Sara could hear Jessie Dobson breaking down into hysterics again. She couldn't leave the woman on her own in that state. She went back inside and sat in the seat next to Jessie.

'It's all my fault,' the sound engineer sobbed. 'I should have reported it sooner. He doesn't deserve to drown.'

* * *

From the end of the pier, Adele heard the familiar rumble of the Tamar class lifeboat, RNLB *Lester*, heading down the ramp. With a huge splash, it hit the sea, and the engine growled with power, carving a neat circle not far from the end of the pier. The lights on the roof scanned the water underneath and followed the pull of the tide. Further down the beach, the D-class inflatable backed into the water from its trailer. It was soon buzzing along the cast-iron structure that held the pier aloft.

Thank goodness it was high tide, Adele thought. *They can get much closer.* She walked quickly down the pier to watch over the rails, along with dozens of other people.

At the end of each arcing sweep, the larger boat returned, getting further out to sea with each pass. It was following the path of the riptide. Lights from both boats scanned the water continuously.

Suddenly there was a shout. The mate on the D-734 pointed underneath the pier, where the sea eddied around the giant cast-iron legs.

The crowd couldn't see underneath the pier. One man leaned right out until his friend grabbed him and told him not to be so stupid. They all heard the lifeboatmen shouting.

'Can you hear me?' yelled one. There was a small pause.

'I think he's waving,' shouted another. 'Has he got a lifebelt?'

The pair mumbled to each other, then the first yelled again. 'Sir, we're going to try and get underneath.'

Adele watched as, buffeted by the waves and crosscurrents, the inflatable moved forward slowly. The driver struggled to keep the boat straight. The mate was fending it off the pier's legs as best he could. Inch by inch, the boat edged out of view.

There was an agonising wait. It felt like hours, but might have been three or four minutes. At last, the boat emerged from the other side, the engine revving triumphantly. Adele and the other onlookers rushed across to see it running clear of the pier. A man lay in the bottom of the boat. The crowd cheered.

Another siren sounded from the Gangway as an ambulance arrived. The inflatable headed at full speed to the beach where Henry and the other fishermen kept their boats, the high tide allowing them to almost reach the ramp that led up to the promenade. The paramedics ran towards them as they unloaded the rescued man.

Out at sea, *Lester* was returning to base. The crowd began to disperse, and Adele headed for the lifeboat station and Henry. As she passed the fire exit doors, she saw the two detectives from the murder inquiry. Lowering her head,

Adele hoped that they would be too busy to notice her and walked on.

* * *

The staff door whooshed open as Pete rushed straight over to Jessie and hugged her. She subsided against his shoulder, muffled sobs still emerging. Outside there was a cheer.

Bowen strode in through the fire exit doors. 'They've got him.'

Jessie's head popped up. 'Is he alive?'

'I'm not sure.' He sounded as if he was trying to curb his excitement. 'The ambulance is waiting for them.'

The door whooshed again as one of the dancers joined them.

'This is Yazza,' explained Pete. 'She lodges with Jessie. I think perhaps they should both go home.'

Sara shook her head. 'Jessie, what did you mean by it was your fault? Can you tell me?'

Dobson looked at her. 'I should have reported him. But I was afraid.'

'I think I can explain some of it.' Pete stood up and waved Yazza over. The dancer took Jessie by the arm, supporting her into the aisle. 'Jessie can give you a fuller statement tomorrow, can't she?'

'Here at ten?' pushed Sara.

Jessie nodded, and Yazza led her away. Sara stood with Pete in the fire exit doorway. They could hear the main lifeboat's engines as it began its reversing procedure to be winched back into the station.

'Well?'

'It's Jessie's personal story to tell for the most part. Larry and I can give you more background tomorrow. But Jessie found something planted underneath her sound desk today. It's not the first time.'

'You mean the dead rat?'

'I'd forgotten you knew about that.' Pete shrugged. 'That was just a bad joke, I suspect. Today's little present wasn't.'

'Do you still have it?'

Pete led Sara back to the theatre bar and collected the house manager. Without questioning them, Charlotte took them into the office, shut the door behind them, unlocked the safe and took out an envelope.

Sara always had spare protective gloves in her pocket. She pulled on a pair. 'May I?'

Pete nodded. He pointed to the seal. 'That's all of us who saw it. We signed over the seal to prove when we lodged it in the safe.'

Sara took out her mobile and photographed both sides of the envelope. The house manager offered her a letter opener. Sara sliced along the top of the envelope, leaving the seal undamaged, and pulled the contents out onto the office desk. It was a small plastic packet, wrapped in a tissue, and full of white powder.

Pete sighed. 'We think Ricky put it under the sound desk. To incriminate Jessie.'

CHAPTER 57

Sara was up early on Friday morning. She still hadn't spoken to Chris about his proposal, despite her mum's advice to contact him and be honest.

'Tell him you're not ready for such a commitment yet,' Tegan had suggested. 'That you want to carry on as you are.'

The trouble was that Sara wasn't even sure that this was true. Perhaps Chris was getting the idea that she wouldn't answer him or call him. It might save the bother of a big scene.

Sara threw her car round one of the corners on the coast road angrily. She'd never been a coward, and that was the coward's way out.

Morning orders had been called in Cromer at eight. She treated them all to takeaway coffees and doughnuts as compensation for the lack of Aggie's cakes. The team gathered in the spare interview room again. Sara's mobile was on speaker so Aggie could hear them.

'I've made an appointment with both the headteacher and the Nash family,' Aggie said. 'What are you eating?'

The rustle of the plastic packet must have given them away.

'It's not as nice as yours,' said Bowen defensively. 'Just a bit of sugar, really.'

There was no reply.

'Can you chase those DNA results?' asked Edwards. Aggie agreed she would. He turned to Sara. 'We'll need to interview the man you arrested last night.'

'I've seen him before, around the town.'

'What made you go after him?'

'I shouted, he ran,' she said with a smile.

'If they run away, they must be guilty of something?' Edwards laughed.

Sara shook her head, eyes narrowed in thought. 'We couldn't hear because of the crowd, so we didn't realise someone had gone over the side. But he had come from that side of the theatre, in a hurry. Then he was throwing some things away in one of the rubbish bins. Forensics have collected the contents.'

'What do you think it was?'

'I only took a glance,' she admitted. 'It was those little plastic bags so beloved of the dealers. I've informed Drugs.'

'Are you sure he came from that side of the theatre?'

'Sure enough to interview him.'

'Aggie, how is our singer?'

'Recovering,' she said. 'Easton's a lucky chap. The tides weren't too strong, so he didn't get too battered floating beneath the pier. The lifebelt stopped him from being pulled down in the undertow. That's how they normally drown, apparently. Easton has a couple of broken ribs and some bruising. They said he'll be allowed home this afternoon.'

'Let's make sure we interview him when he gets back to Cromer.'

'I wonder what they will do about the show?' Bowen seemed to be thinking out loud. 'He's not going to be able to perform with that lot.'

There was a knock at the door, and the desk sergeant stuck his head around it. 'Thought you might like to know this. We've just had a report of a disturbance in the town. A man causing a spot of bother trying to get into one of the fisherman's cottages on Cross Street. A neighbour has rung in and asked for assistance.'

'Why would we be interested?'

'The caller identified the man as Greg Hayward.'

The desk sergeant was nearly knocked out of the way in the rush. They piled into their cars and raced into the town. A police vehicle was already blocking the road at one end. Edwards swung his vehicle the wrong way up a one-way street to reach the other. Bowen followed.

It wasn't hard to see what was happening. Greg Hayward was standing outside one of the cottages. He was shouting and waving his hands at the windows. Two uniformed officers were trying to talk to him, but he was having none of it.

'He's got my wife in there,' Hayward screamed. 'He's got no right.'

'Mr Hayward,' called Edwards as they approached. The tone was calm, even if the volume was loud. 'Calm yourself. What's going on here?'

Hayward swung to face them. 'Fuck me, you lot again. Isn't it enough that you shut me out of my own home? What are you doing here?'

'Just the question I was going to ask you,' said Edwards. Sara, Bowen and Noble stood in a line behind their boss. She glanced at the neighbouring houses. Jessie Dobson was watching them from the upstairs window next door. The young dancer, Yazza, who had taken Jessie home the previous evening, was standing next to her.

Hayward staggered as he waved an arm at the cottage door. Sara guessed that he was already drunk. Or still drunk from last night. 'He's got my wife in there.'

'Who has?'

'Henry bloody Lacey. He's kidnapped my wife.'

Sara laughed. Hayward swung his attention to her. 'You think this a joke, missy?'

'No, I don't, sir,' she said. She couldn't keep the sarcasm from her tone. 'But I don't think standing in the street yelling is going to solve anything.'

'Come away, Mr Hayward,' urged Edwards. He tried to put a hand on the angry man's arm. 'This isn't doing any good.'

Hayward snatched his arm away, pulled it back and aimed a punch. His actions were so uncoordinated, Edwards didn't even have to avoid the bunched fist. It whistled in front of his face, at least twelve inches off target, and Hayward fell over in the road. He lay there without getting up. Sara could hear him whimpering with self-pitying tears.

'I've lost everything, everything,' he muttered. 'Please don't take my wife away too.'

Suddenly he knelt up to vomit in the gutter. Most of it seemed to be liquid. There were six coppers there — none of them wanted to touch the man. Hayward lay down on the ground again, groaning.

'Get the waggon down here,' said Edwards to one of the local officers. 'Then at least if he throws up, you can hose it down.'

'What charge, sir?'

'Disturbing the peace and threatening behaviour. Keep an eye on him for now, in case he chokes.'

The front door of the cottage opened a crack. Sara recognised Henry Lacey from the carnival marquee. She stepped forwards. 'Everything all right, sir?'

Sara heard a woman's voice in the house behind Lacey, asking who had knocked. Sara held up her warrant card. 'DS Sara Hirst.'

'Thank goodness,' the voice said. 'Let her in, Henry. She's the one who was trying to help me.'

Sara glanced at Edwards, who nodded. 'See if you can get to the bottom of this before we have to go to the theatre at ten.'

'Yes, sir.'

Lacey opened the door, and Sara stepped inside. Following him into the living room, she watched Adele Hayward settle onto the sofa. Henry sat next to Adele, took her hand in his and smiled encouragingly. A cat was curled up asleep on the armchair. There were no more spare chairs. Sara leaned on the window ledge, trying not to disturb the lace curtain that kept the room private from the street outside.

'I'm so glad it's you,' said Adele.

'Do you want to lay charges against your husband about all this?'

'Possibly. I want to talk to you about bringing other charges.'

Adele pulled away the dressing on her arm. The marks still hadn't healed properly, and there were new bruises around both wrists. Then she picked up her mobile and punched something on the screen, before holding it for Sara to look at.

'I want my husband prosecuting for abusing me. At home in private. And in public at the carnival marquee. I've been keeping a record of the injuries.'

CHAPTER 58

Jessie and Yazza watched with relief as Greg Hayward was taken away by the police. Jessie provided Adele Hayward with some spare clothes and left her neighbour to sort out the aftermath. She turned down Yazza's offer to accompany her to the theatre to talk to the detectives.

Having spent half the night in her study in a total panic, Jessie had come to a conclusion about her future. She could just about get to retirement age when she finally received her state pension by working part-time at the local care home. It wasn't something Jessie had ever done. Nor was it something she wanted to do. But they were always advertising for staff and needs must where the devil drives, as the saying went. If they sacked her from the theatre, surely it wouldn't be before the end of the season.

Jessie was unsurprised to find four people waiting for her in the auditorium. The two detectives, DI Edwards and DS Hirst sat on front row seats. Larry and Pete sat a couple of rows behind them. She looked at Pete and pointed to the ceiling. He shook his head. There was a pickup mic in the theatre roof, whose only function was to relay any voices in the auditorium to backstage speakers in the dressing rooms. It was how everyone knew what was going on during the

267

show and was commonly called the bitch-switch. Anyone careless enough to be rude about other performers or staff members while warming up would find that their comments were heard by everyone else. Pete had just confirmed that it was turned off. She sat on the front row, several seats away from the police, turning sideways so that her bosses could hear what she said.

After formal introductions, DS Hirst began. 'Can you tell us how you know Ricky Easton?'

Jessie had been expecting this. She outlined their affair all those years ago and the consequences for her. 'I hadn't seen him since. It didn't occur to me he might end up here.'

'You make it sound like the end of the world,' said DI Edwards.

'I don't think of it like that,' she said. 'I love it here. It's just that Ricky's a West End Wendy.'

'A what?'

'A performer who only does big shows or number-one tours. We're not a number-one venue. In time, if he aged gracefully, he could move into character roles in London.'

'How has it been with him here?'

She sighed. 'Difficult.' She looked at Larry. He sat impassively watching. 'He has gone out of his way to make it look as if I was no longer up to my job. I've been frightened.'

Pete shuffled uncomfortably, making his elderly theatre seat creak.

'You felt threatened?' The DI sat up and leaned forward. 'What did you do about it?'

'Nothing. I just had to try and ride it out.'

'You didn't have an argument last night?'

'You mean, did I push him off the pier?' Jessie asked. 'No, it wasn't me. That was his dealer.'

There was a silence. Pete squirmed again. 'They know about the packet, Jessie. I gave it to DS Hirst last night.'

'Perhaps you'd better tell us why you think it was his dealer,' said Hirst.

Jessie weighed up her options. It was still her word against Ricky, whatever happened. These two detectives might not believe her, but the truth was all she had.

'It began a week ago,' she said carefully. 'When I was locking up.'

Day by day, Jessie outlined the times she had seen Ricky with the tattooed man. She pointed to the red scar on her cheek where Ricky had cut it on Sunday afternoon. It was fading but still visible. She told them about the other sightings during the week, how Ricky had threatened her to gain her silence. Backed by Pete, she told them about the bag of drugs. Even Larry nodded in corroboration of that part.

She left out what she had heard on the cans. Pete and Larry would be horrified if they knew she had listened like that. Nor did she mention young Linda, the dancer, taking a packet from Ricky before the parade. That was none of her business, and she could have been wrong about either. Let the police find out if they were interested.

'Last night, we were all on the pier, watching the fireworks. Ricky said he would join us, but he didn't. I'd been drinking. I was at the end of my tether.'

She described how the two men had burst out of the fire exit doors, fighting. How Ricky had been knocked over the side of the railings. That she had run for help and when she returned the tattooed man had vanished.

Pete groaned. 'I usually lock the doors once the auditorium is empty,' he said. 'I was going to do it after the display. My wife and kids were waiting. If I had locked up properly, they wouldn't have been able to get outside.'

'It's not your fault,' said Jessie. 'What was that man doing in here anyway? Ricky must have brought him, surely?'

'Would you recognise this man again?' asked DS Hirst.

'Yes,' nodded Jessie. 'He's hard to miss with all those tattoos.'

Hirst addressed Pete. 'The bag you gave us has been sent to the forensic team. It will be checked for fingerprints, and the contents will be analysed.'

'We have a strict policy here,' said Larry. He sounded cross at the implication. 'No drugs or alcohol backstage. Everyone has to be clean when they arrive for a show, the same between shows if there are two of them. What people do in their own time is not up to us.'

'Ricky Easton seems to have had a bad injury a few years ago.' DS Hirst turned her attention to Larry. 'I am given to understand that crystal meth is favoured by dancers returning to work after a lay-off.'

'It might be in the West End,' snapped Larry, 'but I won't have any of that nonsense here. I can't tell you about the injury. Ricky's agent can. I'll get her details.' Larry walked quickly off through the pass door to the technical office.

DS Hirst turned back to look at Jessie. 'We will need you to give us a statement about this man and about the fight last night. We will also organize an identity parade.'

Jessie winced. Visions of standing behind a two-way window looking at men who might or might not be recognisable played across her mind.

'It's not like it used to be.' Hirst smiled reassuringly. 'It's all done with a computer and photo files. You won't have to see him in person.'

Larry returned with a scrap of paper, which he handed to DI Edwards.

'There's one more thing,' said Edwards. 'Actually, it's a question for all of you. Were you aware of any relationships that Ricky might have formed while he was here?'

Jessie looked at Pete and Larry, who nodded. 'He's been having an affair with Hallie Powell. I think that's over now.'

Larry made a grumpy sound that Jessie could only think was a "harumph".

'Anyone else?'

'You know how people like to gossip,' said Jessie, trying to deflect the question.

'And what did the gossip say?' Hirst asked.

Jessie gazed at her fingers for a moment. She remembered how they felt when Ricky had crushed them in his hand. 'He has a reputation. For being a bit of a loose cannon, sexually, I mean.'

'With who?'

'He tried it on with Yazza at the beginning of the season.' Jessie hesitated, then shrugged. 'And with Daisy. They went out a couple of times before he settled on Hallie.'

'And how did he take his failures?'

'I wasn't watching,' said Jessie.

'What about from your personal experience?'

Jessie took a deep breath. 'He likes to be in control. He likes to be the one making all the decisions. In fact, in my case, I'd say he was ruthless.'

'Ruthless? That's a strong word.' Hirst sounded sympathetic.

'Getting involved with him cost me my marriage and my career in London. All so he could get a lead role that he would probably have been given before long anyway. So, yes. I'd call him ruthless.'

The DI stood. 'I think that's all we need for now. Thank you all for your time.'

Larry showed the two detectives out through the staff door. Jessie turned to Pete and thanked him. 'I appreciate your support. What will happen now?'

'Now?' Pete smiled. 'You need to get a coffee. We've got a long day ahead of us.'

'Yes?'

'Ricky obviously can't perform now,' said Pete. 'You remember Matt from last season? Lucky for us, he was between jobs. He's on his way up as we speak.'

'Of course I do.' Matt and Jessie had become good friends. She was delighted. 'What about the production numbers?'

'The cast are called for eleven. We'll go through the whole show and change what we can.'

Larry was soon back.

'You do believe me, don't you?' Jessie asked him.

For once, the dour Yorkshireman cracked a smile. 'Yes, I do. They'll speak to Ricky as well, no doubt.'

'Will Matt stay for the rest of the season?'

'Definitely.' Larry headed for the pass door. 'I'm not having Ricky Easton back in this theatre ever again.'

It was half past ten. Jessie had half an hour before they began to rework the show. There was only one performance on Fridays, and that was at eight o'clock. They had less than eight hours to replan twenty-seven numbers.

With luck, she thought as she turned on the sound system, *I still have Matt's settings from last summer.*

CHAPTER 59

The warm and sunny morning was a direct contrast to the darkness of their work, Sara felt as she and DI Edwards walked down the pier. The town was gearing up for another busy day. Families with buckets, lines and nets were jostling for positions along the railings for the "World Crabbing Championships".

'Did you believe all that?' asked Edwards.

'On balance, yes I do,' replied Sara. 'I said this was about keeping secrets, and that's another pair of them. The old affair and taking drugs after the injury. Not to mention trying to have an affair with Daisy.'

'I agree.' Edwards's mobile rang. 'Hello? Hang on a minute.'

He fumbled with the screen in the sunlight, turning it onto speaker mode as they reached the prom. Sara perched on the retaining wall to listen.

'Morning, Edwards.' It was Dr Taylor. 'I thought I'd better call you immediately.'

'DNA results?'

'Ultra-fast-tracked,' said the pathologist. 'And two for the price of one.'

'Two matches?'

'This sounds tinny. Are you outside?'

'Yes.'

'Dial it down a bit, will you?'

Edwards reduced the volume. Sara huddled around the phone, so she could hear. 'OK.'

'Firstly, Jacob Marsh. There were traces of his DNA on Daisy's dress.'

'He was her attacker?'

'No. Daisy was assaulted by Alexander Hayward.'

Edwards flicked the phone off speaker mode and jammed it to his ear. Sara was already on her own phone, tracking down Bowen and Noble.

'Get a couple of cars,' she said. 'Pick up the boss and me by the posh chippie. Now. It's urgent. Organize some backup.'

Edwards was striding down the prom. Sara had to jog to catch up. She pointed up to the corner where a set of old stairs climbed the cliff, a remnant of the town's Victorian heyday. Streams of people were coming down them. Sara tucked in behind Edwards as he pushed his way up them against the tide.

Two cars were waiting for them when they reached the road. Edwards got in beside Bowen, Sara jumped into the second vehicle next to Noble. In seconds, they were screaming down the high street and up the hill out of the town towards the Haywards' house. When they turned onto the side road, which wound through the estate, another police car joined them from the other direction.

Edwards was first out. He ran to the front door and hammered on it. Sara beckoned to Noble, and they ran down the path between the house and the garage. Before they reached the side gate to the back garden, it flew open, and Xander Hayward ran out. He hesitated when he saw them, then put his head down and charged straight at them.

Too late, Sara remembered that he was a first-class rugby player. He hit her at full speed, forcing the air from her lungs. Her head snapped backwards as Xander's onrush swung her to one side. She slammed against the brick wall of the garage, her hands scrabbling to grip at her attacker's clothing. Vaguely, she heard Noble shouting for help. Then her fingers hit flesh, and she dug in. Xander squealed as if he had been stung. It distracted him long enough for Noble to wrestle the lad to the ground. One of the uniformed officers pinned down the boy's legs as Noble put on the handcuffs. Sara leaned against the wall with one hand. She felt winded and rather stupid as the DC dragged the struggling and cursing Xander to the waiting car.

At the front of the house, DI Edwards had been having a much easier time of it. It seemed that Jacob was willing to cooperate. Bowen was helping the silent lad lock up the house.

'OK, son?' he asked. Jacob nodded. His face was drained of colour. 'This way then.'

Bowen took him to the other car and put him in the back seat. In Edwards's car, it looked as though Xander had stopped shouting and was now reduced to tears.

'Where shall we go, boss?' asked Noble.

'I think it's time we took this lot down to the custody suite at Wymondham,' the DI said. He turned to one of the uniformed officers. 'We'll take this pair. Can you get back to the station and arrange transport for the other two?'

They were soon on their way. Sara joined Edwards in the lead car for the hour-long drive. Xander Hayward sat next to an officer in the back seat, staring out of the window. There were scratch marks on his arm, where Sara had tried to grab him. Blood had bubbled along the lines. It was already drying into scabs. They matched the older ones on the back of his hand.

Xander sniffed continuously until Sara gave in and passed him a tissue. He grabbed it, blowing his nose violently. The snotty tissue sat in one hand for several minutes before Xander lifted his handcuffed hands onto the back of the passenger seat where Sara sat. Straining against his seatbelt, Xander tried to drop the pulpy mess down Sara's neck. His face pushed against her headrest.

'You think you've caught me, you black bitch,' he growled. 'But we deal with your kind all the time up here. My dad will sort this out, and you'll regret ever laying a finger on me.'

The uniformed officer pulled Xander back into his seat as Sara extracted the dirty tissue.

'I doubt your dad is going to be much use to you,' said Edwards calmly. He kept his eyes on the road ahead. 'We already have him in custody.'

CHAPTER 60

Aggie had managed to find two duty solicitors. Xander Hayward sat in Interview Room One, largely ignoring the man trying to advise him. Jacob Marsh in Room Two was listening intently to his solicitor and occasionally whispering things to her. The entire team stood in the viewing room watching, even Aggie.

'Shall we start with young Mr Hayward?' asked Edwards.

Sara nodded. She was still annoyed at Xander's words to her in the car.

'You going to be OK? I could take Mike instead.'

'No chance. I want him to look me in the face and say it.'

Edwards shrugged, and they went in. Sara started the recording machine.

'Alexander Hayward, you have been arrested for assaulting a police officer.'

Xander smirked.

'You have also been arrested on suspicion of the rape and murder of Daisy Shaw. Do you understand what I have said?'

Xander looked at the solicitor and nodded. 'Yes, I understand.'

'Why did you try to run, Xander?' asked Edwards.

'No comment.' Xander curled his lip in derision.

'Why did you charge at DS Hirst?'

'She was in my way.'

'Where were you trying to go?'

'No comment.'

For a moment, Edwards stared at the young man, who stared back with confidence. 'Let's talk about Daisy.'

Xander leaned back in his chair. 'No comment.'

'We know you had sex with her. We have the evidence.'

Xander's smile widened as if he was remembering the rape with pleasure. 'No comment.'

'We know that you fought over her at the carnival ball. Were you angry with her?'

'No comment.'

Sara knew this was going to get tedious. No matter what question Edwards put to the young man, the reply was always 'No comment.' In the end, Edwards gave up.

'Do you have anything to say at all? No? Then, I'm going to arrange for you to be taken to the cells, pending further investigation.'

'I have a question,' said the solicitor.

Edwards nodded.

'Would you grant police bail if we applied?'

'No.'

'We refute your accusation of murder,' said the solicitor. 'I'll be going over your head to make our application.'

'You can try.' Edwards stood.

'Tut, tut, tut,' said Xander, wagging his finger at Sara. 'Who's been a naughty girl? You can't pin that on me.'

He laughed as the two detectives left the room, which made Sara seethe. Posh white boys like Xander Hayward had a track record in clever lawyers who could get sentences reduced or suspended. The boy had been outright racist and sexist to her, and a streak of anger flashed through her — the motivation to send him down. But that would make her no better than her colleagues, who had been willing to accuse Kit Grice simply because he was a Show Traveller. There was no place for personal bias in this job. She drew a deep breath to calm herself. She had to be strong enough not to let her own prejudices interfere with her work.

Edwards and Sara went to interview Jacob Marsh. The list on his arrest sheet was almost as long as Xander's.

'Tell me about Xander Hayward and yourself,' began Edwards.

'He's my best mate,' muttered Jacob.

'Would you do anything for him?'

'Once I would have.'

'Once? Not now?'

'I don't want to get charged with murdering that bloody girl, do I? It wasn't me.'

'Her name is Daisy,' said Edwards. 'How long have you been friends with Xander?'

'Since I started at Langton Hall. He'd been there since junior school. I joined when I was twelve. We did everything together. I even changed my university application, so we could both go to Oxford.'

Edwards glanced at Sara, and she took up the questioning. 'What are you both studying?'

'Xander is reading geography. I'm doing medicine.'

'Xander must be clever. Perhaps not as clever as you, Jacob.'

'He's going to be a rugby blue,' said Jacob. He sounded jealous. 'I didn't make it through at the trials.'

'Medicine is one of the most difficult subjects, isn't it?' asked Edwards. 'I'd say you are definitely cleverer than your friend. Do you know why I think that?'

Jacob shook his head.

'You said you didn't want to get blamed for this. Why do you think we would blame you?'

'It says there.' Jacob pointed to a note on his solicitor's pad. 'You have my DNA on her clothes. But I didn't attack her. I didn't rape her. That was Xander. I swear it was.'

'So why is your DNA on her dress?' Sara asked.

'I helped to move her.'

They both held their breath as the young man struggled with his conscience.

'Why don't you start at the ball?' Sara suggested.

Jacob nodded. 'It was fun. We got pretty caned. Xander's dad was buying the drinks, so why not? Xander fancied that girl, the Carnival Queen. Daisy. He started chatting her up.'

'Did she respond at all?'

'A bit. She danced with him. She danced with me as well. Then Xander bought her a drink. We'd all had plenty by then, and there was this man at the bar.'

Sara felt her blood begin to pump rapidly. She watched Jacob. His face was contorted with anguish.

'When Xander came back with the drinks, he laughed and said he'd got something to hurry things along because he fancied shagging her.'

'Jacob, is that how you all talk about women?' Edwards asked.

Jacob shook his head and blushed. 'I get too embarrassed. Xander talks about them like that all the time.'

'What did Xander do then?'

'He said he'd just bought some shit from this man and put it in her drink. Said she'd get horny after that.'

'And did she?'

'I don't know. Daisy drank it, and they danced some more. Then this man turned up from the funfair. They seemed to know each other already. Xander was put out. Said she owed him because he'd bought her a drink.'

'Can you describe this man at the bar, Jacob?'

'Older, lots of muscles — like a bodybuilder. He had these tattoos everywhere.'

'Where was Mr Hayward in all this?' Sara asked. 'We know Mrs Hayward left early.'

'He was chatting up some old bird at the bar.'

'Then what happened?'

'Xander tried to pull this funfair bloke off Daisy, but he couldn't. They laughed at him when he fell over. He was livid. Then the security men came and told us all to leave.'

'You left the ball in a group?'

'Daisy and that other chap went off on their own. But we all did.'

'Did you stay together?'

'There was a row.' Jacob shuddered at the memory. 'Xander wanted to go on to the pub. His dad wanted to come too. They started picking on Benji because he wanted to go home. Mr Hayward told Benji to take the car home if he was such a lightweight. Lucky sod.'

'Lucky?'

'Well, I mean, getting to drive a fucking Porsche, just like that.'

The solicitor whispered to Jacob before saying, 'Sorry about the language.'

'Yeah, sorry.'

'The three of you went to the pub? Which one?' Edwards picked up the questions.

'It's on the corner. There was a band on. Xander's dad went to get another round in. Xander said he was off to the toilet. But he never came back. After a while, his dad felt sick and wandered off. I don't know where he went, and I was stuck there on my own. I didn't know what to do, so I waited. I thought Xander would know where to find me.'

'Were you there long?'

'Ages. The band finished, and the bar was closing. I waited outside for a bit, and I saw the girl go past.'

'You saw Daisy?' asked Sara.

'Yeah. She was chatting back to a bunch of lads who were outside. I was pretty pissed by then, but I thought I saw Xander. I wasn't totally sure at first. He had the hoodie on that he'd borrowed from his dad. It covered his face.'

'What did you do, Jacob?'

'There's this footpath. I thought he had gone down there, and I followed him. When I got there, I couldn't see him.'

Jacob's lip was trembling.

'Go on,' said Sara, hoping her tone was kind when, in reality, she just wanted to slap this overprivileged young man.

'It was ever so quiet. There didn't seem to be anyone else at all — just the sea on the beach. Then I heard a noise in one of those dark alleys. A girl's voice and some grunting. And Xander's voice.'

'Did he say anything?'

'He said, "You owe me."'

'Are you sure?'

Jacob nodded. He looked sullen.

'Then what?'

'I could hear him. He was fucking her. Just like he did to Lyra.'

'Just like Lyra?'

'The girl at school.'

'Did you see what happened to Lyra?' Edwards sounded surprised.

'Yes.' Jacob grimaced. 'I knew he had a thing about her. Kept going on about what he was going to do to her when she delivered on her promises. I don't think Lyra said all those things. I think he just made them up. He got obsessed, and I was worried for him.'

'For him?'

Jacob blushed. 'And Lyra, of course. One night, he said it was payback time and went out. I followed him. Xander dragged her around the back of the drama studio. He trapped her up against the wall, his arm across her throat and just went at it.'

'You think he was doing the same to Daisy?' asked Sara. It certainly made sense of the forensic evidence. 'Didn't you try to stop him?'

'It was too late. He'd already . . .' Jacob's voice faltered. 'You know?'

'Climaxed?' suggested Edwards. Jacob nodded. 'Did you say anything then?'

'I asked what the hell he was doing. The girl had collapsed on the floor. He just laughed. We could hear the guys outside the pub. They were moving closer to the alley.'

'You thought they might find you?'

'I was going to run off, but Xander grabbed me. He said if I was going to be a doctor, I would know what to do with a body.'

'You thought she was dead?'

'No, no. The opposite. I checked, and she had a pulse. Unconscious but breathing. In fact, she started making moaning noises. That's when Xander freaked out. He said we had to move her before the drunks got to us. He promised we'd take her somewhere she would be easily found. I wanted to put her shoes on. But Xander threw them in the bin with her bag. Said there was no time.'

'You both moved Daisy?'

'Yeah, like she was just pissed, you know. We carried her between us, her arms over our shoulders. I wanted to leave her in the gardens. It's quite well-lit there — someone would soon see her. Xander said we had to keep moving. Jesus, she was heavy. There was this back alley behind some flats. We turned down that. I said we should leave her on somebody's doorstep. Anybody's doorway would have done.'

He lapsed into silence. None of the other adults spoke.

Jacob looked at Edwards. 'I'm telling you this because I didn't kill her. You understand?'

Edwards nodded. 'Where did you leave her?'

'I left her with Xander. He'd picked her up like she was asleep and carried on down this alley. I couldn't cope with him. I just stood there and cried. Then I ran. I ran down to the beach and along the prom. I ran until I got past the last beach hut, then along the sand until I couldn't run anymore. I didn't see Daisy again.'

CHAPTER 61

Adele and Henry arrived at Wymondham Police Headquarters late in the afternoon. The desk sergeant took them to a family interview room with a sofa and armchairs and gave them cups of tea. They weren't kept waiting long. DS Hirst and her boss, DI Edwards, joined them. Hirst explained that they wanted to record the interview.

'I think we are looking at two separate offences here,' said the DI. 'Your accusations about abuse from your husband will be dealt with by a specialised unit.'

Hirst explained how difficult these cases were and how they handled such complaints in the Norfolk force. Adele agreed to talk to this other unit, though with a sinking feeling that she would be unlikely to get Greg prosecuted for what he had done.

'We're dealing with Daisy Shaw's murder, as you know,' DS Hirst said. Adele could see sympathy in her eyes. 'I'm sorry to tell you that we have arrested your son, Alexander, on suspicion of her rape and murder.'

Adele gasped. Her head swam, and she swayed uncontrollably for a moment. Henry pulled her into the safety of his strong grip.

'Can you carry on?' asked the DS. She sounded genuinely concerned.

Adele drew a ragged breath and nodded.

'We want to ask you about what has happened this week. Can we start with your statement on Monday?'

'At the time, you said that your husband, son and guests all came home in a taxi,' said DI Edwards. 'Do you still stand by that statement?'

Adele didn't know what to say. Henry squeezed Adele closer to him. 'Can we have a few words alone?'

The detectives agreed. The recording device was switched off as they left the room.

Adele looked at Henry as he sat her upright. 'I knew Greg was lying. I remembered that he had gone out again, in the car. Before Xander came home. Greg might have killed this girl himself.'

'Then why have they arrested Xander for it?'

'Clothes,' said Adele suddenly. 'There were clothes in the washing machine the next morning. I didn't put them there. Then they just vanished.'

'Hiding evidence, maybe?'

'Either way. They'll have excuses. It's like this.' She pointed to the burns and bruises on her arms. 'No one will take me seriously. They just palmed me off to another department. I bet I never hear from them.'

Henry chewed his lip thoughtfully. 'I was watching this documentary once,' he began.

Adele couldn't envisage the swarthy fisherman being interested in documentaries. She realised that she still had a lot to learn about him. That he cared for her, Adele had been left in no doubt. Last night he had pledged his support and quietly declared his love for her. Now she would have to trust Henry in a way she'd not trusted a man for years.

'Yes?'

'It was about Al Capone. You know, the gangster.'

Adele nodded.

'They couldn't pin anything on him for the bad stuff. So, they arrested him for something else and made that stick instead. They got him for tax evasion. Don't you see?'

'You mean if I can't get Greg one way, help to get him the other?' Adele said slowly.

Henry held her gaze.

'The trouble is, then I betray my son as well. I'm not sure I can live with that.'

'Perhaps it would help Alexander,' suggested Henry. 'By deflecting some of the blame onto Greg. I don't know. I just want you to be clear about one thing. Whatever you decide, whatever you say, I'm here for you.'

She nodded and pointed to the corridor. Henry called the two detectives back in. Adele sipped her tea as they turned on the recorder again.

'No, Inspector,' she said. 'I don't stand by that statement.'

'Why not?'

'It was forced out of me by my husband.' Adele patted her arm where fresh dressings had been put over her burn marks. 'On Sunday night. When he did this.'

'So, what actually happened on Friday night after the ball?'

'I'd gone home early and was already in bed. Greg's car came back first. I thought it would be Greg.'

'It wasn't?'

'No. Whoever it was went into the spare bedroom where Xander's two friends were staying. Benji told me later that it had been him.'

'When did your husband get back?'

'Later. I was asleep, but Greg slammed the front door, and it woke me up. That's when I heard the taxi. I had to lie still as if I was sleeping. Otherwise, he would have . . .' Adele's voice trailed off.

Hirst smiled sympathetically and waited.

'When he's been drinking, sometimes he . . .' Adele couldn't go on. She sipped more tea to give herself a break. 'Anyway, he fell asleep. Later — I don't know how much later — his phone went off. Some text messages.'

'Can you guess the time?'

'It was still dark,' said Adele. 'Three or something like that?'

'What did your husband do when he got these messages?'

'He got up and got dressed. Went off in the car. He had Xander and Jacob with him when he came back, because I heard them whispering on the landing before they went to bed. Next morning, I was first up because I was worried about my carnival events. Then Henry rang me.'

'About Daisy?'

'We didn't know it was her,' interrupted Henry. 'We'd just heard that the town was being shut down, and we come down to find out what was goin' on. There were all these events on Saturday.'

'And when you got home?'

'They were getting up,' said Adele.

'Just a normal morning?'

'No. There was one really odd thing. There was a load of washing in the machine. When I got it out, I knew I wouldn't have loaded it because it was all wrong.'

'Wrong? How?' Edwards looked confused.

'Things put in together that shouldn't have been, like wrong colours and Xander's trousers that should have gone to the dry cleaners.'

'Did you recognise the clothes?' Hirst sounded eager.

'Yes. They were the ones Xander and Jacob had been wearing for the ball. Plus, a hoodie and tracksuit that belongs to my husband.'

'What happened to these clothes?'

'I hung them up to dry. But when I went back later, they had all vanished.'

'Do you know where they might have gone?'

Adele looked at Henry, who took her hand and squeezed it gently. 'I couldn't work it out at first. Then I remembered that Greg had been putting the drink tins into a sports hold-all just before they'd taken the jet ski out. Maybe the clothes were in there too.'

'What do you think he would have done with it?'

'Knowing Greg, it will either still be in the back of his car, or he would have given it to his secretary to deal with.' She sighed. 'I'm tired. Can we stop now?'

'Just one more thing, Mrs Hayward. How can we get access to your husband's office or your house if we need to?'

Adele reached into her handbag and pulled out a set of keys. 'Here. These are house keys. There are a spare set of office keys on the rack in the kitchen.'

'Don't you need them?' asked DS Hirst.

'I'm never going near that place ever again,' said Adele firmly.

'She don't need to,' said Henry. 'She's living with me now.'

CHAPTER 62

It might have been late on Friday afternoon, but the team sprang into action with their new information. Edwards despatched Bowen and Noble to check Hayward's office for the sports holdall. Aggie chased the forensic reports from the house and car search the previous day. Sara rang their team leader.

'You lot want blood,' he grumbled. 'I've only just spoken to your admin lady.'

'This should be an easy question,' she said. 'When you searched the Porsche Cayenne, was there a bag of clothing in it anywhere?'

'Hold on.' She could hear the team leader tapping at his computer keyboard. 'Doesn't look like it.'

'Or in the house? We're looking for a sports holdall, with trousers, shirts and a black hoodie in it.'

'That's a bigger proposition,' he said. 'We haven't coordinated all the room reports yet. I'll have to get back to you on that. There is one thing of interest for you.'

'From the search?'

'No, from that bag of drugs that you brought, the one from the theatre. The contents have gone off for analysis, but we did a quick dust for prints. There were two sets. One we don't have on record. The other belongs to a known dealer.'

'Who?' Sara raised her arm to signal to the team that she had some special news.

'Drugs have this guy as a person of interest. His name is Tony Moore. They think he's something of a kingpin on the Surrey Road estate. Been after him for ages. And guess what else?'

'Go on.' Sara jotted Tony Moore in capital letters on a scrap of paper and held it up.

'Do you remember there was a bag of ecstasy tablets in Daisy Shaw's handbag?'

'I do. Don't tell me they were the same.'

'Both of them. The unknown and Tony Moore. Seems to be a middleman somewhere here.'

It was more than ample to keep their suspect in the cells waiting for an interview. What they needed to do was identify this other man. Sara trusted her instincts like every copper had to. Right now, they were telling her that the other fingerprints most likely belonged to Ricky Easton.

The DI agreed with her. 'You think this fight on the pier could have been a falling-out among dealers?'

'Perhaps. Where is Ricky Easton now?'

'He left the hospital at lunchtime,' said Aggie.

'Looks like we're going back to Cromer,' said the DI.

* * *

Ricky Easton was indeed at his untidy flat above the news-agents. He let them in, and they followed him to the living room. He slumped into an armchair, looking like a beaten dog.

'They've sacked me from the show,' he said. 'First job in three years. Now what will I do?'

It was funny, mused Sara. This man had just been attacked and thrown off the pier by a known drug dealer. He could have been killed or badly injured. But all he was worried about was losing this job. Performers were a whole different breed.

'We need to talk to you about the man who attacked you,' the DI said. It didn't sound as if he was about to take any prisoners. 'We have a witness to the incident.'

'I bet.' Ricky snorted. 'Jessie Dobson, I suppose.'

'If it hadn't been for Miss Dobson's prompt action, you could have drowned.' Sara was losing patience with the man.

Ricky frowned. Sara explained how Jessie had brought help and a lifebelt, then got them to call out the lifeboats.

The story seemed to hit home with Ricky. 'I think I've got this terribly wrong, haven't I?'

'This man is called Tony Moore.' Sara produced a photo on her mobile and showed it to Ricky. 'Recognise him?'

'Yes.'

'Is this the man that attacked you?'

'Yes.'

'Why would he do that?'

Ricky looked shamefaced. 'We had a falling-out.'

'Because of Daisy Shaw?'

'Yes. I was going to tell you, really I was.'

Sara doubted that. The DI cut across her next question with one of his own. 'What about Daisy?'

'We sometimes chatted in the pub,' said Ricky. 'She was really nervous about giving that speech at the ball. I said I could get her something to help with it.'

'And that was?'

'A couple of ecstasy pills. Just to bolster her confidence. Make her feel happy.'

'And you got these pills from?'

Ricky pointed at the picture.

'How did you come to know him?'

'I had an injury,' said Ricky. His voice was full of self-pity. 'I was out of work for three years. When I got offered this job, I thought it would be my way back. A friend said I should use this little helper. Said he used it to get him through a season of Les Mis.'

'Which little helper?'

'Ice.'

'You mean methamphetamine?' Edwards wasn't holding back.

Ricky nodded. 'The season is so long — I knew I would need something to get me through it. My friend made a couple of calls, and this man contacted me. I met him in Norwich a few times. Then we got really busy on the show, and I needed more than ever. He came out to see me.'

'He visited you regularly?'

'Yes. And I'm not the only one.'

'Oh?'

'I get some for Linda too. She's finding the season too hard. It's her first long job.'

Sara looked at the singer in amazement. She wondered if he understood what he had just done. Not only was he admitting to being their middleman, but he had also just dumped another cast member in the shitter.

'We're going to need a full statement, sir,' she said. 'We're also going to need your fingerprints and DNA. We can do it at the station this afternoon, if that's convenient.'

Ricky whimpered. 'I have no choice, do I?'

'Not really, sir. Besides, we will be bringing charges against your attacker. I'm sure you want to help us do that.'

They left the singer to his hospital-prescribed painkillers, forlornly ordering a takeaway and clearly feeling sorry for himself.

'If his prints are a match, then we can be sure he also put the bag under the sound desk to incriminate Jessie Dobson,' said Sara.

'Spiteful little bugger, isn't he?' said Edwards.

Sara's mobile rang. It was DC Bowen.

'Yep?'

'Tell the boss, we've found it.'

'The holdall?'

'Yes. Mrs Hayward was right. The secretary at the office still had it. She'd been told to take it to the clothes bank in Holt, where the agency is. But because her boss hadn't been in all week, she hadn't got around to it. We're taking it back for Forensics to go over.'

'The thing is—' said Edwards casually as they got back into his car — 'people don't realise. They think that washing clothes will get rid of all the evidence. But it doesn't.'

CHAPTER 63

Greg Hayward's face was an open book. His features changed with almost every sentence. Sometimes it was anger, or arrogance, or complacence. Sara wanted it to register fear. They had kept him in the holding cell for a second night, with the permission of a magistrate. She had hoped it would have a salutary effect on him. It didn't seem that way, with his solicitor sat next to him.

'Can you tell us exactly what happened on Friday night?' Edwards asked.

Hayward stuck to his familiar story of the pub followed by a ride home for all four of them.

'We have witnesses that say otherwise.'

'No comment,' said Hayward.

'What happened in the middle of the night?'

Hayward briefly wrinkled his brow. 'What do you mean?'

'We believe that you received a text message and went out in your car. At about three o'clock.'

'We have requested your phone records, sir,' added Sara.

'All right, yes, I went to collect Xander and Jacob.'

'Where had the young men been?' Edwards continued.

Hayward hesitated.

'We're checking the town CCTV for your vehicle,' said Sara.

'I met them at the Gangway. They'd been at the beach.'

'How long had they been there?'

'I've no bloody idea,' snapped Hayward.

'When you got home, what did you do with your clothes?' Edwards sounded like he was reciting a shopping list, there was so little emotion in his voice.

'No comment.'

'We have a witness who says one of your party put some clothes on to wash.'

'You can't believe a word my wife says.' The man's face turned puce.

'What happened to these clothes?'

'How would I know?'

'We've spoken to your secretary,' said Edwards. 'In fact, we've recovered the bag from your office. It's with Forensics.'

Hayward grimaced. 'No comment.'

Sara took a deep breath. 'Mr Hayward, do you know that we have also arrested your son?'

Hayward stared at her, scrunching up his face, before turning his gaze to Edwards. 'Is this true?'

'It is.'

'Damn it.' Hayward turned bright red and slapped his hands onto his thighs. 'Fuck it.'

'Sir?' asked Sara.

The man let out a long stream of breath, like a balloon deflating. 'After all I did to protect him.'

The solicitor raised a finger. 'Perhaps I could have a word with my client.'

'I think you should,' said Edwards. 'Explain how good forensic science is these days.'

In the viewing room, the team was joined by DS Ellie James. Ellie was Sara's best friend on the force. They had worked together on a case when Sara had first moved to Norwich. Ellie had subsequently been promoted as a Detective Sergeant to the drugs team. She was brimming with excitement. In Interview Room Two, Tony Moore sat with a man in an expensive-looking suit.

'We've been trying to pin something on this man for months,' she said.

'Don't get too excited,' warned Edwards. 'We want him for assault as well.'

'Good. That stuff you saw him put in the bin? Dozens of bags of illegals. Coke, crystal meth, weed, you name it. Covered in the bugger's prints.'

Sara smiled at Ellie's enthusiasm. 'We also want him to help us with the murder.'

'You think he murdered this girl?' Ellie slowed down a little.

'No. Someone has already been arrested on suspicion of that. We still need to question him about it, though, as a possible witness.'

The DI lay a photograph of Xander Hayward on the table and identified it for the tape. 'Mr Moore, do you recognise this young man?'

Moore shrugged. 'No comment.' The professional criminal's reply sounded far more convincing from the dealer than it had from Greg Hayward.

'We have your fingerprints on several objects, linking you to drugs sold to the cast at the Pavilion Theatre.'

Moore's face remained impassive. 'No comment.'

'We also have witnesses that will testify to your assault of Ricky Easton on the pier on Thursday night.'

This time Moore didn't bother to reply.

'Including the victim.'

Silence.

'Are you sure you can't identify this young man?' Edwards tapped the picture.

Moore looked at his solicitor. The man leaned forward and whispered to his client. It was too low to be caught by the recorder.

'May we ask the context of this inquiry?' the solicitor asked.

'Certainly. It is in connection with the murder of Daisy Shaw in Cromer a week ago.'

'Would my client be considered a witness in this context?'

'He would be helping me with my inquiries,' agreed Edwards. Moore folded his arms and looked to be considering his options.

'If my client were to cooperate, could this be taken into account at another time?' persisted the solicitor.

'I can't guarantee that,' he said. 'I might be prepared to write a letter in confidence for the judge to consider.'

The solicitor whispered to Moore again. The dealer stared at Edwards before unfolding his arms to point at the picture.

'Yeah, I know this one.'

'How?'

'I was at the carnival ball.'

'The ball that opens Cromer's carnival week?'

Moore nodded. 'I got there quite late. This one had been drinking with his mates. Looked pretty pissed. Knew who I was, though.'

'How come?'

'I don't know.'

'Go on.'

'Came straight up to me and asked if I had something he could buy. By the look of him, I thought he'd be after ecstasy. You know, clubbing happy pills.'

'Which you deal in?'

'No comment.'

'What did he ask for?' asked Sara.

Moore looked at her closely before answering. 'Special K.'

'Got him,' Edwards breathed.

Sara sincerely hoped her boss was right. It was down to the barristers now.

CHAPTER 64

The show had gone as well as could be expected on Friday night with Ricky's hastily engaged replacement. More rehearsals had been held during the morning on Saturday, and the two shows yesterday had been an improvement on the first. Jessie went to the theatre on Sunday morning, even though it was her day off. Matt had asked her to help with his solo numbers, which she was happy to do. It was hot outside, despite it only being ten in the morning. She was glad to get inside the cooler dark of the theatre.

Jessie had agreed to turn on the systems, so Matt and Larry could have an hour or two together. It also allowed her to learn the numbers and properly balance Matt's mic and backing tracks. She should have been the first one there, but someone, possibly the bar manager, seemed to have got there before her. She walked unhurriedly around, firing up the bits of the system they needed. Taking fresh batteries, she went backstage.

Matt's dressing room door was open. The rest were all locked, as they should have been. Jessie went in to greet their replacement singer, but recoiled when she saw Ricky Easton. Her feet had made no sound on the carpeted corridor, and he was unaware of her presence until she started back, knocking into the door with a clatter.

He jumped with surprise. 'Fucking hell, Jessie. You didn't half give me a fright.'

'What the hell are you doing here?'

Ricky cut a somewhat pathetic figure. He was dressed in an old baggy tracksuit, and there were plasters on his face and hands. His movements were stiff and slow.

Jessie almost felt sorry for him. 'You look a mess.'

Ricky winced. 'Thanks for that.' He pointed to his side. 'Broke a couple of ribs.'

'From falling off the pier?'

'Yeah.' He looked embarrassed. 'I owe you for that, don't I?'

'What?' Jessie was instantly on her guard. What was he going to try and accuse her of now?

'You saw it. Saw that man push me over. The police told me that you went for the lifebelt and called the lifeboats out.'

'Yes.' Jessie's tone was nonchalant.

'I might have drowned if you hadn't done that, they said.'

'Underneath there? Yeah, it happens. Or you could have got carried out on the riptide.'

'Thank you.' Ricky held out his hand. 'I mean it. I owe you my life. Thank you.'

Jessie stared at it, before shaking his hand a couple of times, then let it go as if it had stung her. 'I have to ask. Why did you do all this to me?'

Ricky sat on the dressing room chair, looking at his reflection in the mirror. Jessie waited.

'I'm washed up,' he finally said. 'Three years without work. A serious injury that the physio can't improve. I'm forty-four. Past my prime. This was my last chance.'

'I doubt that.' Jessie wasn't prepared to fall for the self-pity that poured from Ricky in waves. 'Not unless you allow it to be.'

'My agent knows about my problems.' He patted his hip and winced. 'Says it's why I'm not moving into character parts as I should be. And I couldn't bear the thought of not being in theatre anymore. People don't understand, do they? This isn't just a job. It's our whole lives.'

'I get that. But why did you take it out on me?'

'This stuff I've been taking.' He pulled a small plastic bag of white powder from his jacket pocket. 'I didn't think how addictive it would become. Or how much it would change my behaviour.'

'That happens with addiction. What did you expect?'

'I thought I could beat it. Now everyone will know, and I'm finished.'

'Do you want to know the truth?'

Ricky looked at her in the mirror. 'What do you mean?'

'Do you want to know why you don't get the work?'

'Go on then. If you're so clever.'

'You don't get work because you have a reputation.'

'Like what?'

'Oh, come on.' Jessie snorted. 'For moaning, for being difficult and for being a shag bandit.'

'That's cruel,' said Ricky after a pause.

'A lot less cruel than you've been to me the last three months. Or all those years ago. You think what you did to me wasn't common knowledge at the time? It made me a laughing stock. The middle-aged female techie conned by the handsome, young, ladder-climbing singer. Dumped by my even-more-ambitious husband for a younger model.'

Jessie could barely hold in her anger now. Ricky hung his head as she ranted on.

'It took me years to play it down. I lost my home and my career. I lived in crappy digs until my not-overly-generous divorce settlement came through. I worked on the road for more than ten years, you bastard. Trying to get people to trust me again. While you—' Jessie pointed angrily at him — 'You went from the chorus to the lead in one single job and never fell back to earth.'

'Until I broke my hip,' he said. Turning on the chair, he faced Jessie. 'I'm sorry. I really am.'

There was a long silence, which Jessie knew was up to her to break.

'Then I got this job,' she said quietly. 'It's perfect. The team is great. The shows change regularly. My work is appreciated. I could even afford to buy a home at last.'

'Then I came along and spoiled it for you,' said Ricky. 'Look, I didn't know you were here, and I was shocked when I saw you. I thought you would have it in for me, try to get me sacked.'

'You decided to attack me before I could do it to you? Jeez, Ricky. How spiteful was that?'

'Well, I've paid for it. The police are going to question me for other stuff as well. I've got to stay around the town until they've finished with me. I may well be arrested.'

Jessie knew how hard that would be. Not just waiting to see if he got arrested, but knowing that the show was carrying on without him. Being excluded from the red-and-gold world while someone else took his spotlight.

'Will you tell me one thing?' she asked.

'You can ask.' Ricky sounded weary.

'What was it you did to Daisy?'

'I gave her some pills,' he said. 'She was frightened about making that speech, so I got her some happy pills. I thought it would help her. But maybe I just made it worse. Maybe it was my fault she wasn't careful enough and got attacked.'

Jessie let the guilt hang in the air. It wouldn't do Ricky any harm to feel it for once. The sensation would, no doubt, soon fade.

'What you doing here?' she suddenly thought to ask.

'I came for my stuff.' Ricky pointed to a small suitcase, randomly stuffed with make-up bags and dancing shoes.

'You're making a hash of that, aren't you?'

'It's harder than I thought. I can hardly move without my ribs killing me.'

Jessie knelt next to the suitcase. 'Come on then. Let me help you.'

CHAPTER 65

DI Edwards insisted that the team take Sunday off. Sara had spent the day in her garden, basking in the sun, washing flapping on the line. Her body rested in a lounger while her mind raced. Her phone had rung a couple of times, but she still hadn't spoken to Chris.

On Monday, they began the paper trail that would prepare the CPS cases and their court attendance later on. The team handed Tony Moore over to the drugs team, and Edwards took Sara out on two final interviews.

The first was to see the headmaster at Langton Hall. The man snubbed her entirely. He ignored any question that she put and spoke directly to Edwards and only Edwards. The implied sexism and racism made Sara grind her teeth. No matter how hard Edwards pushed, the headmaster fended him off.

'It would have ruined that young man's career,' he said, his lips pursed in annoyance.

What about the young woman's future? Sara thought. *Doesn't that matter?*

It seemed not. No wonder his pupils didn't expect to be held accountable for their actions. She wondered what the headmaster would say of Kit Grice and the accusations

302

against him. He'd probably say it served the Traveller right. The irony didn't escape her.

There was no way the headmaster would cooperate in any accusations against Xander Hayward, no matter what happened or how many witnesses there were. All he wanted to do was bury the rumour and protect the reputation of his school.

'He's not worth the effort,' Edwards said. They drove to their next appointment. 'Don't let him get to you.'

Lyra Nash and her parents were equally reluctant, though for different reasons. Sara thought the young woman looked hollow-eyed and far too thin. She barely spoke, and it was her mother who answered all their questions.

'This has been so traumatic for Lyra,' said Mrs Nash. 'The school were very unhelpful. Pretty much said she had brought it on herself.'

Sara could just imagine the conversation between the distraught parents and the headmaster with his rumour-burying shovel. Despite the promise of testimony from a witness, neither she nor Edwards could persuade them to bring a prosecution.

'Lyra is only just recovering,' insisted her mother. 'It would mean her having to remember and talk about what happened.'

Only then to have her honesty and level of sexual experience ripped to shreds in the witness box, Sara suspected. The CPS were notoriously cagey about bringing rape prosecutions, partly because of predatory defence barristers. The incident had happened so long ago, there was no chance of forensic evidence that might corroborate Lyra's version of events.

'How have your exams gone?' she asked.

Lyra shook her head. Her mother glared at Sara. 'They haven't. Lyra left before Easter and didn't take her A levels.'

'No university to go to?' asked Sara.

'Not yet,' said Mrs Nash. 'We've been fortunate. The girls' high school have been sympathetic. Lyra is going there in September to complete her course by doing the year again. She'll get extra tuition. And it's an all-female environment.'

Sara wished Lyra the best of luck.

By Friday, Hayward, father and son, were in Norwich prison awaiting their trials. Edwards had argued in court that they were a flight risk, and the judge had believed him. Jacob had been released on bail but would stand in the dock beside his friend on several charges.

Sara went home feeling an equal measure of joyful anticipation and trepidation. Her mother, Tegan, and stepfather, Javed, were to be waiting at the holiday cottage for her.

* * *

They walked around the village, past the striped red-and-white lighthouse and down to the beach. The evening was warm, and the light was fading when they reached the pub. Javed went inside to get some drinks as Sara and her mother settled in the beer garden.

'Have you spoken to Chris?' asked Tegan.

'Mum! You don't waste any time, do you?'

'Well, have you?'

'Not yet.'

'I know I'm in no place to preach. I made a mess of my life like that. I don't want you to do the same.'

Sara reached for her mum's hand and squeezed it. 'Will you come into the cottage? I've kept some of the photos of him.'

'Yes, I will. Not tonight, though.'

'And will you visit Dad's resting place with me?'

'Later in the week. Give me time between the two.'

'Deal.'

'Now,' said Tegan. 'You go ring that nice young man. Go on.'

She waved Sara away as Javed returned with their drinks.

The Norfolk Coastal Path wound its way through Happisburgh by the side of the pub. Sara walked along it in the setting sun's glow until she thought she was out of hearing distance. Her mum was right. She had kept Chris waiting far too long. She dialled his number, and he answered after two short rings.

'Hello, Chris,' said Sara. 'Can you come over to mine soon? There's something I'd like to say to you.'

THE END

ACKNOWLEDGEMENTS

I would like to thank my beta readers — Antony Dunford, Karen Taylor, Louise Sharland and Wendy Turbin — for their notes and encouragement, as well as Clive Forbes, a former DI, for his police procedural advice and thoughts on whodunnit. Any incorrect procedures are there because I made an executive author's decision (or mistake!).

My gratitude goes to Jasper Joffe for welcoming me to Joffe Books — I'm still pinching myself! My especial thanks to Emma Grundy Haigh, Cat Phipps and Matthew Grundy Haigh, all of whom have helped me improve the novel with their edits and picking up on timeline errors. My grateful thanks to the rest of the Joffe Books team for all your work and support.

Much of an author's life is spent in front of a computer and online. I feel very lucky to have joined this merry and generous gang of authors, publishers, bloggers and online party organizers. I raise a virtual glass to you all. Your support is invaluable.

Last but not least, my family. My husband, Rhett, and my daughters, Gwen and Ellie. Thank you for your continued support and love.

THE JOFFE BOOKS STORY

We began in 2014 when Jasper agreed to publish his mum's much-rejected romance novel and it became a bestseller.

Since then we've grown into the largest independent publisher in the UK. We're extremely proud to publish some of the very best writers in the world, including Joy Ellis, Faith Martin, Caro Ramsay, Helen Forrester, Simon Brett and Robert Goddard. Everyone at Joffe Books loves reading and we never forget that it all begins with the magic of an author telling a story.

We are proud to publish talented first-time authors, as well as established writers whose books we love introducing to a new generation of readers.

We have been shortlisted for Independent Publisher of the Year at the British Book Awards three times, in 2020, 2021 and 2022, and for the Diversity and Inclusivity Award at the Independent Publishing Awards in 2022.

We built this company with your help, and we love to hear from you, so please email us about absolutely anything bookish at: feedback@joffebooks.com.

If you want to receive free books every Friday and hear about all our new releases, join our mailing list: www.joffebooks.com/contact

And when you tell your friends about us, just remember: it's pronounced Joffe as in coffee or toffee!

THE PROMISE OF
WILDERNESS
THERAPY

Jennifer Davis-Berman, Ph.D.

&

Dene Berman, Ph.D

Association for Experiential Education
3775 Iris Avenue, Suite 4
Boulder, CO 80301-2043
303.440.8844 • 866.522.8337
www.aee.org

ISBN: 978-0-929361-16-1

This publication is sold with the understanding that the
publisher is not engaged in providing psychological, medical, training,
or other professional services. Its contents is not intended
as a definitive guide, but as a resource.

association for
experiential education
A COMMUNITY OF PROGRESSIVE EDUCATORS & PRACTITIONERS

Published and printed in the United States.